An Eddie Pannoni Thriller

STREET BUSINESS II

BY

ERNIE LIJOI Sr.
&
LAWRENCE MATTHEWS

W & B Publishers
New Jersey***North Carolina

W & B Publishers

For information:
W & B Publishers
Post Office Box 193
Colfax, NC 27235
www.a-argusbooks.com

ISBN: 978-0-6922418-8-2
ISBN: 0-6922418-8-4

Book Cover designed by Dubya

Printed in the United States of America

DEDICATION

Street Business is dedicated to my wife and to all of
the wives of undercover Police Officers around the world
for their understanding which allows their men to stay on
the street protecting the public at large.
Ernie Lijoi Sr.

DRUGS

People study drugs
Like others study bugs.
People use drugs
As a drinker downs the suds
People enforce drugs
Like a dike with plugs
It leaks from the bottom to the top
Will it ever stop?

Some spend a lifetime
In the dirt and grime
To protect the public
From all of the crime

To the youth it's like candy
To the adult like brandy
To a junkie it's handy

Society is taking the flop
Will it ever stop?
Will it ever stop?

By: Ernie Lijoi Sr.
March 21, 2014

INTRODUCTION

This story is based upon real events that occurred in and around Quincy, Massachusetts in the first half of 1978. Some of the events of have telescoped to improve dramatic flow; others are close to how they really happened.

The characters in this book are fictionalized versions individuals who may or may not have a relationship to a real individual. No one character is based upon a single real individual, with one exception.

Ernie Lijoi Sr. is a real police officer whose deep undercover work was the primary element in the elimination of a major drug and weapons operation in New England during the 1970's and 1980's.

His investigation resulted in dozens of arrests, a major disruption of drug traffic, and weapons seizures. At least six murders followed the police roundup that came at the end of this particular operation and more cases would follow that can be located in The Pannoni Files.

Our main subject is the well-known Eddie Pannoni, drug dealer and gun runner who in reality is the unknown Detective Ernie Lijoi Sr.

Chapter 1

Into the rat hole

Friday, November 18, 1977

As part of his work with the transit police, Ernie had been riding a train known as the Red Line through the gloom most of the day. The rain drew lines along the glass when the trains rose up to the daylight as he watched the crowds from Alewife to Harvard Square and Park Street train stations. It was the end of the week and the riders had a worn look about them, their faces saying, *"just get me home for the weekend."* It had been raining since midweek and Boston was damp and cold as the Thanksgiving holiday approached. Office Ernie Lijoi Sr. was in uniform, wearing the badge of Massachusetts Bay Transit Authority. His attention was on watching and scanning the train for threats to the general public such as pickpockets, thieves and more.

He got off at the North Quincy station to stretch his legs and grab a cup of hot coffee. It was late in the afternoon and the crowds were growing as the work-week ended and the station filled with commuters who stared straight ahead, no expression on their faces, as they stuffed themselves onto the trains or fought their way up the stairs and out the doors into the drizzle. Officer Lijoi held his coffee cup in both hands and leaned against a side wall, watching the crowd and well out of the way of anyone trying to get to the trains. He was looking forward to his own weekend and wondered whether it was too cold and rainy to take his wife and sons to Maine, where they could get away from the Boston crowds.

A young man came in through the Newport Avenue entrance and scanned the crowd as he walked to the turnstiles, his dark eyes energized and flashing. Officer Lijoi thought he looked excited or even intoxicated, and placed his coffee cup on a concrete ledge along the wall. He made mental notes as the young man looked left and right, moving past the other commuters, never noticing Officer Lijoi standing off to the side. The young man was a tall, thin, white male, dark hair, late teens, sporting a very thin beard.

Lijoi moved away from the wall and waited to see what the kid would do. The young man did not see the policeman and he easily jumped the turnstile and ran to the top of the stairs that led down to trains. Kids did it all the time and almost always got away with it. Officer Lijoi never made an arrest for this, he usually just explained that all the kid has to do is tell the money collector his name and address and he can travel free. That was usually!

"Hey! You! C'mere!" Lijoi pointed to the teenager and moved toward him, trying to cut him off as the kid moved down the stairs to the train platform. He kept moving, trying to insert himself into a knot of people who were attempting to board a train going south to the Wollaston station. Lijoi took the stairs three at a time and grabbed the kid by the belt before he would reach the platform.

"Leave me alone! I ain't done nothing," he whined as Lijoi pulled him out of the crowd and into a small room that was available to the transit police for such purposes as interviews and holding suspects.

"You jumped the turnstile without paying the fare. That's a crime, its larceny," Lijoi had the young man against the far wall and he was standing back a distance he judged to be about the length of his night stick. He did not want to give the young man an opportunity to hit or grab him.

Kid: "Fuck you," the kid said.

Ernie realized that he had a little fireball on his hands.

Ernie: "Excuse me?" Lijoi stood back and reached for his handcuffs.

Kid: "I said, fuck you."

Lijoi had been prepared to let the kid go if he would leave his name or pay the fare. Most turnstile jumpers were warned, paid the fare, and went on their way. Lijoi was in no mood for this kid's attitude.

Ernie: "Do you realize that you can be arrested?" he said, turning the young man's face to the wall. "You gotta weapon? Tell me now before I find something."

The young man stared at Lijoi. "No, nothing'"

Lijoi patted him down, and then he searched his pockets. He found some bills and small change in one. Then he found a lumpy bag. He took the bag from the kid's pocket which turned out to be a small bag of blue pills.

Ernie: "What's this?"

The kid stared at him, his cockiness draining away.

Ernie: "Looks like some Nembutal pills to me. Do you have a prescription for this?" No reply from the boy.

Lijoi held up the bag and picked up the telephone in the small room to call the Quincy PD to send a car to transport the kid on what was now a narcotics case, but before he could dial the number the kid said:

Kid: "I need to talk to Detective Churn. Do you know him? Detective Churn, Quincy. I wanna talk to him before you take me in."

Lijoi put the telephone down. "How'd you know him?" It was common for suspects under arrest to blurt out the names of police officers in hopes of sliding out of charges.

"I work with him. I give him things, you know, information and shit, I'm kind of doing something for him right now. Can you call him?"

Ernie: "What's your name?"

Kid: "He knows me, I'm Johnny Aiello, I work with him."

Lijoi looked at the kid for a moment, and picked up the telephone and dialed. Detective Churn arrived about fifteen minutes later, wearing a business suit and carrying a wet umbrella. He knocked on the door and opened it without waiting for an answer to his knock. Lijoi and the young man were sitting at a small table and Lijoi was holding the bag. He briefed the detective and gave him the small bag of blue pills.

Det. Churn: "How you doing, Johnny? Got you again."

Det. Churn turned to Ernie: "I'll take him," the detective said, and led the young man out of the room.

Lijoi sat there for a moment, wondering whether to check the station again or just call it a day. He had no way of knowing that collaring the kid would change his life, bring down drug kingpins, result in hundreds of arrests, and end in the murders of six people in a card room. That evening, as he rode home, he looked forward to a weekend with his family.

***

Thursday, December 1, 1977

It was another cold, rainy day along the New England coast. The MBTA bus depot in South Boston was busy as the drivers made their shift changes and vehicles needing repair were shuttled, or towed, into the massive garages where transmissions would be fixed or windshield wipers made to work again. Busses were brought here from all over the city and the parking lot was littered with parts and old vehicles that were being cannibalized. The driving rain made the gloom even deeper as the weak winter sun sank low in the sky, silhouetting the busses against a small brick building in the corner of the lot. Uniformed men were coming and going, holding their hats against the weather. They entered the building and climbed a flight of stairs to a small room, walked past the sergeant's desk and ambled into a larger roll call room where they would be inspected and prepared for duty.

Officer Lijoi was ready for another evening shift riding the busses and trains, staring down gang bangers and smiling at old ladies and commuters. He wanted out of transit and into something that offered better pay and benefits, and less riding around. He waited for roll call by reading a small green and yellow pamphlet titled. '300 Most Abused Drugs'. He scanned the glossy pages and tried to store the images of Mellaril's yellow tablets against Darvon's yellow tabs. *Millaril is round, Darvon is oblong.*

Another officer walked by and saw the pamphlet in Lijoi's hands. "What's with that? Why do you study that shit? Leave it to the pros." He punched Lijoi in the shoulder and laughed, pointing a finger in Lijoi's face.

"That's how you become a pro, studying this shit," replies Ernie.

Sgt: "Roll call, is everyone ready?"

The men all stood in a row and waited assignments for the night.

Sgt: "Lijoi! Lijoi!"

Ernie: "Here, Sergeant."

Sgt: "Report to the Chief's office. He wants to speak with you."

The room erupted into jeers and catcalls. "Ernie, what did you do now?" laughingly. The other men whooped and ooohed and pointed at him as he made his way to the door and down the stairs to the office where an assistant chief named Eli Murphy was waiting behind the desk. Lijoi did not like Murphy, but kept that fact to himself. His feeling about the man was rooted in an incident two years earlier, when Lijoi asked for time off to deal with a family matter and Murphy had responded by saying, "Your family ain't my problem". Murphy was running the department at the time as chief, because the actual Chief was very ill and possibly dying of cancer.

Now Lijoi stood at the desk and waited for what Murphy had to say. As he stood there he asked himself what this could be about and whether he had done anything that could have gotten him into trouble. He thought about his recent arrests and wondered if any of them had involved someone with connections at the police department.

Murphy had a folder in front of him.

Murphy: "You arrest a guy at North Quincy station a couple weeks ago? The guy had some pills on him?"

"Yeah," Ernie replied. "Quincy detective took the kid, he seemed to know them and they knew him."

"Well, you made a good impression on him. Your knowledge of the drugs impressed them. The detective liked your attitude; He thinks you got street smarts." Murphy stared at Lijoi for a moment and saw what the Quincy detective had seen; a cocky Italian kid from Brooklyn. Ernie was in his early thirties but he looked ten years younger. His profile on a police report would have read: white male, dark skin, curly black hair, five feet eight inches tall, 185 pounds a scar across his face, nose and eyebrows. He looked like what he was, a former street fighter. His gaze said he was one step ahead of you.

Murphy: "Quincy Police have a proposition for you. Would you be interested in working undercover? Quincy needs somebody to work deep undercover for a narcotics investigation. The job should last no more than thirty days. It's a dangerous job, Very dangerous."

Ernie had two reactions. The first one was immediate, but he kept it to himself. He wanted the job, the second he shared with Murphy.

Ernie: "I need to talk this over with my wife," he said. "I can't make this decision without talking to her."

Murphy: "I don't blame you for that, it will concern her as well as you in many ways, I'm sure. Let me know as

soon as you can and good luck no matter what you decide."
With that, Murphy motioned to the door to indicate that the
meeting was over.

Officer Lijoi's feet were light as he thought about the
offer. *Out of uniform, on the streets, and off the trains and
busses, this could work out in a lot of ways,* he thought to
himself.

Quincy's police department had better benefits, assuming he could turn a temporary assignment into a permanent
job. He had his entire shift to figure out what he would say
to Teresa to get her to accept the assignment. He would tell
her about the danger of the job, but he would not emphasize
it. He knew it would have an impact on his family, but at
that moment, he had no idea how profound it would be and
what his decision would mean to Teresa.

***

Ernie spent the next few hours riding a bus, lost in
thought about deep undercover work. A small African-
American girl, who appeared to be about 8 years old, got
on alone and quietly went to the back, where she sat by
herself. The bus driver, also African-American, glanced at
her as she got on and then he began his runs. He stopped
often; every eight, ten, fifteen blocks. The little girl did not
get off. She sat by herself in the back, never speaking,
never showing interest in where the bus was going or where
it stopped.

Finally, the bus driver's shift ended. The girl was still
sitting in the back. Lijoi walked to her and saw that she was
holding a twenty-dollar bill. She had marks on her arms
and neck and stared at the policeman. The bus driver came
to the back of the bus where the girl was sitting at Ernie's
request. He wanted a witness to this little girl being alone.

"What are you doing here alone?" Lijoi asked of the
little girl.

Girl: "Riding the bus," she replied.

Ernie: "How old are you?"

Girl: "Seven."

Ernie: "Why are you riding the bus late at night?"

Little girl: "My mommy gave me money and told me to go out because her boyfriend is there."

Lijoi noticed the girl's arms and saw round, red marks. He and the driver carefully pulled the top of her dress away from her neck and back area and saw that her back was covered in the same red circles.

Ernie: "What are these marks on you?" he asked.

Girl: "That's what my mommy does when she gets mad at me. She touches me with her cigarettes."

Lijoi and the driver looked at each other. They were both very upset at hearing this and could only look at each other in amazement. Ernie could see the hatred for the little girl's mother in the eyes of the driver.

Ernie: "I'll take her to the station and see what I can do."

***

Lijoi took the little girl to the transit police station and tried to contact a social services agency, but was told there was nothing that could be done. He told the duty sergeant that he wanted to take the girl home with him, but the sergeant said he could be charged with kidnapping. In the end, he took the girl back to her own home and threatened her mother with arrest if it ever happened again. She promised that it would not.

Ernie: "If I ever see this child out late at night or with burn marks on her body again, I will find a hundred ways to arrest you," he said.

Mother: "Yes, sir," she replied.

Ernie handed the little girl a business card with his personal phone numbers on it, but he never saw the girl again.

That night, after his shift on the bus, he went home and told Teresa, his wife about the girl.

Ernie: "By the way," he said, "I got an offer to go undercover for Quincy." He told her what Murphy had said and in an off-hand way, mentioned that it might be a little more dangerous than working as a transit cop.

Ernie: "Teresa, remember that this could be a very big opportunity for us. If I can do a top job there, maybe they will offer me a permanent position with the Quincy Police. We would have better income and better benefits for us and the kids. It's definitely something to take into consideration.

Teresa could see in his face that he wanted the job and knew he could take care of himself on the street. Neither she nor Ernie had any way of knowing what the life of a deep undercover cop was really like. At that moment, it was just another job, an opportunity for Ernie to maybe make more money and provide more benefits for her and their two boys. *If it makes him happy, why not?* She thought.

The next day, Lijoi told Assistant Chief Murphy he would accept the temporary assignment to work undercover for the Quincy Police Department.

"Report to a Lieutenant Walter Lyme at the Quincy Police headquarters right after the holidays," Murphy said. "Take care of yourself."

Chapter 2

First Meeting

Wednesday, January 4, 1978.

Officer Lijoi drove his car to the Quincy Police Department and looked for a parking spot in the lot that had been cleared of the previous night's snow. By nine o'clock the temperature had climbed only to the mid teens, but the morning sunshine had begun to melt the glaze left by the plows in the parking lot. Lijoi was nervous and reminded himself to offer a firm handshake to the lieutenant who ran the Quincy narcotics unit. He wanted to make a good impression.

The lieutenant's name was Walter Lyme. He was a tall, thin Irishman in his mid to late fifties, whose hair was thinning. He had a friendly, open face but his eyes had the look of someone accustomed to sizing up others very accurately.

"C'mon in," he said, motioning Lijoi to follow him down a short hallway to an office marked, Narcotics. Lyme unlocked the door and entered, passing several unoccupied desks as he walked to a small office at the back of the room, where he sat down and opened a folder.

Lt: Lyme: "Lijoi. What kind of name is that?"

Ernie: "My people came from Italy, but we have a French name," he replied.

Ernie related a family story that went back hundreds of years to the centuries when France ruled Italy and the formation of what has become known at the Mafia, which, Lijoi said, was formed by the Italian people to fight and take the government out of the hands of the French so that Italians could rule Italy and this was back in the 1100's.

Lt. Lyme let Ernie tell his story and when he had finished said, "That's an interesting story, Ernie. You're articulate, that's important in this business. Now let's get to the point. Do you know why you're here?"

Ernie: "Yes, sir, to act as an undercover agent for the City of Quincy."

Lt. Lyme: "Can you tell me your ideas about the job?"

Ernie: "Well, sir, I expect that it will be a job in which I must contact drug dealers and make buys from them and establish as much as I can about them." Lijoi was unusually formal in his speech, hoping to impress the lieutenant.

Lyme looked at the officer and explained the assignment. "You should know that if you are accepted for this job, there will be only four people who will know exactly who you are. I'll make sure that you will always have a backup crew available whenever you need them. We have a lot of information that we will be funneling to you so that you can be at the right places to meet people that are dealing the most. We have several people that we are aware of right now. The detectives will go over that with you when they meet you. At times, you will leave the city because people you meet will have contacts outside Quincy and there will be many variations on the job. But right now I want you to understand one thing. This is a very dangerous job, Ernie. Never forget that a bullet is waiting around every corner and do not underestimate the drug people, the dealers or the suppliers.

"You probably already know this, but you must never put a drink down. If you do, someone may place some drugs in it and you can be seriously injured. You don't know what the bad guys know and who may be telling them the information about what we may be doing. The only people you can trust are right here and NEVER trust anyone else as long as you are working this deep cover job."

Lt. Lyme paused to let it all sink in, watching Lijoi's reaction. The officer looked back, his street stare from his youth in Brooklyn saying little about what was on his mind. Ernie acknowledged what was being said.

The lieutenant continued with his questions:

Lt. Lyme "Any restrictions? Duty restrictions?"

Ernie: "No, Sir."

Lt. Lyme: "Any family issues or reasons why you can't take this assignment?"

Ernie: "No, Sir."

Lt. Lyme: "Any problems with alcohol or anything like that?"

Ernie: "No, Sir."

Lijoi had a secret. It was a secret that could end his career as a cop. The secret was something his doctor called Arteriovenous Malformation. It was a knot of veins in his left frontal lobe that had formed during his development in his mother's womb and would remain hidden until the night Lijoi and his partner arrested two drunks, one of whom hit Lijoi on the head with a magnum of champagne, causing the malformation to become active. After the drunks had been cuffed and transported to a precinct house in Boston, Lijoi stood before the duty sergeant and experienced an aura, then a seizure. The aura was a sense that Lijoi was speeding up as the rest of the world slowed down. Then he experienced nothing at all. When it was over, he found himself on the floor, staring into the faces of his fellow officers. Two days later he was released from the hospital. The department classified the seizure as a result of the blow to his head. Lijoi's doctor told him it was epilepsy and prescribed a drug called Dilantin, an anti-seizure medication. Lijoi lived with it privately, fearing that the word "epilepsy" would cost him everything he had worked for. His doctor told him the seizures could return, but he had not had one on the job, and the ones he had in his private hours did not prevent him from leading a normal life. He was forced to limit his exposure to alcohol and drugs. He stood before Lieutenant Lyme, accepting a job involving both, and explained, "I don't drink much."

Lyme laughed. "A cop who doesn't drink? Imagine that!" He closed the folder and put it aside.

Lijoi's face remained expressionless.

Lt. Lyme: "Ernie, there are some very important points that you must comply with. These are very important points:

"#1) you will, I repeat, you will supply me with a report each and every day.

"#2) you will not go anywhere without someone in this unit knowing where you are going, why and with whom. Am I clear?"

Ernie: "Yes sir,"

Lt. Lyme: "We're gonna give you a cover name with a driver's license, and put a special phone line in your home under that name. We'll give you a few hundred dollars buy money to start out with and we'll make arrangements for whatever you need down the road."

Ernie: "Yes sir."

Lt. Lyme: "We have to start by changing your name. Pick something you will answer to. Think about it and pick an address, something on the other side of Boston, take a ride this afternoon to look around. We'll get you a new license and a new car. Change your appearance. Don't shave or cut your hair for a while. Look at the people you see in the dives and dress like them."

Ernie: "Yes sir." Officer Ernie Lijoi Sr. was about to disappear.

Lt. Lyme: "Ernie, why'd you take this job?"

Ernie: "Well, sir, I'm very interested in narcotics for one, and for another, I may want to transfer to the Quincy

Police Department some day and this will be good for my background."

Lyme smiled. "Okay. Be here tomorrow morning and ask for Tommy. He'll set everything up for you. After that you will not come into the station again until after this job is completed which should be in about thirty (30) days and when you do come in tomorrow, come in the back way. Good luck."

***

That afternoon Ernie Lijoi Sr. became Eddie Pannoni of 1066 Center Street, Boston; a street thug who bought drugs and guns in Boston and sold them in New York. He picked the address at random while he and Teresa drove the streets, looking for a place where a guy like Eddie Pannoni would live. They had no idea at that time what they were getting themselves into.

Teresa was a small, cheerful woman whose Italian family had settled in what was then the small town of Dedham, near Boston. She met Ernie in Falmouth on Cape Cod during beach week following her high school graduation, and was swept off her feet by the street-wise New Yorker who was stationed at a nearby Air Force base. He was brash and outgoing, and he walked over to her table at a pizza joint to invite her and her friends to a party that night, just like that. Four months later they were married. She was eighteen. He was twenty-one.

Thirteen years later she rode with him to help him become someone else, a street guy named Eddie Pannoni, gun runner and drug dealer. Some of those years were hard. He had struggled to support his family and had worked at a number of jobs before he became a police officer. Things were stable now. They owned a home in Dedham and often spent weekends in Maine. The boys were still young and they agreed that they would try not to let the boys know exactly what Ernie was doing. They felt it was best to keep the children safe from the street garbage that Ernie would encounter in the new job.

***

Thursday, January 5, 1978.

The streets of Quincy were slushy as the snow melted. The wind came in off the Atlantic Ocean at nearly thirty-miles per hour at midday, picking up the moisture from the melting snow and creating conditions that residents of eastern Massachusetts call "raw". The wet, cold air would cut through even layered clothing and drove most people indoors.

The man who would now be known as Eddie Pannoni, drug dealer and gun runner, parked his car at the Quincy police station and went inside to ask for Tommy, the office manager, a guy who took it as a personal mission to take care of the officers in the detective unit, especially those who worked undercover.

Tommy asked "Eddie" for his new name and address which Ernie supplied. Tommy then contacted the motor vehicles registry to get a driver's license under the new name. He then made arrangements for a special telephone line to be installed in Eddie's house.

Tommy: Your all set with one exception, follow me."

Ernie followed Tommy down the back stairs to the garage area where he pointed out the new car that Ernie would be using and gave him the keys to a new white Ford Thunderbird convertible.

"This is your car," Tommy said. "You need to meet a couple of narcotics officers tonight so they can show you some hot spots. Detective Churn and detective Rule, meet them in the parking lot of St. Catherine's in Milton about seven o'clock. Go to the registry and speak with the supervising clerk, he will give you your license under the new name. If you need anything, let me know, but don't come by here. Lieutenant Lyme instructed me to give you this." He handed the brand-new Eddie Pannoni an envelope containing three hundred dollars. "This is to get you started on your drug buys." He then gave Eddie a small card with a telephone number written on the back. "This is the number to call to get around the switchboard. It rings on Lyme's desk. Call it when you need something or when you report to him. Good luck, you'll need it, you're about to enter into one of the toughest jobs and thankless jobs there is. "

***

By seven o'clock Officer Lijoi, now Eddie Pannoni was a licensed driver in the state of Massachusetts. His official photograph showed a scruffy looking, dark complexioned man who needed a shave. He was wearing a hooded sweatshirt, but his head was bare and the image revealed dark, curly hair. He stared into the camera with a slight smile that someone so inclined could describe as a smirk. He did not look like a cop. He could claim to be Italian, Latino, and any number of other ethic identities. He looked like a man who was confident of himself.

Eddie Pannoni 1978

Eddie drove the new white Ford convertible into the parking lot of St. Catherine's church and saw a beat up four-door sedan parked under a light post. It looked like a car that had a lot of hard miles on it. Two men were inside, smoking and waiting for Eddie. He pulled into the spot next to the sedan and got out, walking to the driver's side, where the window was slowly being wound down. The driver was Detective Abraham "Abe" Churn, the man who put forth the name of Office Ernie Lijoi Sr. for the undercover job.

"Nice wheels," he said, extending his hand through the window. "Welcome to Quincy. Get in back."

Eddie opened the door behind the driver and settled into the back seat, which was littered with food wrappers and two spare sets of handcuffs.

"Sorry for the mess," Churn said. "We don't get many passengers we give a shit about." He laughed. "We gotta clean it out at the end of the shift." He introduced the man in the passenger seat. "He's Detective Bob Rule."

Rule: "My name is a derivative of a much longer Swedish name." as he extended his hand. "Like his name is really Churn?"

They both smiled, Churn began conversation, "How ya doing? We're gonna take you round to show you some shit holes. Ready for a little ride?"

Eddie sat back and listened as the two men in the front seat explained the drug business in Quincy and the rest of the Boston area.

These men had no idea that Ernie grew up in a drug infested area of Brooklyn and that his first view of an overdose was at the age of twelve (12) years old. He saw a young man, about fifteen (15) years old laying at the bottom of a stair well with a needle sticking out of his arm. He would never forget that sight.

"Shit comes from everyplace," Bob said, waving at the windshield of the car. "We get it all, Heroin, Cocaine, Pills,

Marijuana and more by the ton. We got guns coming in. Bikers and shit bags buying and selling. It's a fucking rat hole."

Ernie: It may change, but in my opinion; not all drug users are bad people. Many of them are good people at heart; they are just in a bad business."

Rule: That could be and this is where you come in." Churn glanced at him from the rear view mirror. "You're going into the rat hole to get some rats. Take us to the head rat and let's bring them all down. Clean out the sewer, so to speak."

Ernie: "I grew up in Brooklyn, New York. Drugs are not new to me; they have been around as long as I can re-member. I've lost many friends to this danger."

Rule: "My first contact with any druggies was when I started this job."

Ernie looked out the window as the car slowed in a neighborhood of older, rundown buildings.

"We got problems right here," Bob said. "See that place? Ray's Place? The one with the fucked up sign? The "s" is missing. That would be a good place for you to start. It's a biker's bar where they and their friends hang around. We get information constantly about the drugs being sold in this place. We could go in there right now and get high just breathing the smoke in the air. You can get anything you want in there."

"Guns, too," said Churn. "That's our biggest problem right now. Guns, we got word that some guy named Bill or Billy is dealing guns or renting them out for jobs. We don't know who the hell he is, but we do know that he hangs out there sometimes. I don't think he's a biker, but he may be one of those guys who like to hang around them to pretend to be bad asses."

Ernie: "Yeah, well, if you're dealing guns, maybe you are a bad ass."

Churn laughed and said, "You better watch your own ass around here. We don't know who this fucken Billy is or where he gets his shit and we certainly don't know what he is capable of, so be careful. We need you to find out. We're gonna be around to back you up, but you're gonna be doing this on your own as much as possible. We have other work to do and we could only ruin it for you if we are observed, you understand? I think you've got the stones for this, but you gotta remember to cover your ass at all times."

Ernie looked at the neighborhood and thought about where he grew up. There was nothing in Quincy that was tougher than Brooklyn, New York, during the 1950s. Punks, he thought, these guys are punks, and I know how they think. *Most of these guys are typical drug users and what they call today gang bangers who break into cars to steal radios and break into homes to steal anything they can.*

The detectives drove him back to St. Catherine's in Milton.

Ernie: "Ray's have a pool table?" he asked.

Bob: "Yeah, couple, do you play?"

Ernie: "Yeah, a little. I used to play quite a bit, as a kid, you know." In fact, Eddie, as Ernie Lijoi, had been a pool hustler as a teenager and had cleaned out more than a few "well connected" neighborhood characters. A local don had cautioned him to miss a shot now and then, just to keep the peace. Later, in the Air Force, he made good money on the pool table.

Bob: "Good place to start," Churn pulled into the parking lot and stopped at Eddie's new convertible. "Good luck, we'll be available if you need us and we'll be in touch with Lieutenant Lyme about your reports. Meet us right here at midnight every night for the next two weeks. We won't be in the same car, but you will, so we'll find you. We're here to back you up. Welcome to the team, keep your head down and stay safe."

***

Eddie drove the new car home and thought about his new life. The telephone company was coming the next day to install a red phone in Eddie's bedroom. He had received permission from Lieutenant Lyme to connect a tape recorder to monitor all of the calls from the rats he would stir up. This recorder was for Ernie's protection; in the event that he disappeared, the police would have somewhere to start. The recordings would be evidence if Eddie disappeared.

Teresa was waiting for him when he got home. "How'd it go?" she asked.

"Good. It was good. It looks like I'm just gonna be shooting pool for awhile. A lot like being back in Brooklyn when I was a kid. Should be fun."

"Tough life," she teased, "I think you can handle it/ You're right, It'll be like being back in Brooklyn."

He sat in his easy chair, the one that faced the television as he waited for dinner to be ready. *Yeah*, he thought. *Just like Brooklyn.*

Chapter 3

The old days

Friday, August 15, 1958
Brooklyn, New York
The heat rose off the pavement on St. Mark's Avenue and swept into the open windows where the women were sitting, watching the boys outside as they tried to open the fire hydrants. It was 91 degrees at LaGuardia, but the city seemed hotter. The air did not move and Brooklyn experienced a summer tropical mood, with the neighborhood mothers slowly fanning themselves as they perched in the windows watching the kids on the street.

Occasionally a woman would shout at one of the children, threatening to tell the mother that he or she was misbehaving.

Neighborhood Women: "Hey, Ernesto! Be good, I tella you Momma."

It was how the neighborhood worked in the 1950's. It was a big family with thousands of Italians living and working together, watching each other's children, knowing each other's secrets, going to the same church, and dealing with the "mustachios", the "Connected Ones", known to the outside world as The Mafia. They functioned as senior overseers. The mustachios ran numbers games and the bars and restaurants and had their own ways of enforcing the neighborhood rules. Most of the trouble in the neighborhood was caused by the kids, and that is why the women watched from the windows and the man meted out what they felt was proper punishment in the form of a smack or a swat. It was an Old World social system that relied on force or the threat of it to maintain the order of the streets.

Ernie Lijoi Sr. was almost fifteen. He was a rising leader in the Washington Avenue gang, a group of boys who acted as enforcers of neighborhood security from outsiders; the Irish on one side, the Jews on the other. Most of the neighborhoods had gangs of their own and street fights were part of life in the city. Ernie never shied away from a fight, but he was not drawn to a life of violence and crime, as some of the other boys were. He had no desire to be an enforcer for one of the mustachios or a numbers runner, although he had run a few errands for them and had been well paid.

Ernie's love was playing the game of pool or billiards as it is more commonly known. He began playing the game at age twelve and discovered he had a talent for the game. He had to change his birth certificate so that he could get into the pool hall legally. He went to the church, St. Teresa's, and obtained a copy of his baptism record. In those days they wrote them out in hand with ink. He soaked the certificate in milk over night and the next day he had a certificate with nothing written on it. The ink was taken away by the milk. He re-wrote the dates and signed it. He was now sixteen years old and could play pool. Many of his friends did the same thing.

He played in the recreation room at St. Theresa's Catholic Church with the other boys at first, but the real action was in the pool halls and bars, where the men played for money. As a teenager, Ernie moved up fast in the pool crowd. New York City required that anyone entering a pool hall be at least sixteen years of age. Proof of age was required, but it could take many forms.

Andy's Pool Hall offered six nine-foot tables covered in green felt. Most of the players were in their teens, like Ernie, carrying baptism certificates that had been soaked in milk. The boys wore jeans, or dungarees, rolled up at the cuff, sneakers and short-sleeved shirts rolled to reveal their upper arms. Some of them wore "duck tail" hairstyles, combed back on the sides to meet in the back, and held in place with shiny hair oil. They kept their cigarettes in their rolled up sleeves or one single cigarette behind their ears.

Andy's was stifling in the summer heat. Air conditioning was not common in those years and aging ceiling fans that were brown from accumulated dust and cigarette smoke slowly rotated the hot air. Andy was a tall, thin man who walked with limp caused by an artificial leg that was the result of an injury during World War Two. Prosthetic devices were not as advanced as they would become in later decades, but the one Andy wore was enough for him to get around without crutches or a wheelchair and it allowed him to run his pool hall. The hall was set up and started by the mob as a neighborhood gift for this war hero because of his sacrifice while in the service of his country.

Andy ran a bookmaking operation from the pool hall and he set up large exhibition games in which real money was on the table and the players were often from outside the neighborhood. These games filled the pool hall and side bets mixed with the beer and cigarettes that the patrons brought in. Today, it was just the neighborhood kids and change on the table.

Four of the boys gathered at the head of one of the tables to determine who would get the break on the rack. The game was "8 ball". The cue ball was placed about six inches from the rubber bumper. Each shooter hit the ball to the far rail, where it bounced and rolled back to the head of the table. The order of shooting during the game was determined by who came closest to the head rail without hitting it. Experience had given Ernie a fine touch and on this afternoon his shot came within an inch of the head rail before it stopped. He won the break, but lost the game. He placed a quarter under the bumper on the table, which Andy scooped up, and played again. This time he won. Ernie played into the evening and went home.

The next day, Saturday, was cooler and offered a welcome relief from the city summer. Ernie worked as a delivery boy for a neighborhood grocery store. The orders were telephoned in and filled by Ernie and the owner, who put the canned goods, produce, meat and other items into cardboard boxes. Ernie carried two boxes, one on each shoulder for several blocks, then, typically, up eight or ten flights of stairs. The customers tipped him usually a dime or fifteen cents, at times a quarter per delivery, very rarely, only in the rich neighborhoods he may get fifty cents if they felt generous, and the grocer paid him a dollar an hour. He made twenty to thirty dollars on a good weekend, and he used the money to gamble at pool and, as he got older, to buy beer and sometimes cheap booze for the Friday night dances at St. Teresa's school.

After work, he went to Andy's until around ten o'clock and left with more money than he went in with and thought it had been a good weekend. He walked down St Marks Avenue in the cool summer evening and felt like the world was at his feet. Women were sitting in windows, calling out to him, telling him his parents were waiting at home and to be a good boy. He waved and laughed.

He heard shouting near his building and saw several people running to two men who were fighting. They were both in their early twenties and they were trying to kill each other, first with fists, then with knives. One of the men was from the neighborhood, the other an outsider from the Irish area. The Irishman rushed the Italian and stabbed him, then ran for his life. The Italian was bleeding on the sidewalk and the people from the neighborhood called an ambulance and the police. There was talk of vengeance and finding the Irishman and taking care of him and his friends.

Ernie stood on the sidewalk and watched as the ambulance crew placed the wounded man on a stretcher then placed him into the back of the ambulance. He watched as the police officers questioned the witnesses, whose memories were blurred and amounted to we-didn't-see-anything. The neighborhood would take care of the Irishman and leave the police out of it. At least that is what many people on the sidewalk and in the windows were thinking.

It was midnight before Ernie walked into his family's fourth floor apartment. His father was waiting and angry.

Mr. Lijoi Sr. "Ernie, where the hell have you been? We've been worried about you?" he shouted. He was no man to cross.

Joseph Lijoi had been born in Sant' Andrea, Calabria, Italy in 1921 and he came to America at the age of 7 years old. He was a Golden Gloves champion fighter before the war and saw action as a navigator on a B-29. He broke his back in a crash of the plane that he was navigating. He pulled out the Pilot and Co-Pilot both before he collapsed with a broken back. He was in a full body cast for over six months after that incident. After the war, it was a short leap from being an expert in radio to the newest thing on the market, Television. He learned the new business of television and built the neighborhood's first set in the basement of the apartment building where he lived, and he invited the neighbors over to watch fights on the set's five-inch screen. The room was filled with neighborhood men during fight night.

Joseph was an Old World parent and was, to use a phrase that was popular at the time, quick with his hands. Kids needed a good smack now and then to keep them in line, he thought. His boy Ernest was strong willed and given to violence and trouble. At least that is now Joseph thought of the young man, so he tried to keep him on a short leash. He demanded that Ernie be home at the time he set and tonight was an example of what happens when the boy thinks he can get away with being late.

It was loud and emotional and when it was over Ernie promised himself that he would leave his father's house when he could find a way out. It took him two years.

**

Friday, October 7, 1960
Brooklyn, New York

Ernie Lijoi had become one of the war lords and leader of the Washington Avenue gang, a group of over one hundred neighborhood boys and the ones who protected the Italian-controlled blocks from outsiders. Violence was common. Today, (in the year 2014) Ernie would say that he and his friends were the stupid ones.

He had the scars to prove it. He had had over three hundred stitches all over his body with (57) fifty seven stitches on his face alone, yet he was still days away from his seventeenth birthday. On his right ankle the letter "W" proudly proclaimed his membership in the gang. The tattoo had been there since he was nine, when he and some other boys obtained a bottle of India ink and a needle. Some of the boys tattooed a "W" their ankles, some tattooed their hips. It was a badge they would wear for the rest of their lives. The "W" signified Washington Avenue, their gang and area.

Perfect autumn weather greeted Ernie as he walked out of school that afternoon. It was dry and cool and Ernie stopped to comb his hair as he breathed the city air that hinted at diesel and garbage. He walked with an air of confidence that someone who did not know him might consider arrogance, but it was his way of showing the world he was no one to push around. He had worked his way up to the top of the Washington Avenue gang by being tough and loyal, and ready to fight for his turf.

He was worried about life in the neighborhood, but he did not tell anyone. People lived in violence and some of them died. Others just gave up and nodded off to the power of the heroin that was available to anyone who looked for it. They were found dead, sometimes with the needle still in their arm. The block where Ernie lived had an undercurrent of controlled rage that boiled over in ways no one could predict.

He had almost killed a man in such a rage. He was walking home, waving to neighbors and thinking about a girl when he saw his seven-year old brother being beaten. A grown man was holding the boy's arms as another boy hit him in the stomach. His brother was yelling and trying to break the man's grip, but the little boy was no match for the man and was helpless as the other boy pounded him. Ernie ran down the block as the man held his brother, and punched the man in the side of the head, knocking him out. The man fell to the sidewalk and Ernie was on him, stomping him, trying to stomp the man's head. He was out of control with rage. He would have killed the man right there on the sidewalk if neighbors had not intervened and grabbed him, pulling him away.

"You touch him again, I'll kill you," Ernie said, as he was pulled down the block. The man was barely conscious. His little brother was shaken, but not seriously hurt. That night his father told him he had done the right thing.

He had been thinking about his life as his birthday approached. What were his options in life, in the neighborhood? He looked at the older men who had lived all their lives along Washington Avenue and he saw men who ran numbers operations, tended bar, or worked for the mustachios. His father had a good job and worked as an engineer for a defense company, but Ernie did not relish the idea of staying at home to go to school. He and his father were constantly at odds and argued daily about just about everything associated with Ernie's life.

Ernie had been flouting his father's rules and the previous week had gotten drunk on something called "PM", a mixture of liquor and beer. His friends carried him home where his father exploded on his drunken son, who wound up in a heap at the bottom of the stairs.

Remaining at home was not an option, in Ernie's mind. He had been a runner for the mustachios and knew he could find work with the connected ones, but he did not see a future for himself in organized crime. He did not want to be a street fighter all his life.

He walked to Andy's pool hall and played a few games of Chicago Rotation, winning a few dollars. He looked at his friends and wondered where they would be in ten or twenty years. Would they still be here playing pool? Would they be in jail or worse? Would he still be delivering groceries for tips?

His answers came that night and they came in the form of a gang fight.

The Washington Avenue gang had formed a loose alliance with the neighboring Irish and Jewish gangs. The alliance meant fewer fights and a larger territory to move about. However, no such alliance existed with the African-Americans who lived one block down St. Mark's Avenue. There was a candy store on the block that was a cover for a bookmaking operation. Ernie walked to the candy store with a friend. He went inside to look around while his friend remained on the sidewalk. As Ernie looked out through the front window, he saw his friend being beaten by several black kids. Ernie ran outside and threw metal trashcans at the kids who were beating up his friend, but, in the end, both of them had to run because they were outnumbered by about (40) forty to one.

It was Friday night and there was a dance at St. Theresa's school. Ernie ran to the school and banged on the door, yelling that there was a war underway with the black neighborhood. He was a war lord a leader and the kids at the dance listened and acted. Over one hundred boys poured out of the dance and down the block and a mass fight between whites and blacks was underway. Ernie made what he later decided was a stupid move. He ran up a set of stairs to a stoop, where a black kid was holding a milk bottle, as Ernie approached the boy smashed the bottle into Ernie's face, splitting open his cheek, eyebrows, nose and forehead. Ernie did not notice the cut and continued to fight. When it was over his cousin told him his nose was hanging off as Ernie walked away from the area with his cousins Larry and Vinny. They took Ernie to the hospital where he was treated after his Father arrived. Ernie received (57) fifty seven stitches.

Those stitches later affected Ernie in many ways. He glanced in the mirror and saw himself swollen, bruised and looking as though his face had been repaired by a bad tailor. Was this the life he was destined to live? *I gotta get out,* he thought. *I gotta get out of New York.* He would quit high school and find a way out.

His father agreed and suggested the Air Force. Joseph had served in it when it was called the Army Air Corp and believed it would be a good place for his eldest son to learn to become an adult. Following Ernie's seventeenth birthday, Joseph Lijoi signed the papers that would allow Ernie to get out of Brooklyn. There was only one problem. Ernie looked like he had been in a traffic accident. He still had stitches in his face and the Air Force doctor who gave Ernie a physical wanted to classify him 4F, physically unfit for service. Ernie told the doctor that the Air Force was his only chance. If he did not get out of the neighborhood, he would either become a junkie or a drug dealer if not dead. The doctor took one last look at Ernie's face and signed a health form stating that Ernie Lijoi Sr. was fit for duty.

It changed his life.

Chapter 4

Knock-out punch

Wednesday, July 10, 1963
Brooklyn, New York
Airman Ernie Lijoi Sr. was home on leave after serving two years in Germany. He had filled out during his time in the service and he was clean cut and wore his black hair short, but his swagger remained as he walked the streets of his neighborhood, shaking hands. Nothing had changed except Ernie. The same faces looked out of the same windows. The grocers, the bartenders, and Andy at the pool hall were all the same. He felt at home, but strange at the same time, as though he was looking back into his childhood. His friends had moved on in life, some worked with organized crime, others were on drugs and still others were working in regular jobs trying to live an honest life. Ernie didn't know exactly which of his old friends was on drugs and which were not, not yet. He would find out.

The summer had been mild in New York and the air was soft but not hot. It smelled of car exhaust, garbage and Italian cooking. To Ernie, it smelled like he was ten years old. He saw an old man he had known all his life coming out of a candy store. The man had run numbers as long as Ernie had been alive. The old man waved. Ernie waved back and shouted some random numbers at the man, which made him laugh.

Ernie stopped at a small neighborhood bar to order a beer. The drinking age in New York in those years was eighteen. It was the first time he had legally consumed alcohol in Brooklyn. He stood at the bar and enjoyed the moment, watching customers come and go. He saw an old friend come into the bar, a young man Ernie had known all of his life. His real name was Robert Louisa, but Ernie knew him as Chinky.

"Jesus fucking Christ!" Chinky said, smiling and shaking hands with Ernie. "Look whose back in the neighborhood."

The two men talked about everyone they knew, and Chinky told Ernie about some parties that were coming up over the weekend. Ernie said he had report to Otis Air Force Base on Cape Cod but he would be back in Brooklyn soon. They talked easily, like old friends. Ernie saw that Chink's eyes were glazed a sign that he was on drugs, but Ernie didn't say or ask anything. He was happy to see Chinky, one of his old corner singing partner's.

Ernie saw an older man at the other end of the bar drinking and laughing with a women and with his son. Ernie knew who this man was because Ernie had been to his apartment several times with his father to repair his TV set, but Ernie didn't know what the man did for a living. The Lijoi's, father and son, would carry large boxes of tools and parts up the stairwells of Brooklyn apartment buildings. Ernie at the age of (11-14) would help his father in the work by getting tools, holding mirrors, etc. as his Dad, Joseph fixed broken TV sets.

The man stared at Ernie and Chinky and his face reddened.

"You gonna try and sell your poison here? You fucking assholes!"

Ernie ignored the man, assuming he was speaking to someone else, but Chinky grew nervous and began to look around for a fast way out of the bar.

"Hey! Assholes! I'm talking to you." The man was standing next to his son, Jimmy Jr., who was silent.

Ernie recalled that the older man, Jimmy, had lost another son to drugs, but he still did not make the connection
that the man was yelling at him and Chinky, until he came
down the bar and stood directly in front of Ernie. He was in
his late forties, heavy, and wearing a suit.

"I'm talking to you and your junkie friend. You his
supplier of that poison?" he said, glaring at Ernie and
Chinky.

"You're not talking to me," Ernie replied, "I don't do
drugs."

Jimmy: "Then you're a supplier, you fuck."

Ernie ignored the man, which infuriated him.

Ernie looked at the bartender. "Can you do something
about this guy?" he asked.

"I'd better go," Chinky said, heading for the door.

The older man said something Ernie couldn't hear and
he bent his left arm up to adjust his watchband with his
right hand. Ernie recognized the move as an old trick to
sucker punch someone to knock him out. Ernie struck first.
The man went down and did not get up; he was out like a
light for a few seconds. Ernie left the bar and when he was
about two hundred feet away, the man came out of the bar
and threw a glass at Ernie, who kept walking, he didn't
need any trouble. He had to return to the base on Cape Cod
where he was assigned.

Two weeks later, Ernie was home again, having hitch-
hiked from Cape Cod to New York. He went to Andy's to
shoot some pool and meet old friends. As soon as he
walked into Andy's, a school chum named Anthony Peroni
saw him. Peroni was a man that Ernie grew up with and
would later in life become well known as Tony Two
Scoops , but that is another story. Tony rushed up to Ernie
and yelled at him: "What the fuck are you doing here?"

Ernie: "I'm on leave. What do you mean?"

Tony: "Remember that guy you hit? Do you know who
he is?"

Ernie: "Of course I know Jim, but he must be a drunk, it's over."

Tony: "He's no drunk, Ernie. He's a lieutenant. He's Jimmy Bendetti. He's connected. He's got a contract on you. You better get the fuck outta here."

Ernie stared at Anthony. "You're crazy. I used to fix his TVs with my father. He knows me. Why would he get a contract on me?"

Tony: "Well, he didn't recognize you, after all you've been away a long time, and no one is telling him who you are in an effort to keep you alive."

"I'll talk to him," Ernie said.

"No," Anthony looked Ernie in the eye. "You don't talk to him. Get out of here and go back to your base. I'll talk to my dad, maybe he can straighten this out."

Ernie left Brooklyn that night and returned to Otis Air Force Base on Cape Cod, Massachusetts. He wondered why Jimmyy Bendetti would want him killed over a simple bar fight. The man was obviously drinking and insulting and he even tried to sucker punch Ernie.

Ernie resolved to work things out with Bendetti, he would talk to him and do his best to keep peace in the neighborhood, when he came home the next time.

***

Saturday, August 31, 1963
Brooklyn

Labor Day weekend emptied out many neighborhoods of New York as families went to the beach or Coney Island for hot dogs and rides. Traffic on Washington Avenue was heavy at mid day as cars stuffed with coolers and folding chairs moved slowly as the children in back seats screamed at each other and pedestrians on the sidewalks.

Ernie had hitched a ride from Otis and had arrived at his parents' apartment after midnight. He slept in his old bed and arose late in the morning to drink a cup of his mother's coffee. His mother Marie Ann was the youngest of (14) fourteen children, stayed at home to raise her children and she endured the strict standards of her husband. She was born Marie Ann Pannoni. Her maiden name would be used by her son years later to create a deep undercover identity. But on that day in Brooklyn, she served him a cup of coffee and looked at him with love. *Such a strong-willed boy*, she thought. *God help him.*

***

Ernie dressed and went to Andy's pool hall to shoot some pool and hang out with friends. He had plans to go to a party that night to meet some girls and maybe have some fun. He stood in front of the pool hall enjoying the summer air and watching his neighborhood, the women in the windows, the kids on the street, the families loading their picnics into cars. As he turned to enter Andy's, he saw a man come rushing across the street. He recognized him as a "connected one" known as Archie who used to give nine-year-old Ernie ten dollars to go to the candy store to get him a twenty-five cent pack of cigarettes.

"Bruno! Hey, Bruno!" the man yelled. Ernie knew the man as "Archie". Archie had always called Ernie by the name of Bruno because that was his uncle's name. Archie and Bruno grew up together in that same neighborhood so Archie called Ernie by his uncles name Bruno. Archie always said that Ernie looked exactly like Bruno as a boy. Ernie's uncle was also connected.

"Bruno! Geez! What the fuck did you do?" Archie was fair-complexioned with the very light skin of a red-haired northern Italian. He always dressed well and today he wore a well-tailored suit.

Ernie: "You talking about Jimmy?"

Archie: "Yeah, I'm talking about Jimmy. Do you know what you did?"

Ernie: "I guess not. What's goin' on, Archie? I need to get this straightened out.

Archie: "Come with me and don't argue." Archie grabbed Ernie by an elbow and moved him across the street to a small neighborhood bar called THE GRAND MARK. It was a bar run and owned by mob bosses. This was where The Appolino Brother's, Vinny and Joey, ran that section of Brooklyn. Everyone in the neighborhood had heard stories about those who walked in the front door of the Grand Mark Bar and went out the back door, feet first, never to be seen again. Others had been made to see the errors of the ways by whatever went on in the bar's back room.

Archie led Ernie to the front door, opened it, and told Ernie to follow him to the back. They walked past the bar and a few curious patrons who were watching Ernie. Their faces had no expression and no one spoke a greeting.

Two men sat at a table in the back. Ernie recognized both of them as the new Don and Capo for the Family, they replaced Johnny Robert who was shot and killed with two shots to the head. Ernie did not recognize the two bodyguards who stood behind them. They were the largest men Ernie had ever seen. He guessed that they were about six feet seven and heavily muscled. They wore expensive tailored suits that did not hide their massive arms and shoulders.

The Brothers were in their sixties and both were balding, with steely grey hair. One of them spoke. Joey was about two years younger than Vinny.

Vinny: "Do you know who you hit?"

Ernie: "Yeah. I hit Jimmy to protect myself and before he could hit me."

Vinny: "Who are you?"

Ernie: "You don't recognize me?" Ernie paused to let the man examine his face. The scar across his cheek, nose, eyebrows and forehead was no longer red, but it defined Ernie's face. "I used to shovel your car out. Me and Anthony. You used to give us twenty dollars when we were done."

Joe: "Anthony, he's the son of one of our people. What's your name?

Ernie: "Ernie. Ernie Lijoi. I'm Joe Lijoi's son and Bruno Lijoi's nephew."

Joe: "Joe the television man and his Brother Bruno who runs a small club with us?"

Ernie: "Yes, that's my old man, Joe Lijoi and my uncle Bruno."

Vinny: "I don't recognize you, kid."

Ernie: "I've been in Germany with the Air Force for two years."

The Brother stared at Ernie for a moment, looking him over.

Vinny: "Tell me what happened," he said.

Ernie told his story, about coming home on leave, going to the bar, running into Chinky, Jimmy's insult, and the punch. He left out the part about how Jimmy threw a glass at him on the street.

Ernie: "What was I supposed to do? Let him hit me and call me a junkie dealer?"

Vinny: "Yes!" The brother replied. "Then you come to us. Don't ever raise a hand to any of our people again. You understand?"

Ernie: "Yes, I understand." Ernie looked at the man and wondered what would happen next. He knew and had heard stories about men that walked in the front door of this bar and were carried out the back door.

Vinny looked at the goons behind him, waved his hand and said: "Call it off," returning his gaze to Ernie.

Vinny: "Young man, I like you. Keep your hands in your pocket and when you get out of the service I have something for a ballsy guy like you." He lifted his chin at Ernie to indicate that the meeting was over and the matter of the contract on Ernie's life was settled.

Ernie and Archie walked back through the bar, past the stares of the men who had observed the meeting, and walked out the front door. Ernie was relieved. Outside, Ernie thanked Archie for his help.

Archie: "You know you're lucky he took a liking to you. There is a back door to that bar."

"I know," Ernie replied. He saw a man approaching from a nearby building. It was Jimmy's son, the one who had remained silent during the outburst in the bar weeks earlier. The young man walked up to Ernie and stared at him.

Jr. "Why did you hit my father?"

Ernie: "That's a stupid question. You were there. If I didn't hit him, he was going to do a job on me."

The young man looked at the sidewalk, then back at Ernie. "You were wrong to hit him. You should have let him get it out of his system. He lost a son, my brother, to that shit."

Ernie looked the man in eye. "I'm not involved with drugs, I'm in the Air Force, home on leave and it's over now, unless you want to create a new problem."

Jr.: "No. No. It's over."

The two men did not shake hands. Ernie turned and went back to his parents' apartment, where he spent the afternoon before going to a party that night.

Chapter 5

The Game Starts

Friday, January 6, 1978.
Quincy, Massachusetts

Ray's Place was everything Ernie Lijoi, now Eddie Pannoni, thought it would be, a complete dive. The glass on the right side of the door had been broken in the distant past and covered with a piece of cardboard from a beer box. The door had not been painted in years and whatever color it had been was long gone to weather and the hands that had pushed it open. Inside, the bar was on the left, along the wall, and motorcycle items were hung from the ceiling and stacked behind the bar, mixed in with whiskey bottles. Formica-topped tables were pushed against the right wall and metal chairs were scattered across the floor where patrons were smoking and pointing at each other. The ceiling disappeared into the smoke and the dim light from the lamps along the wall made it difficult for Eddie to see the back of the place, but he could hear the slap of pool balls coming from the area beyond the bar, so he moved through the smoke to the pool tables. Few people looked up as he moved past them. The smoke reeked of marijuana and an odd odor that Eddie could not place.

A couple of fat, bearded bikers were playing a game of eight-ball at the back table, smoking and drinking beer as two young women watched them. The women were very thin and their skin was pasty in an unhealthy way, as though they had not eaten right for a long time. The bikers were not very good at the game and were frustrated to the point of taking wild shots that sent pool balls onto the floor. They paid no attention to Eddie.

A group of five men had gathered around a second pool table where a game of eight ball was taking place. Money was on the side of the table next to the center pocket and the men had the serious look of gamblers, although slightly stoned. Two men were playing; the others were drinking beer, talking and swearing, either for or against the players.

The first man takes a shot and misses:"Fuck!"

The second man takes a shot and misses: "God dam it!"

First man shoots, makes the shot: "Yes! Fuck yes!"

This is what passed for conversation as Eddie moved closer to the group to watch the game. One of the players looked like he knew what he was doing a good player and possibly a hustler. He seemed set to run the table, but Eddie sensed that he was still in the setup of his hustle. As it played out, the man missed key shots, giving his opponent the false sense that he was not as good as he was. The hustler lost the game and the twenty dollars he had placed on the table. He also seemed drunk and his mark was quick to agree to a rematch for one hundred dollars. The hustler seemed to sober up as the game progressed and ran the table when the mark missed his first shot. The hustler picked up his money, staggered a little for effect, and left. The others stared at him and muttered "What a lucky bastard," behind his back.

"Some fuckers do that and end up dead," muttered one of the men who had watched the game and the hustle.

Eddie was wearing a sweatshirt, short jacket, jeans, and ankle-length black boots with elevated heels. He had a growth of beard, which called attention to the scar that ran across his left cheek, over his nose, and into his left eyebrow. He could have been any street fighter from any big city. He looked at the table and walked over to the wall where he examined a cue stick, holding out straight to determine if it was bent. He then examined the felt tip.

Ernie heard a voice yell towards him: "You a playa?" The questioner was the man who had just lost the hundred dollars, a man Eddie would describe in his report to Lieutenant Lyme as "w/m, 180lbs, blond hair, blue eyes, and tattoo on his right forearm".

Eddie: "Yeah, some," he moved toward the man and held out his hand. "Eddie," he said.

The man took his hand and responded, "Peter, let's play." He racked for eight ball and laid a five-dollar bill on the table. "Break?" he said.

Eddie put his own five on the table and said, "Go ahead."

One of the other men shouted to the bartender, "Hey, Joey, get this man a beer, me, too, bring them for everybody. We can't shoot pool without beer."

He looked at Eddie. "Loser buys the round, you know that." The other men nodded and smiled as the bartender grabbed longneck bottles from a cooler, opened them, and put them on the bar.

Eddie's opponent walked to the bar with the self-important attitude of a man about to accomplish great things for the first time in his life. He gazed at the other men, then at Eddie, and strode to the table to break the rack. He was too intoxicated to hit the cue solidly and the cue ball careened off the left side of the triangle of balls and into the corner pocket.

"Scratch!" The small gallery of beer drinkers spoke as a small chorus.

Eddie saw the man's face redden and he did not want to risk an incident involving a drunk with a cue stick. "Your stick's fucked up," he said. "Get another stick and try it again."

Peter: "Yeah, that's right. It's the fuckin' stick."

The man went to the wall, elaborately chose another stick and returned to the table. This time his break was better and he hit the rack solidly, scattering the balls. Eddie watched the man shoot and altered his game to allow him to win. He was not there to win pool games; he was there to get to know everybody else. After Eddie lost the game, the man took his money, held it up to his friends like he just won an award and left. Eddie stayed there until after midnight, losing four games and winning two, for a loss of ten dollars on the night, plus the cost of four rounds of beer. Eddie nursed one beer all evening.

~ ~ ~

The next morning Eddie went to a fast-print shop in Dedham and picked up two hundred business cards that read, "Eddie Pannoni" and beneath that was the telephone number the police had given him for the red phone that now occupied the bedside table where Eddie and Teresa slept. Beneath the table was a reel-to-reel tape recorder.

That night Ernie gathered the boys in the bedroom and pointed to the RED telephone.

Ernie: "This is Daddy's special work phone. Never answer this phone. Understand? This is Daddy's special telephone. Never answer it. Our family will never get calls on this phone, only Daddy's work calls, and if Daddy is not home, let it ring." Eddie's great fear was that his family would be identified with him as Eddie Pannoni and the words of Lieutenant Lyme rang in his head: "This is dangerous, very dangerous. Be very careful, I cannot stress this point enough."

He spent the rest of day with Teresa and the boys, and went back to Ray's around nine o'clock that night. He played a few games of pool, making sure to lose about half of them. He bought three rounds of beer and introduced himself to everyone he could, passing them his business cards. Several of the men who had been in the place the night before were there and they welcomed Eddie as a friend, making him appear to be a regular. Several of his new friends asked him where he was from and he replied with his New York accent, "I'm originally from New York".

Late in the evening one of men he was shooting pool with named Robby produced a marijuana joint and lit it, offering it to Eddie.

Eddie: "I can't right now, I gotta meet somebody, but I'd like to get some, you know, for later."

Robby: "I don't know, man, this is all I got. I might know somebody's got a little something, but not tonight, you know, it's late, if you're around Monday?"

Eddie: "Yeah, sure." Thinking to himself, I have to start small and this may be a start.

Robby: "I can get you, maybe quarter ounce, something like that."

Eddie: "How much?" Eddie was entering the rat hole.

Robby: "Maybe twenty-five."

Eddie: "Sounds good. You got my card. Call me Monday and I'll buy you a couple beers and pick the shit up."

Robby: "OK, we'll talk Monday."

***

Monday, January 9, 1978.

The red telephone rang around noon. Eddie was sitting at the kitchen table, making notes about the weekend. His first report to Lieutenant Lyme was due and he was writing on a lined sheet of paper. Teresa had agreed to type the report later that day. Eddie moved to the bedroom and stared at the phone as it rang.

Eddie: "Yeah," he said, as picked it up.

Robby: "Eddie?" the voice at the other end was unsure and a little too loud.

Eddie: "Yeah," Eddie said, "Who's this?"

Robby: "Robby, you know, we met the other night at Ray's. You wanted something."

Eddie: "Hey! How ya doin'? We okay with that?"

Robby: "Listen. I know a guy's got something; He is gonna be around this afternoon, maybe four, five o'clock. I don't know if it's any good. He wants twenty dollars for half bag. I need five for myself, kind of a finder's fee, you know. You okay with that?"

Eddie: "I'm okay with that right now, it depends if it's any good. I'll see you at Ray's, about four o'clock?"

Eddie hung up the phone and watched as the tape recorder stopped turning. He closed the bedroom door and went to the closet where he kept a .38 caliber snub-nosed revolver locked in a box and on a high shelf in his closet. The gun was equipped with a trigger guard to prevent it from firing if one of the boys found it. He took it down, checked to see that no shells were in the cylinder, and cleaned it. It was not a common police model and had no markings that would tip off anyone that the weapon had been issued to Eddie by law enforcement. It was the kind of weapon that a street thug would carry, if he could get his hands on one. It would be useful in a close situation, but nearly worthless at any distance where its accuracy and stopping power would be limited.

He went to the closet near the front door and grabbed a light jacket, placing the gun into his belt at the small of his back. The day was unusually warm but the wind was picking up, and the TV weather girl said a front was coming through and conditions would change by evening. He told Teresa he had to go out and would be back late. Then he went to the Thunderbird and placed the .38 revolver under the driver's seat and headed for Quincy, where he drove through neighborhoods, memorizing street patterns and examining the houses and the people who walked the neighborhoods. He waved at everyone who looked at him and twice stopped to introduce himself to men whose cars appeared broken down. He handed out his card and said he was a mechanic who could repair vehicles right in their driveways.

He saw young men and women, about twenty years of age, hitchhiking and gave them rides. He struck up a conversation getting them to talk about themselves.

Eddie: "I'm up from New York, doing some business, you know, street business." He winked, "You know what I'm talking about." He gave them his card and asked: "What are your names?"

"I'm Louise and he's Trip" the young girl replied.

The young men asked, "What you got?" He was thin, brown hair, brown eyes, army field jacket and black boots with well worn heels."

Eddie saw an opportunity to try out his back story and see how it worked.

Eddie: "What you mean?

Trip: "What you selling?"

Eddie: "I don't have anything to sell right now, but I'm looking. I got customers in New York. You know about anybody selling something for the head, you know what I mean. I'm interested in quantity. Plus, I can fix cars," he laughed.

Trip: "I'm on my way to get some grass right now," said the hitchhiker.

Eddie: "Maybe I can buy some from you," Eddie said.

Trip: "You drive us there, but you can't come in. Just give me the money. I'll get it and give you the grass."

Eddie: "Right, I'm just gonna give you some money to watch you walk away."

Trip: "Park in front, you can watch me go in."

Eddie drove the young man to a duplex and parked on the street. There was an old chain link fence in front of the house and the gate was held open by a stick jammed into the hinges. The rain and wind were picking up. Eddie gave the man twenty dollars and watched as he went to the door, knocked and went inside. Five minutes later the man came back and handed Eddie a small bag of marijuana. The man went back into the house without waving to Eddie, who drove away after noting the address, time, date and the names the young man and women had given him.

Eddie parked his car on the street near Ray's and stepped out into a driving rain and gale force winds. A front was moving through Boston and the temperature was dropping. An awning over a shop window ripped and flapped in the wind. The rain turned to snow and he regretted his choice of a light jacket. He walked into Ray's, forcing the door open, and allowing it to slam behind him, as a tall biker looked up attracted by the door slamming and smiled at Eddie.

Robby was at the bar, nursing a beer and looking a little stoned. Eddie walked over to him and sat down, but Robby jumped up and asked," You got a car?"

The two men left the bar and went back into the weather. They drove to an address on Burns Avenue where Robby told Eddie to pull over. By now the wind had died down and a steady snow was failing.

"You got some cash?" Robby asked?

"I'm supposed to give you money and wait around to see if you come back?" Eddie said, "Maybe I can see where my money is going."

"I'll be right back," Robby said, as he opened the car door and walked through the snow and up the stairs to a porch, where he knocked on the door. He spoke to a man at the front door, gesturing at Eddie, and nodding his head. He waved at Eddie to join him and both men walked into a living room, stomping their feet on at a mat near the door. There were two men in the room. One of them was sitting on a chair, looking at the two men who were shaking the snow from their clothes. Another man, the one who had answered the door, was standing back, looking at Eddie.

"Who're you?" he asked.

Eddie knew he was being examined by someone who had a lot to lose if he made bad social choices, such as dealing with cops.

"Eddie," he said, offering his hand. "And you are?"

The man did not take Eddie's hand or answer, offering instead a seat on the sofa. Eddie made quick mental notes. W/m, 5'10", 140lbs, brown eyes, dark brown hair, cuts over left eye, late 20s. The other man was younger but heavier and had lighter hair and a mustache.

The man went into the kitchen and Eddie heard a cabinet door opening and closing. He came back into the living room with two joints, which he lit and passed around. Robby was as excited as a child, grinning stupidly as the marijuana was shared. Eddie simulated smoking the joint by putting to his mouth and inhaling loudly without sucking on the joint, allowing his face to redden as though he had taken a deep drag, he then passed the joint to the heavy man, who gazed at it without looking at Eddie.

"Tony, I'm Tony Cole, nice to meet you." The voice came from the man with the cuts over his eyes. "That guy over there, he's Pauly. You can call him asshole." He laughed and pointed at the heavier man.

"You can kiss my ass," Pauly replied, scratching at a tattoo of a bull on his arm.

Eddie could not tell whether Tony was being friendly or sarcastic, but at least he was speaking to him and that was an opening.

Eddie: "What are you getting for this shit?"

Tony: "Twenty five a half," Tony pointed to the joints that were being passed around.

Eddie: "Robby said it was twenty."

Tony: "Its twenty-five, take it or leave it."

Eddie knew the going price for a half-ounce of marijuana was less than twenty dollars. It was common knowledge on the street and the two detectives who had briefed him mentioned a going price of seventeen dollars.

But he was not here to haggle over a bag or a couple of bucks. He had been prepared to give Robby his five dollar finders' fee, but that was out of the question now. If he paid the twenty-five to Tony and another five to Robby, he would look like a chump, or worse, a cop looking to score at any price for a cheap bust. Ernie was not after small dealers, he wanted to get the suppliers, the ones responsible for bringing in the poisons that kill these kids.

Eddie: "I'm good with the twenty-five for a taste, but Robby, you ain't getting nothing outta this." Robby shrugged and opened his hands in a what-are-you-gonna-do? gesture. Eddie used the street term "a taste" as a way of telling Tony that he would be willing to pay a premium to sample the product, but the implied agreement was that future buys in bulk would be subject to a discussion about a lower price.

Robby was lost in the joint he was sucking on and had forgotten the finder's fee for the marijuana. He glanced at Eddie to acknowledge that he had spoken, but had no reaction to what Eddie had said.

Tony: "I only got one for you. I'll see if I can do better in a few days. We'll talk then."

Eddie handed his twenty-five dollars and Tony gave him a half-ounce bag of marijuana.

Eddie: "That's fine, but I will need about three bricks to take care of my people in New York."

Tony: Maybe I can help you out with that order, if you have a couple of grand to spend?"

Eddie: "I'm not worried about the money; I need product and more than just grass. I hope that you can help out. We'll talk soon." Eddie left the house, leaving Robby behind.

He drove to St. Catherine's Church parking lot in Milton and pulled his convertible under a light. A dark two-door sedan pulled in next to him and Detectives Churn and Rule waved him over. Eddie climbed into the back seat and explained what had happened and produced the marijuana, which Rule said would be tested. After some small talk, Eddie went back to the Thunderbird and both vehicles left the church lot.

Later that night, as the boys slept, Teresa typed Eddie's report to Lieutenant Lyme.

Sir,

*At approx. 5:30 pm this date I entered the home of one Tony Cole....*It outlined what had taken place and ended:

On this date, I gave the ½ oz. of marijuana that I purchased from Tony Cole for twenty Five dollars U.S. Cash to Det. Abraham Churn sealed in an evidence envelope.

Respectfully submitted,

Ernie Lijoi Sr.

***

In the following days Eddie Pannoni cruised the bars and streets of Quincy, shooting pool, picking up hitchhikers, and passing out his cards. Three people called him about repairing their cars. He tuned one vehicle, fixed a broken window crank on another, and cleaned the spark plugs on a third. He never charged more than ten dollars. Eddie Pannoni was becoming known as an all right guy. He was getting to know the neighborhoods and who was selling small amounts of marijuana, heroin and cocaine. He bought drugs and turned them over to Detectives Church and Rule during their nightly meetings, along with the reports Teresa was typing for him. He was also receiving reports on the quality of the drugs he was buying. The street level heroin and cocaine was only fifteen to twenty per cent pure. The quality would rise along with the level of dealers as he worked his way to the sources. It was a beginning. He was not targeting small time dealers for arrest; he wanted to work his way up the supply chain. These were small fish and only of interest in that they would lead Detective Ernie Lijoi Sr., aka, Eddie Pannoni to the big fish. These people were more in need of help then in being arrested. Ernie wanted the big guys.

Chapter Six

Citizens Band Radio

Monday, January 16, 1978.

His report to Lieutenant Lyme, typed by Teresa, began:

Sir,

*At approx. 7:30 pm this date I entered the house of To-ny Cole...*He described the two other men in the house that evening and ended:

While leaving I stated that I am interested in investing money. At which time Tony stated that I could buy a pound of marijuana and make $2200.00 by cutting it with rag-weed. I stated that I would be in touch.

Respectfully submitted

Ernie Lijoi Sr.

***

He was at Tony's house for two hours before the subject of marijuana by the pound came up. Pauly was there, smoking weed and complaining about the snow, which was a foot deep on Tony's steps. Tony wanted to know if Eddie liked the half-ounce marijuana he had purchased the previous week, and Eddie told him it was all right, and he told Tony he had sold most of it to a friend who was going to New York.

Tony: "Need some more?" Tony asked.

Eddie: "Yeah. How much you got?" Eddie responded.

Tony: "Are you looking for some quantity?"

Eddie: "I got some money to invest, yeah."

Tony: "I got a little secret for you, this stuff we're smoking here. It ain't cut, at least not by me. But the retail stuff, you can cut it with ragweed and make some real money, like maybe twenty-two hundred a pound. See what I mean? I know you got people you sell to, so maybe you can, you know, make some walking around money."

Eddie: "You mentioned that before. I need to talk to my money guy. But it sounds good."

Tony: "Hey, you fix cars, right?"

Eddie; "Yeah, what do you need?"

Tony: "The antenna on my car is broken; the radio won't get decent reception. Can you help me out?"

Eddie: "Too much fucking snow right now, but maybe in a couple days we can, you know, fix the antenna and take care of some other business." Eddie got up and went to the door. "You ever think about shoveling the steps?"

~ ~ ~

The next day Quincy was covered in deep slush, but Tony managed to shovel his stairs and some of his drive-way. Eddie discovered that the wire on Tony's antenna had separated from the connection on the underside of the car's fender. He reattached it and went inside, where he and To-ny drank beer. Eddie nursed his and confessed to Tony that he was subject to seizures if he drank too much. That ad-mission seemed to calm Tony, who said, "Well, I guess that means you ain't a cop."

Pauly arrived with Robby and the two of them helped themselves to Tony Cole's beer and asked if Tony had any marijuana to smoke.

Tony: "This look like a charity kitchen to you?" he said. "You here to buy or just bullshit?"

Eddie: "Speaking of that, how about those pounds or bricks that we talked about Monday? How's that look?"

Tony: "It's looking very good; you got some buyers in mind?"

"Yeah, well, you know, I do some business in New York. Whatever you can get I'm in. It will be helpful to me and my people in New York; it's been very hard to make a buck since the big crack down in the New York area."

Pauly sat back in his chair and pointed to Eddie. "You interested in coke?"

Eddie: "Now that's a product that I can make money on. You got some to sell?"

Pauly: "Nothing around right now, but give me a couple days and, yeah, I can get some for you. Small amounts, though. I ain't got the cash to invest in big amounts."

"Listen," Eddie said, "Like I said to Tony, I can use anything. My people in New York will take it all. So, ah, get me what you can."

"Okay, give me a few hours. Come by tonight, I'll have something for you." Pauly had the overly sincere look of someone who was shoveling pure horse shit.

Eddie went back to Tony's three times that evening, but no one was home. It was all in his report to Lieutenant Lyme.

***

The red telephone in the Lijoi house rang at noon the next day.

"Eddie," was all he said as he answered it.

"Eddie, Tony", was the response from the caller.

"Where were you?" Eddie asked. "I came by like three times to meet Pauly," The tape recorder slowly turned under the table where the phone was kept.

Tony: "He's an asshole. I don't know. I got something for you and I wonder if you can get me something."

Eddie: "Sure, if I can, yeah. What do you need?" Eddie asked.

Tony: "You know where I can get a CB radio?"

Citizens Band radios were popular in the late 1970s, nearly as popular as cell phones would become decades later. The CB radio was a simple, two-way communications device that allowed anyone to share designated frequencies to talk back and forth. Husbands could talk to wives. Bosses could talk to workers. Drug dealers could talk to their customers in a coded vocabulary. There was no formal examination or competence required to operate a CB radio. A ten-dollar fee and application to the Federal Communications Commission was enough to obtain a federal permit, so anyone who could find the on switch could talk to anyone else on any given frequency. Truckers used them to communicate with each other and the usefulness of portable communications systems on CB's spread from truckers to suburban dads to drug and arms dealers.

Truckers moving up and down the East Coast occasionally padded their loads with bales of marijuana or kilos of cocaine and had developed a code to use on the CB radios to alert dealers that shipments were on the way. They were easy to monitor if you knew the frequencies being used. All anyone had to do was listen. Police were wising up. Eddie was in a position to place one of the radios in the hands of a drug dealer. The Quincy police had permission from the courts to use the confiscated CB radios so there was no need to purchase a CB radio, they had them. They listened to traffic as they sat at their desks in the police station. Ernie acted as translator when a message was heard but not understood.

Some of the codes went along these lines:

A meatloaf was an ounce of Marijuana, a Cola was cocaine, a hopper was heroin a mat was methamphetamine and this simple coded list went on and on.

Eddie contacted Tony about the radio: "I can get you one. I got one right now. I'll work a deal with you. I'll exchange the CB for an ounce." Ernie made a note of the time called and what he was asking for.

Tony: "Can you meet me at the Donut Hole on Sea Street at 7 tonight?"

Eddie: "Yeah. See you there." He hung up the telephone and watched as the tape recorder stopped turning.

Eddie had installed a CB radio in the Thunderbird and often listened to Channel 19, a popular band in Quincy, as truck drivers, businessmen, housewives, street thugs and drug dealers talked to each other. They all had "handles", or identities they used only on the CB radio, calling themselves "King of the road" or "Badass" or "Honey on the vine" when they talked to others. Eddie's handle was "Mr. Blue" and he wondered if anyone who talked to him over the CB would put Mr. Blue together with "cop". No one did. They thought the name was from the popular song.

~ ~ ~

He met Tony at the donut shop and followed him down Sea Street to a parking lot next to a market. Tony owned a thirty-foot camper and he wanted a CB so he could talk to other drivers on the road and have a way to summon help if his camper broke down on the highway. Eddie did not have a new radio for Tony, but he wanted another drug sample from him, so he used the ruse of a CB to arrange the meeting.

Eddie; "I got one here in my car," he said, adjusting the knobs on the radio he had mounted under the dashboard of the Thunderbird. He turned the dial and adjusted the volume, turning the radio on and off, acting as though he were testing it. "Fuckin' thing doesn't work," he said. "I can get another one, brand new. Right out of the box. Tell you what. I'll buy the stuff you brought. Give you cash and we can work something out for the radio when I get it."

"I don't know what it is with that shit," Tony said, looking at what he thought was a dead radio in Eddie's car. "A couple hours ago I had three color TVs, they all worked fine at my house, but one of them went bad at the guy's house where I sold it. You never know with this stuff."

"You got TVs?" Eddie asked.

Tony: "Yeah, sometimes, and other stuff."

Eddie: "Listen, if you get some more I would be very interested in buying one." Eddie now knew that Tony and his friends were involved in more than drugs.

Tony and Eddie walked to the camper where Tony had left the marijuana. As he reached under the passenger seat to grab a small paper bag, Tony motioned for Eddie to come closer and he whispered, "My, ah, camper was stolen awhile back and I had a lot of stuff in it, merchandise, you know what I mean? Receipts, too, I had some receipts for all this stuff but they're gone now. Can you help me out?"

"You need some receipts?" Eddie asked.

"Yeah, you know, regular receipts for stuff like TVs."

"I don't know. I'll see what I can do, but I don't know if I can help you out with that." Eddie gave him two twenty-dollar bills for the grass.

Eddie: "You owe me five in change," he said.

Tony took the twenties and gave Eddie a ten-dollar bill as change.

Tony: "Now you owe me five," he said, handing Eddie a bag of marijuana.

Eddie: "I'll get you a thirty-two channel CB in a couple of days and I'll put it in for you," Eddie said, as the two men parted.

On January 18th, 1978, I gave the marijuana, which I purchased from Mr. Cole, to Det. Abraham Churn, sealed in an envelope.

Respectfully submitted,
Ernie Lijoi Sr. #62

~ ~ ~

Two days later the man Tony Cole knew as Eddie Pannoni installed a thirty-two channel citizens band radio in Tony's family camper. Eddie was alone in the camper as he installed the radio and he took the opportunity to examine the vehicle. He discovered two hidden compartments, each large enough to hold thirty or forty kilos of cocaine or about forty or fifty bricks of Marijuana. The CB radio came from the police evidence room and was considered un-claimed. In payment, Tony offered Eddie one ounce of ma-rijuana, a five-dollar bill, and a promise of another twenty-dollars at a later date.

"Call me tomorrow," Tony said. "I'll have something for you."

Eddie waved to him as the snow began to fall. The forecast was for a major storm.

~ ~ ~

The storm came up from the south, gathering moisture as it moved along the Atlantic coast. A cold front came down from Canada and collided with the wet air that sat along the New England coast. The snow piled up and the hardy Massachusetts highway workers could not keep up with it. Before it was over, more than three and a half feet of snow was on the ground at Logan International Airport. Nothing moved. Not even drugs. Eddie spent the day at home, listening to the CB radio bands, amazed that some of the people he had been working on the streets were talking to each other as if they were all in the same room.

Pauly: "Gunfighter this is Bat Masterson, over."

"Gunfighter here, you got anything for the head? Over" The static from the signal mingled with the words, giving the quality of an old-time long distance telephone call.

"Nah, nothing moving today. Playing my own head games, if you know what I mean. Over."

Eddie recognized Pauly's voice on the radio.

Eddie: "Hey, Bat Masterson, Mr. Blue here. Got any-thing for me? Over."

Pauly: "Mr. Blue, call me at The Snake's house later. I got something to talk about, Over."

Tony Cole had taken The Snake as his handle. He got it from a glass pipe he used to smoke marijuana and PCP. The pipe was three-feet tall in the shape of an attacking co-bra.

The conversation was choppy and the messages were mixed in with other CBers who were complaining about the roads or lack of milk at the grocery stores because deliveries were shut down for the day. Eddie sat back and listened to the chatter and wrote down the names of drug dealers and users who were communicating with each other, despite the weather. One name caught his ear. A CBer whose handle was Bent Bobby called Gunfighter "Billy", then "Stine". The two men talked in an easy, loose way about a deal they were working on, but the conversation was chopped into small pieces by the interrupting traffic on the CB network.

Eddie had been trying to connect with Billy Stine since his first day as an undercover detective. Billy was the man thought to be a gun dealer who both sold and rented handguns and rifles to local thugs. He was also rumored to be in the drug business. Eddie now knew Billy was in the area. He also knew that Tony Cole had done business with him. It was time to move up the ladder again.

Ernie was at home listening on his portable CB radio, The Red Phone rang:

"Hello, yeah." Cole's sleep voice sounded distant as Eddie checked the tape recorder to be sure it was rolling on the call.

Eddie: "Hey, Tony. You asleep, you called me. It's Eddie. How ya' doin'."

Tony: "Okay, Eddie. What's up?"

Eddie: "You got your CB working today?"

Tony: "Yeah, yeah. It's in the van."

Eddie could tell that Tony was riding out the storm with drugs and was barely conscious.

Eddie: "Hey, look, I'm interested in some quantity. Remember, we talked about it. I gotta guy who wants something, you know. Can you help me out?"

Tony: "I don't know. I'm pretty stoned right now. I don't want to talk to anybody."

Eddie: "I might want something else, too. You know Billy? Billy Stine? Maybe he can help me as well."

Tony: "Yeah, yeah. I know him. In fact, he was asking me if I know anybody can fix his car. That might be a good way to get to know him." Tony's voice trailed away from the telephone. "Call me later."

Eddie: "I heard Pauly on the CB, Bat Masterson is his handle. He said I should call him at your house and he's got something for me. Is he there?"

Tony: "He's kinda fucked up right now. Hey, Pauly, it's Eddie." His voice was distant as he passed the phone to Pauly, who kind of moaned as he took the call."

Pauly comes on to the phone:

Eddie: "Pauly, Eddie. You got something for me?"

Pauly: "Pretty good stuff, Coke." Pauly's mumble was punctuated by a small laugh, a high-pitched giggle that was directed at Tony, who could be heard snoring in the background.

Eddie told Pauly he would call him Monday when the roads were clear, around noon. He hung up the phone and watched as the tape recorder stopped. He spent the afternoon making notes about the deals he was hearing on the CB radio, listing to everyone who claimed to be buying or selling. They spoke in a code that he understood.

He spent Sunday sledding with his boys and met with Detective Churn at St. Catherine's parking lot after dark. The two men drank coffee as Eddie passed reports and notes to Churn and told him about Billy Stine and his plans to meet Pauly to discuss purchasing cocaine in quantity. Churn had some news of his own.

Det. Churn: "You're getting noticed," he said. "All those buys of yours are pissing off the state boys. You're network is getting bigger than theirs. The coke you brought in last week was twenty-per cent pure. You're moving up the pipe." He laughed at his own joke. "I heard talk the bosses may be talking to you. The state police may want

you to work with them. No good deed goes unpunished."
He laughed again. "Keep your head down. Meet you here
tomorrow night."

Eddie drove back to his home in Dedham and thought
about the state police and what they might have in mind.
There was no traffic. It was Sunday night and the roads
were plowed, but sidewalks were deep under the snow and
most of the cars were still buried. He saw men with snow
shovels and brooms digging out here and there, but most
people were warm in the homes, unaware of the under life
of their city and the contest that was taking place for control of the streets they lived on.

Near his home, Eddie stopped to help a neighbor and
his son dig out their car. The boy was about ten. He wore a
knitted cap down over his ears and his face was red with
the cold. He laughed and jumped in the snow as Eddie and
the boy's dad threw snowballs at him. Eddie thought about
his own boys and their red faces as they sledded through
the deep snow, laughing and rolling in the drifts.

He also thought about Tony and Pauly, stoned, and all
of the junkies and lowlifes who would poison the world if
they could. Some of them were just lost, not bad people,
just lost. They had no idea how to lead a normal life with
all of its challenges and rewards. They only knew how to
stagger from one moment to the next, hoping for a fix or
score of some kind, accepting a constant state of near mis-
ery and periodic degradation. On the other hand, there was
no shortage of shit bags that fed off the lost and took all
they could get from them.

Shit bags came in all shapes and sizes and some of
them wore very nice suits. That night they were snug in
their homes or ski lodges, working on their deals and contacts. They knew that they were being stalked, but they did
not know who the stalkers were. They had no idea that a
deep undercover cop using the name Eddie Pannoni was, at
that moment, catching their scent. He would, in time, track

them down and leave no footprints. But that was to come. Tonight, the streets of Quincy were empty and the snow kept falling and piling up.

Chapter Seven

Billy Stine

Monday, January 23rd

The clear, blue sky allowed the sun to shine on the weekend's snowfall, nearly blinding Eddie as he carefully stepped through the narrow opening that Tony had shoveled from the driveway to his porch stairs and up to the front door. The rush hour had just ended, what there was of it, and traffic was returning to normal. Pauly answered the door, wearing a plaid hat with earflaps. Thermal underwear was visible under his checked shirt.

Pauly: "Tony ain't here," he said, by way of greeting. "C'mon in."

Eddie left his boots by the door and stepped into the room, soaking one of his socks in a puddle that had been made by melting snow from Pauly's boots.

Eddie: "When's he comin' back?" he asked.

Pauly: "Few minutes. He's pickin' something up. He usually gets his stuff on Thursdays, but somethin' happened last week, so he's pickin' it up today. Listen, I got something for you." Pauly went to his coat and reached into an inside pocket, removing a small bag. "It's a full gram. Hundred bucks."

Eddie looked at it. "How do I know it's any good?"

Pauly: "Believe me, it's good shit."

Tony came into the room through the back door, stamping his feet. With him was a well-dressed man wearing a suit, tie, overcoat and rubbers over his leather shoes. Tony wore a leather bomber jacket over a wool sweater, which was loose over his jeans. He had left his boots at the kitchen door.

Tony: "Hey, Eddie. I've been using my CB. I think it needs more power." Tony walked and patted Eddie on the shoulder. "You know how to do that?"

The power of CB radios was regulated by the government to prevent signals from overlapping from one community to another, and a small industry had developed to add illegal power to the radios that were sold to the public.

"I think I can take care of you," Eddie looked at Tony, then at the other man.

"This is Billy," Tony said, by way of introduction. "Billy Stine."

"How you doin'?" Eddie said, offering his hand. Billy was in his twenties, dark complexioned, clean-shaven. He had the smile of a salesman, all teeth and handshakes, but his eyes were staring into Eddie's face.

"He's alright," Tony said to Billy. "Eddie took care of me and he's here for some shit. He can take care of your car as well."

Billy sat back and made a motion as though he were putting a key into the ignition of a car. "I don't know. It doesn't turn over right. Sometimes it takes forever to get it started. What do you think it is?"

Eddie nodded his head and reached into his shirt pocket, removed a card, and handed it to Billy.

Eddie: "Give me a call. I'll take a look at it."

Tony sat down on the sofa and reached under it to retrieve his snake pipe. He propped it on a small carpet, where Eddie could see the dark-stained bowl and the lines of residue left on the shaft of the pipe, all the way to the snake's mouth. A tube protruded from the snake. Upon sucking through the mouthpiece, the tube pulled the smoke through the water from the pipe into the mouth of the person who sucked on it. He opened a plastic bag of marijuana and loaded the stained bowl, lit it, put the tube into his mouth and took a deep drag of the thick smoke into his lungs. He held his breath as the smoke worked its way into his blood stream, his eyes bulging as his faced swelled. He let it out with a cough and passed the tube to Eddie.

Eddie could never allow himself to become disoriented by drugs, even if police regulations had allowed it, which they did not. He risked seizures from exposure to drugs and alcohol, and he had therefore become very good at faking it. He mimicked the loud sucking noise of a "toke" or drags on the pipe, and held his breath. He quickly passed the tube to Billy; the tube was almost black from all of the residue that had built up within it. Billy did not notice that no smoke had passed up the snake. Billy took his own drag and passed the tube to Pauly.

Tony got a grin on his face and announced that he had a surprise. He stuck his hand under one of the cushions on the sofa and produced a .44 caliber magnum revolver.

Tony: "I'm fuckin' Clint Eastwood," he said, waving the huge handgun in the air.

Eddie stared at the gun and leaned back into his chair and felt the pressure of his own .38 snub-nosed against his spine where it was tucked into the waistband of his jeans.

Pauly was holding a breath full of marijuana smoke at that moment and coughed it out, nearly choking.

"What the fuck is that?" Pauly asked, almost at a whisper because he had blown his voice with his coughing and gagging.

"My new friend," Tony said. "Eddie, tell Billy about your little gun business."

Eddie had told Tony that he sold drugs and guns to customers in New York.

"We can talk about this some other time." Eddie smiled at Tony and Billy. They relaxed and took another hit on the snake.

"You got something for me?" Eddie asked Tony.

"Yeah, he does," Billy responded, pointing to Tony.

Tony put the gun back under the sofa cushion and went into the kitchen. Eddie could hear a cupboard open and close and the sound of a paperbag being blown open. A minute later Tony came into the room and handed a large package to Eddie.

Tony: "Full pound. Good weight. Good quality."

Eddie took the bag and looked inside. A musky, sweet smell filled his nostrils, a deep, wet scent. They were buds, no sticks or leaves. It was higher quality than the stuff the common street smoker was getting.

"Can we talk a minute?" Eddie asked, motioning to the kitchen.

The two men went into the other room where Eddie pulled Tony aside.

Eddie; "What's with Billy?" he asked.

Tony: "Like I said, he's good. He's got friends, if you know what I mean."

Eddie; "Friends?"

Tony: "You know, friends. As in the type of friends you got in New York. Italian friends. Capice?" He smiled at his use of the Italian word for "do you understand?"

Eddie: "He's got friends—he's good as far as I'm concerned."

Eddie counted out cash for the marijuana and handed it to Tony, who patted Eddie's arm and went back to the living room, where he reloaded the pipe and passed the tube around.

Eddie motioned for Pauly to come to the kitchen, where he paid for the gram of cocaine and put it into his shirt pocket. He went back into the living room, faked another hit on the pipe, put the packet of marijuana into his jacket and left, reminding Billy to give him a call to talk about the car that needed work.

Chapter Eight

The Candy Store

Wednesday, January 25th

The red phone rang; the tape recorder began its slow spinning as Eddie picked up the telephone.

"Eddie. It's Billy,"

"Hey, Billy, what's up?" Eddie's voice betrayed a slight annoyance, as though the call had come at a bad time. In fact, Billy had called while the undercover officer was spending some time with his children and enjoying their company.

Billy: "Eddie, this dam car is a real problem. It's like it won't start. I think it's the distributor. I don't know what's going down with that. I was wondering if you can come on down with your light or something."

Eddie paused, as though thinking it over. "Is she turning?"

The two men talked about Billy's car and its problems and whether the gears were damaged.

Eddie: "Don't do anything; let me take a look at it. I'll be down in about an hour or so."

Billy let out a sigh. "Beautiful. Thanks, man."

Eddie drove through the streets of Quincy, carefully navigating the low spots where the melting snow had created ice holes in the roads. There was a light rain. The warming temperatures had created fog that gave the city an eerie, pearly appearance. He found Billy's and pulled into his driveway, where Billy was poking under the hood of his car.

"Fuckin' thing," Billy said. "I need it for my business. I gotta pick somethin' up this afternoon."

Eddie looked at the new distributor Billy had purchased and installed it, but the vehicle wouldn't start.

Eddie: "What kind of business are you in?" he asked.

Billy grinned. "I'm in the dope business," he said. "I have to move around. I got a little marijuana and Coke business. I have some great connections and I supply only people that are close to me, that I trust."

Eddie looked surprised. "By the way, I'll take an ounce while I'm here."

Billy motioned for Eddie to follow him into the house, where he went upstairs and returned with an ounce of marijuana.

Billy: "Thirty-five dollars," he said. "I can get quantity for you if you want, all that you can handle."

Eddie took the marijuana and handed Billy the cash.

Eddie: "You got anything else? You got any coke?"

Billy: "Yeah, Not right now, though."

Eddie:"How much?"

Billy: "Hundred, Hundred ten a gram."

Eddie: "I can go a hundred, Billy, no cuts. I want clean stuff."

Billy: "Okay, yeah. No problem, Eddie. I'll call you. Thanks for trying to get the car going. I don't know what's going down with that."

Eddie drove to a parking lot about a mile from Billy's house, placed the ounce of marijuana in a sealed envelope, and put it in his glove compartment. He had another appointment, this one with a man whose CB handle was Grayboy, known on the streets as Sanyo. Sanyo was one of a growing number of mid-level drug dealers and criminals who were seeing Eddie Pannoni as a familiar face, but who did not trust him, yet. Sanyo, like Billy Stine, wanted Eddie to work on his car. Sanyo tested Eddie. The meeting took place at a coffee shop on Sea Street.

Sanyo: "Where do you live? Did you say West Roxbury?" Sanyo was smiling and being friendly.

Eddie: "Yeah, near Dedham."

Sanyo: "You married?"

Eddie: "Yeah."

Sanyo: "No shit. You got kids?"

Eddie: "Yeah, two." Eddie wanted to present a credible story that could reasonably match his own life without offering any details that could help Sanyo or anyone find his home and family.

Sanyo: "That's great, good luck with your family. Maybe you can help me. I'm trying to get the part that I need for the car. I called three dealers, but no one's got it. What's it called? A controller thing right?"

Eddie: "It's a control switch, that's right."

Sanyo stared at Eddie for a moment. "I'm a little confused."

Eddie: "What's the problem?"

Sanyo: "I don't know."

Eddie tried to steer Sanyo back to the vehicle. "How much is the part?"

Sanyo: "I don't know. I didn't ask them." Sanyo appeared to be unfocused.

Eddie told him the problem with the controller was probably caused by the weather. Sanyo then asked about ways to improve his gas mileage. The conversation drifted around problems with Sanyo's car until he asked Eddie if he knew a man named Bobby Laronda.

Sanyo: "He's a good friend of mine. He owns a shop of his own." Sanyo mentioned the name of an auto repair and body shop that was believed to be a chop shop for the Mafia, a place where stolen cars were turned into parts.

Eddie: "Bobby Laronda. Gee, I don't know." Eddie shrugged his shoulders.

Sanyo: "Opened up last year. He sells used cars, trucks, you know. He also fixes trucks, cars, fire trucks, everything, he's a diesel mechanic. You don't do that kind of work?"

Eddie wondered what Sanyo had in mind when he said "that kind of work".

Eddie: "I do, yeah," he said.

Sanyo: "I should introduce you to him. Maybe you could do a couple of days a week in there, you know, beats loafing around and doing nothing."

Sanyo leaned in and lowered his voice. "I know you been talking to Bingo and The Judge on the CB. Be careful. They're into some serious stuff, you know, like stolen trucks, drugs and shit." He looked at Eddie to check his reaction.

"Yeah, okay," Eddie said. The network was growing.

"Okay, so I'll get the part, the controller, and I'll give you a call." Sanyo stood up, placed some money on the counter, and left.

That night, Eddie met Detective Rule in the parking lot of St. Catherine's, handed him the envelope containing an ounce of marijuana and a report that was typed by Teresa. Eddie was moving up in the world.

~ ~ ~

The next day, Eddie was back in the coffee shop to meet Tony Cole to talk about buying some pills with the street name of crossroads, amphetamine sulfate in ten milligram tablets. The tablets were indented with a cross that allowed them to be cut into four equal segments. Eddie had told Tony he wanted crossroads in bulk for his friends in New York, and Tony had said he had a friend who had a large supply.

Tony: "I'll take you to the source," Tony said. "This guy has everything. You don't need to deal with low level guys. This guy lives in Randolph. You drive."

The two men drove to a small apartment building on Reeds Street in Randolph.

Tony: "Guy's name is Waylen Beyer. You won't believe the shit this guy's got."

They parked in the parking lot of a large apartment building. Tony led Eddie up a flight of stairs to the second floor, where a line that Eddie estimated at fifty people snaked down the hall to an apartment door at the far end. Eddie couldn't believe his eyes. There were numerous kids from teens to twenties standing in this line all waiting for the door to open and the dealer to start business. It was like a candy store, the first on the block back in Brooklyn and the kids were waiting for their supply of candy.

Eddie: "What the fuck is this?" Eddie whispered, as the two men surveyed the line of young men and women who leaned against the walls and doors of the building.

Tony: "I told you, man, this guy's got some shit."

Tony led Eddie past the customers who were waiting to see Waylen Beyer and marched up to Beyer's door and knocked. It was opened by a man Eddie noted as w/m, 5' 6", mid twenties, 130 pounds, blond hair, moustache, very sparse van dyke beard, dungarees and striped shirt.

"Hey, Tony," the man—Waylen—said, opening the door. "Come on in." He turned to the people waiting, "Be right with you," he said to the people who were lined up against the wall.

Eddie followed Tony into the apartment, where a half-dozen people were gathered around a table that was piled high with pills of various colors, shapes and sizes. Eddie estimated there were thousands of pills in that apartment and available for sale.

Tony: "Eddie, this is Waylen. Waylen, Eddie."

The two men shook hands as Eddie looked around. A girl Eddie guessed to be around nine years old was sitting on the sofa, watching television. A toddler wandered around the room, staring at the grownups. A distinguished looking man who appeared to be in his late forties stood talking with two customers. The man wore a white pullover sweater, dungarees and boat shoes. Eddie thought he stood out from the others, who looked like standard issue drug users wearing un-pressed and well-used clothes. Many of them needed a shower. This guy did not fit in. The man reminded Eddie of one of his uncles, a man who was always sharply dressed and had a reputation as a ladies' man.

"Eddie is looking for some crossroads," Tony said. "I told him you're the man to see."

Waylen: "I can take care of you. How many are you looking for?"

Eddie: "Hundred now. Maybe more if those are OK."

"No problem." Waylen waved his left hand in the direction of the table, which was divided into piles of different types of pills.

"You got any Quaaludes?" Eddie asked.

Waylen: "Whatever you need, quantity is not a problem."

Eddie purchased one hundred crossroads and left with Tony, walking down the hallway past the line of druggies who were waiting patiently for their turn to buy something on that apartment.

That night Ernie met the Quincy detectives in the church parking lot and gave them a sealed envelope with the amphetamine pills. He also gave them a typed report on Waylen's operation and his address.

The following morning a task force of police officers raided the apartment, seizing thirteen thousand dollars in drugs and over eight thousand dollars in cash. Any one of the druggies in line could have been the source of the information, but Quincy police wanted to make sure Waylen did not suspect Eddie. It was decided that Eddie would order up some quantity, so he called Tony to say he wanted to buy Quaaludes from Waylen.

Tony: "Didn't you hear? He's been busted. Fucking cops got him this morning." Tony sounded stoned. "Confiscated the whole fuckin' thing."

Eddie: "Geez! He in jail?" Eddie acted surprised.

Tony: "Not for long. He'll be back in business as soon as he can restock."

Eddie: "When's that?"

Tony: "He'll get himself bailed out and in a day or two he'll be back in business. I'll let you know."

Eddie hung up the red telephone and watched as the tape recorder stopped turning.

~ ~ ~

By Monday, Waylen was back in business and the lines were forming outside his door. Tony called Eddie to tell him Quaaludes were available in quantity. That night Eddie reported to Detective Churn that Waylen's suppliers had him up and running. Quincy detectives set up twenty four hour surveillance on Waylen's apartment, noting the level of business during various parts of the day. Evening hours were busiest, with lines going down to the bottom of the stairs. They raided him again and seized drugs and money.

This time they moved in late in the afternoon to shut him down before the busy evening business lined up. Quincy uniformed and plainclothes officers knocked on the door, announced a warrant, and were preparing to knock down the door when Waylen opened it and let them in. The kitchen table was covered with pills. Social services workers moved in to remove the children while the police searched the apartment. Waylen's telephone rang constantly and one of the officers picked it up.

Officer: "Yeah."

Caller: "Waylen?"

Officer: "Yeah, what do you need?"

Caller: "Crossroads."

Officer: "C'mon up," the officer said.

He put the telephone down and it rang again.

Officer: "Yeah, what do you need?"

Caller: "'Ludes."

Officer: "C'mon up."

The telephone kept ringing and the officer invited everyone up. In all, fifteen drug buyers were arrested while the officers searched Waylen's apartment.

Eddie told Tony he was shocked. "I coulda been there when the cops came!" he said.

"No shit," Tony replied. "Give him a week and we'll go back. He'll be in business again by then. There's other stuff going on, Eddie. You interested?"

Eddie: "Like what?"

Tony: "You never know. Stay by your phone." Tony laughed and hung up.

~ ~ ~

Sunday, February 5

Eddie spent the weekend as himself, Ernie Lijoi Sr., family man. The red phone had rung but it was mostly nuisance calls from the junkies who were looking for something to keep them from getting sick. He had to put them off, saying he had nothing at the moment but might early in the week, "If you can't find what you need, you should go to the hospital and turn yourself in, It's better than suffering." He told the users and junkies that called. He spent Saturday and Sunday with Teresa and the boys, watching the Celtics and the Bruins, and enjoying Teresa's Italian cooking of a dish called Gnocchi's which is handmade and takes hours to prepare.

It was cold in Dedham, but the snow was almost gone. Television weathercasters were talking about a huge storm in the Midwest that was dumping record amounts of snow. The storm was moving east. Forecasters in New England issued a Winter Storm Watch because three air masses were merging over the region. One was moving from the west, the second was over northern Georgia, and the third was over the Mid Atlantic. That Sunday night, when Ernie and Teresa watched the late news, the television weather forecaster said he would have more news about the storm in the morning.

By dawn, heavy snow warnings were out for southern New England and television weathercasters were warning of imminent blizzard conditions.

Tony called the red phone around eight. "Do you believe this shit?" he asked. "Fuckin' snow. Geez. I don't know why they're making such a big deal. It's fuckin' New England."

"I got a four wheel drive," Eddie responded. "I can get out. We already had deep snow this winter. This ain't gonna stop me."

Tony: "Listen, you interested in something?" Tony moved to the business at hand.

Eddie: "Yeah, sure."

Tony: "I might be getting some coke in quantity in a day or so. You in?"

Eddie: "Kilo?" Eddie wanted to know what the word 'quantity' meant in Tony's latest deal.

Tony: "At least; maybe more."

Eddie: "I'm in—if it's any good. I don't want junk. My people don't want junk."

Tony: "This is a good source, Eddie. It's not junk. I'll call you and we can make a deal."

Ernie hung up the telephone and watched as the tape recorder stopped. He went to the window to check on the storm.

Outside, the wind was picking up. The storm was growing stronger, driven by a high pressure area off Canada and trapped the now-merged air masses over southern New England, creating bands of heavy snow that looped continuously over eastern Massachusetts, Connecticut and Rhode Island. Tails of the storm went as far south as New

York City, creating a nightmare of blinding snow and wind for hundreds of miles. Winds topped seventy-five miles per hour. Heavy snow fell for thirty-three hours, sometimes at a rate of four inches per hour. It was accompanied by thunder and lightning.

By mid day state and local governments told their employees to go home. Major businesses closed and ordered their workers to leave. It was already too late. Thousands of cars were trapped in ever-deepening snow. Interstate 95 and Route 128 quickly became impassable. Cars were stopped with no hope of moving forward.

The governor announced that Massachusetts was closed and ordered everyone to stay home. Anyone caught trying to drive would be arrested. Cross country skiers tried to evacuate Route 128 and save the people who were dying in their cars because the snow was so deep it prevented exhaust from escaping from their idling vehicles.

Owners of four-wheel drive vehicles were asked to help rescue stranded motorists and deliver emergency medical workers to hospitals. Eddie called Lieutenant Lyme's private line at Quincy police.

Eddie: "I got a Bronco with a CB, I can help," he said.

Lt. Lyme: "You need a pass to go out, but you gotta go as Eddie Pannoni. I can't risk you driving around as Ernie Lijoi Sr., the shit-bags can dig out and see you."

Eddie: "That sounds good. I can dig out here and meet Churn or somebody to pick up the pass."

Lt. Lyme: "Can you get to Quincy emergency services? I can have a pass waiting for you there."

~ ~ ~

And so Eddie Pannoni, the drug and gun dealer from New York, joined the rescue effort. He drove the streets of Quincy and other communities, delivering doctors and nurses to hospitals, pulling stranded motorists from cars that were buried in snow drifts as deep as fifteen feet, and helping to pull cars free of deep snow. He talked to the state police on his CB.

He also talked to Tony and other drug dealers, who laughed and assumed that Eddie had pulled a fast one to get his hands on a pass that allowed him to be on the streets during the crisis. His street credibility shot up and junkies and dealers called each other to talk about him. "Can you *believe* that guy?"

It never occurred to any of them that Eddie Pannoni was driving around a closed city because he was a cop. Eddie Pannoni had been accepted as a drug dealer and gun runner and never, ever thought of, by street people, as police officer.

Chapter Nine

The courtroom

Saturday, February 11

Eddie's red telephone was ringing at all hours. He was spending time with Mafia lieutenants, mid-level drug dealers, and people who had an interest in guns both buying and selling. In a world of what-can-you-do-for-me, Eddie had something to offer. The people of the night believed that he was a walking marketplace, the guy who had money to buy whatever was for sale to supply his people in New York City where he made great profits. Enough profit to be able to buy and sell anything. This false belief, all worked in his favor.

He was insulated from blame when an arrest was made. Going to jail was the cost of doing business on the street and Eddie acted as surprised and shocked as everyone else when the police took a drug dealer into custody and took him into custody along with everyone else.

He was seen as an okay guy, one of the boys. Even the street people who did not know him well seemed to trust him because of his reputation, at least as much as they trusted anyone else. He said the right things, he looked the part, and he knew the streets.

The red telephone rang at two o'clock in the afternoon. Eddie was hoping to spend some time with Teresa and the boys, and had planned to watch television with them because it was too cold to do anything outdoors. He answered the phone.

Bobby: "Eddie, its Bobby, Bobby Bee, how ya doin'?"

Bobby Bee was a street-wise hoodlum who had connections all over the Boston area and knew what was coming in and going out. His contacts went beyond the usual pool hall hustlers and dealers who traded rumors about drug shipments and weapons buys.

"Hey, Bobby. What's up?" Eddie saw that the tape recorder was rolling.

Bobby: "Want to hear a good one?"

Eddie: "Yeah, sure."

Bobby: "State Street Bank was robbed last night."

Eddie: "No shit, I didn't hear anything about a bank robbery on the TV news or in the paper, what'd they get?"

Bobby: "I'm told they got some bonds. Nobody even knows exactly how much yet."

Eddie: "What do you mean?" Eddie took out a pad of paper and a pen that happened to have the State Street Bank logo on it.

Bobby: "You ain't gonna hear anything on the news or anywhere else either. They had somebody inside. No one's gonna know the bonds are gone until Tuesday or Wednesday, when the bank's bond auditor comes to check them out. The best part is, the Mafia is trying to sell the bonds to some people in Rhode Island and they've run into some problems. They are negotiating over price and who transports the bonds."

Eddie thought about what Bobby Bee was saying and decided to make an offer to buy the stolen bonds.

Eddie: "Bobby, you know I have people in New York that will definitely be interested in something like that."

Bobby Bee paused. "You do?"

Eddie: "Yeah, that's what I do. I buy and sell for all kinds of people."

Bobby: "Shit. That's pretty good, Eddie. Listen, why don't I have Tony Fats give you a call. He's Angelo's key guy. You know who I'm talking about? I don't wanna know nothin'. These are the kind of people that you just do not fuck around with. You know what I mean?"

Eddie: "Yeah, I know. Have him call me anyway."

Bobby: "Tony Fats is Italian, like us. He's about sixty, six-three, three hundred pounds. You'll know him when you see him. I'll give him a call and give him this number."

Half an hour later the red telephone rang again. Eddie picked it up and paused before he said anything. The voice on the other end did not wait. "Eddie, this is Tony, Tony Fats."

Eddie: "Yeah, hey, Tony."

Tony Fats: "Bobby Bee asked me to give you a call."

Eddie: "Tony, I'm glad you called. Can you give me some information about this deal?"

Tony Fats: "Okay, Bobby says you're good, so here's what happened. This fuck from the North End fucked me outta some big money awhile back and I think I can get him back for it by getting a clean piece for myself. You understand?"

Eddie: "What do you have, Tony?"

Tony: "Last night a delivery was made to State Street Bank. These guys own the driver, so he looked the other way while a large pile of negotiable bonds disappeared off the delivery platform. The thing is, the bank won't know about it until the bond auditor comes Tuesday morning to check them out. A couple of guys from the North End have a connection in Rhode Island. You know what I mean?"

"Yeah, sure." Eddie was making notes.

Tony Fats: "They have an offer of two million for the ten million in bonds."

Eddie: "Tony, listen. What if I knew a bank vice president in New York that, you know, could have connections to wash the bonds overseas? I can make these guys the same offer, maybe better."

Tony Fats: "Are you the vice president of this bank?"

Eddie: "No, but my partner is."

Tony Fats: "I think I can sell that, but, Eddie, I want enough to get outta here and take my mom to Florida maybe."

Eddie: "How much are we talking about, Tony?"

Tony Fats: "Twenty-five thousand."

Eddie: "That's a lot of money, Tony. I don't know if I can do that much?"

Tony Fats: "It's worth it, your bank friend should pay it after you have the bonds."

Eddie: "Let me see what I can do."

Tony Fats: "Get back to me fast so we can set up a meeting."

An hour later, Tony Fats called back.

Tony Fats: "Eddie, they want to know where and when."

Eddie: "I'll call you in the morning. What's your number?"

Eddie wrote the information down, and then he called the FBI office in Boston. A duty agent took the call and Eddie told him he was Detective Ernie Lijoi Sr. of the Quincy PD and he needed to talk to either Agent Blaine or Agent Jones right away.

Ernie: "It's very important that they get back to me, I have a bank robbery situation where I can buy the proceeds," he said. "We need to move fast."

Five minutes later Agent Blaine called the red telephone and Eddie explained the details of the bond robbery and the deal with Tony Fats. Blaine said to reduce the money for Fats to ten thousand dollars ($10,000). "Push him down, he's a piece of shit looking for a free ride." Blaine said.

~ ~ ~

At noon Sunday, Eddie called Tony Fats and told him he would not get twenty five thousand dollars. Eddie explained that his people would only pay ten thousand dollars for the deal and he would get paid after the meeting and the close of the deal to purchase the bonds.

Tony Fats: "That sucks, it's worth the twenty five grand."

Eddie: "That's the best that I can do. Take it or leave it. I need a decision."

Tony Fats: "I guess I'll have to take it, but I trust you, Eddie, I want the money when it's finished."

Eddie: "Now you're being smart, don't worry, you'll get paid."

Eddie: "I want the meeting to be someplace where I feel safe," Eddie said.

"These guys are crazy, but they're logical," Tony Fats replied. "Just say where and when."

Eddie: "Let's make it tomorrow morning at eleven, in the Dorchester District Courthouse, inside the courtroom. Nobody can bring guns inside, so it will be safe for every-body. What do these guys look like?"

Tony Fats: "Are you crazy? That's a court house and you want to bring this deal in to the court house. You want to negotiate a ten million dollar deal in a court room? You must be crazy?"

Eddie: "Look Tony, I am not a tough guy, these guys are tough. I'd rather be safe than sorry. No one would be crazy enough to bring a weapon into the court house. So I'll be safe and can negotiate freely. If we don't make a deal I can walk away."

Tony Fats: "I guess that makes sense. You can't miss 'em. They're both Italian; full head of hair, clean shaved. They wear very nice suits and they both weigh about three-hundred-fifty pounds. One's Jerry, the other one is Carl. I'll be there to point them out but I will not be part of the nego-tiation. How do I know you?"

Eddie: "I'll be wearing a grey pinstripe suit. I'm Italian and I have a lot of hair. I'll trim my beard so I won't scare anyone. I have a large scar across my face. I'll meet you under the statue out in front of the building."

Tony Fats: "Eddie, one thing. Once I make this meeting and you guys meet, I'm out of it. All I want is my money."

Eddie: "No problem, see you then, Tony."

Eddie called the FBI and advised them that the meeting was all set to negotiate the bonds. He then called his boss, who promised to have men at the courthouse to cover him along with the FBI.

~ ~ ~

Eddie's police cover was in place well before eleven o'clock Monday morning. Only one of the drug unit detectives was informed of the meeting. FBI agents were in place with cameras to photograph the Mafia members who went to the courthouse to meet with Eddie. He shaved his beard, but his Afro hairstyle remained. He wore a pinstriped suit and shined leather shoes. Teresa laughed until she cried as he walked out the door of their home in Dedham that morning, calling him her husband, the banker. The boys just stared at their father's beardless face.

Tony Fats met Eddie at the courthouse and looked him over.

Tony Fats: "They're waiting inside," he said.

Eddie and Tony Fats walked into the courtroom where over one hundred men and women were sitting in the seats waiting for the court to start the trials for the day's session. Tony pointed to two men sitting near the back of the room, and left.

As Eddie went to a bench directly in front of the men that Tony Fats pointed out, the court was called into session, the first case was called. Eddie turned and introduced himself. All three men looked at each other for a moment, "You with Tony Fats?" Eddie was asked.

In the background, Eddie could hear the discussions in the court as they called and argued the cases.

Eddie: "Yes. Let's get to the point. You have any buyers?"

One of the men who introduced himself as Jerry leaned forward. "We have a buyer in Rhode Island that offered us two million for the package."

Eddie: "I can match that, but it's high. Maybe you should go with them. However, you will not have to transport the package. I will do that."

"Yeah, maybe we should go with Rhode Island." The man paused, looking around the courtroom at the people who were waiting for their cases to be called. "That's a long trip to where they are. If we had some financial incentive to do the dealer closer to home, it would be better and easier." His voice was low and his eyes followed Eddie's scar across his face.

Eddie: "Let me make a call. Maybe I can go a quarter more. Wait here. I'll call New York."

Eddie left the courtroom and walked through the front doors of the courthouse to a pay phone on the sidewalk. Police officers who were covering Eddie took note and the FBI took photographs as he picked up the phone, inserted a quarter, and called Teresa to say hello and ask about the boys. A large Italian-looking man in a suit came out of the courthouse to watch as Eddie made the call. Eddie hung up the phone and re-entered the court room and the man watching him went back into the courtroom right behind him. Eddie observed that man give Jerry the Nod, indicating that a phone call was made.

Eddie: "If you will accept a quarter more than two million, we have a deal, but there are a couple of contingencies. First, my expert has to look over the merchandise. Second, I pick the spot for the deal. I will have the money and if there is no problem, we never have to see each other again. We'll do the deal tonight. You guys want to talk it over?"

The two men looked at each other and one of them had a smirk that suggested he had just made the deal of a life-time.

Carl: "Jerry, it sounds good to me, let's make the deal." he said.

Jerry: "OK, we have a deal two and a quarter million for the package."

Eddie offered his hand to seal the agreement, they shook hands and he replied: "I'll call you later, between three and four. Give me your number."

Carl wrote a telephone number on a piece of paper and handed it to Eddie.

Carl: "Allora Vedilo," he said. Which is Italian for, See you then.

~ ~ ~

Later, Ernie met with the FBI agents. The FBI agents said they needed an hour to set up a surveillance system in the room where the buy would take place. Agents Blaine and Jones met Eddie at a street corner in Quincy and rode with him to arrange two adjoining hotel rooms in Braintree. Blaine, who was in back, lay on the floor of the car and Jones hid on the floor on the passenger side in front.

"What the hell are you doing?" Eddie asked.

"We don't want anybody to see us with you," Blaine responded from the floor in back.

"Nobody knows who the fuck you are," Eddie said, laughing at the agents, who looked ridiculous.

This had become an FBI operation and Eddie was act-ing as an undercover investigator. The FBI was supposed to be picking up the tab for the hotel rooms and other expens-es, including Tony Fats' fee. Eddie pulled into the parking lot of a hotel in Braintree and three men went inside. Blaine showed the desk clerk his badge and said he wanted adjoining rooms that had a door between them that could be opened to allow access to each room. The clerk looked at a floor plan of the hotel and said he had two such rooms on the fourth floor. Blaine said he needed the rooms right away and gave the clerk an FBI credit card. The clerk took the card and called a number to verify the charge. A moment later he gave the card back to Blaine and explained that the charge was denied.

The three men left the hotel and went to another, this one in Weymouth just off Route 128. On the way, Blaine explained that there must be something wrong with the card, but he had another that he could use.

"Why didn't you use the second card in Braintree?" Ernie asked.

"I didn't want to make a fuss," Blaine responded from his spot on the floor in the back.

This time, it went that same way, the explanation to the clerk that the men needed adjoining rooms immediately. The second card was rejected. They went back to the car.

"What the fuck is going on?" Eddie asked, wide eyed.

"I don't know," Blaine said, sitting upright in the back. "I'll check when I get back to the office."

"It's getting late," Eddie said. "I have to call these guys and set up the take down and I have to let my boss know what's going on."

Blaine: "Don't worry. We have plenty of time."

They went to a third hotel and Blaine produced yet another FBI credit card that was rejected.

"Now we'll do it my way," Eddie said, clearly upset.

Eddie drove to the Presidential Motel in Quincy, where he called his boss, who arranged two rooms, side by side, immediately, paid for by the citizens of Quincy.

It was dusk. Eddie called the two Mafia men and told them to meet him at the motel at seven o'clock.

Carl: "We know where it is. We'll meet you there at seven."

A few minutes later, a U-haul rental truck pulled into the parking lot and FBI technicians unloaded a container of electronic equipment and rolled it into one of the rooms, where tables were set up. An agent Eddie had never met examined the wall between the two rooms and inserted a very finely pointed long needle into the wall near the floor. He plugged a wire into the needle and Eddie was amazed to see a live television image of the adjoining room appear on a screen that had been set up on one of the tables.

The door between the rooms was opened to allow another agent to walk around the room in a sound and video check. The agent walked from corner to corner and Eddie could hear his footsteps and watch his every move.

FBI Agent: "We're set."

The time was nearing 7 PM. Eddie and Blaine went into the adjoining room and waited. Blaine would pose as the bond expert. Shortly after seven there was a knock on the door. Blaine opened it and four men walked in. Two of them were the men from the courthouse. The other two wore coats over their arms and Eddie and Blaine assumed they had guns under their coats. One went to the back of the room and stood by the window. The other man sat in a chair by the bed. Neither man acknowledged Eddie or Blaine. Jerry and Carl walked in after the first men entered and were set in their place.

Eddie nodded at Blaine. "He's my expert on bonds. If he's OK with them, we have a deal."

The two men from the courthouse nodded, but said nothing.

Eddie: "Where are the bonds?"

The man who had been identified as "Carl" stood up. "In the car, I'll get them."

Everyone else remained where they were and said nothing until "Carl" returned with a briefcase, which he placed on the bed and opened. Eddie could see the bonds inside and bent to examine them. He then called Blaine over to offer his opinion. Blaine picked them up and searched the lines and markings with a magnifying glass, asked a few questions about the numbers on the bonds.

Carl answered Blaine's questions.

Blaine looked at Eddie: "These look perfect to me. They are the real thing."

"That's all I need," Eddie said. "I'll get your money. I hope you don't mind hundred dollar bills. I got a lot of them."

Carl smiled. "Fuck no. We don't mind that weight at all."

Eddie walked to the door and opened it. He stepped aside as FBI agents filled the room, guns drawn. The two mafia gunmen made brief moves with their hidden hands but thought better of it. They dropped their guns and raised their arms. The agents pointed to Eddie and took him into custody, announcing to the Mafia men that they had been watching him and had followed him to the meeting at the motel.

The Mafia men were taken to the FBI office in Boston and charged. The bonds were recovered before the bank was aware that they had been stolen.

~ ~ ~

On Tuesday, Eddie met Tony Fats at a diner in Weymouth.

Tony Fats: "I heard you all got arrested."

Eddie: "Yeah, that's right, the FBI got wind of it somehow. That's what I think, but you earned your money. I have to protect my street reputation. So I'll pay you, Happy Valentine's Day."

He handed him a paper bag that contained ten thousand dollars in cash. The two men never met again.

Chapter Ten

Whitey

Wednesday, February 15

Teresa could not sleep. She glanced at the red telephone and wondered if it would ring. It rang at all hours and, if he were home, her husband would answer it, often leaving their bed to meet the person who had called. He had been gone for several hours and it would soon be dawn. She tossed in the bed, trying to find a comfortable position and fall asleep, but her mind kept wandering to the man she had married and who now was God-knows-where with God-knows-who.

She did not know it would be like this, although she admitted to herself that she had no idea what the life of an undercover detective would be like for him and for their family. The man she had married had become someone else. He had taken on a new name and a new personality and he came home with both and was always, it seemed to her, this man named Eddie Pannoni. She missed Ernie Lijoi, her New York boy. She missed his coming home and leaving his work behind.

Now their lives were ruled by the red telephone. Even their weekends were gone, she thought. He went out to meet people on Saturdays and Sundays and came home distracted. The only glimpse she got into his world was typing the reports that he submitted to the police department, but they were dry and spared the details of his encounters with the street life. She tried to distance herself from the details she typed, from the man who offered to sell pounds of marijuana and cocaine in kilos and the man who thinks he has hepatitis because he shared needles with another addict. She tried to wipe away the thought of people who were selling guns or using them in crimes. Were they calling her husband? *Is he safe?* she wondered, and answered her own question. *Of course he's safe. He's a tough guy and he can take care of himself.*

She thought about the young man who had swept her off her feet in the summer of 1964. She had never met anyone like him. He was so confident of himself. She had just graduated from high school in Dedham, then a small town on the edge of Boston. She was engaged, sort of, to a high school sweetheart, a nice boy, but he was not very sure of himself or his place in the world. He let her push him around, which she thought was fun. She also thought he was weak. Then she met Ernie at a pizza shop on Cape Cod during beach week.

She was sitting with her friends in THE LEANING TOWER OF PIZZA in downtown Falmouth. They had rented a small beach place to celebrate their liberation from high school. Ernie was in the air force and he and his buddies had rented a small house for the summer and partied there every weekend. Ernie and his buddies came into the pizza shop and flirted with the girls and invited them to a party at the beach house that night. It was a magical week for Teresa. She had met the man of her dreams and the boy from Dedham was history. Teresa and Ernie were married in November of that same year, 1964..

Dedham was a small town when Teresa was growing up during the fifties. She was the youngest of five children, three girls and two boys. Her parents were born in Italy and settled in one of the oldest towns in America. Dedham was Old Yankee. Its oldest families had been in the town since 1635, when Pilgrims, spooked by rumors of an impending Indian attack, moved up the Charles River to settle. In some ways, newcomers were considered outsiders and the Italian community tended to stay to itself, going to the same churches and living in the same neighborhoods. Teresa grew up in a two-story colonial style house, but her family life was rooted in the old country.

On Sundays, her mother cooked large Italian meals for the family. It was a place where everyone knew everyone else, and that is one thing she shared with Ernie, whose Brooklyn neighborhood was like a small town. Where he was rough and ready for a fight, she was soft and intellectual. She graduated with honors from Dedham high school and was a member of the National Honor Society. A week later, she met Ernie, a high school dropout from the big city. He would eventually (years later) complete high school and go on to college, as they raised their boys together.

She laughed to herself as she recalled his young, scarred face and his Brooklyn accent. She felt safe with him. She thought he would protect her if anyone tried to hurt her. He was a good father and had kept his vow to be kind and gentle and not like his own dad, who was hard and physical with Ernie.

Teresa met Ernie's father and saw where Ernie got his strength, but she knew the man to be difficult, as well. That was when she and Ernie lived in Brooklyn for several months after he was discharged from the air force. Brooklyn was not for her and Ernie came to know that it was not for him, either. They moved back to Massachusetts where they struggled until Ernie got a job with the MBTA police. They were not rich, or even comfortable, but they had a home and two fine boys.

She already missed the life they had led when he worked shifts for the transit police. He worked eight hours and came home. They went to Maine on some weekends and others, attended the boys' sports games. He left his job at the station and never brought home any problems that he had on the job. Now, he never left the job, it followed him home and even into their bedroom where the red telephone rested on the nightstand.

Teresa was in bed and dozed off. She woke when Ernie climbed into bed and fell asleep next to her. His hair had grown into a large Afro style that collapsed against the pillow. The closet door was ajar after he had locked his gun in a strongbox on the top shelf. His clothes were on the chair next to the bed and his sox were on the floor.

She lay back and watched as the dawn broke, slipping from black to grey in the cloudy winter morning. The boys would be up soon and she would make them breakfast and send them off to school. Maybe, she thought, the red telephone won't ring until noon and this man next to her can get some rest from whatever or whomever he is dealing with.

She felt alone there in bed, even though her husband Ernie, known as Eddie now, lay there next to her. They were living in different worlds now, she and the boys in one; Eddie Pannoni and the dealers and junkies in another. Ernie belonged in her world, not the world of Eddie Pannoni. *Come back to me,* she prayed.

***

Thursday, February 16

The diner was across the street from the Quincy Police Department. The two uniformed officers who were sitting at the counter drinking coffee did not recognize Eddie Pannoni. Another uniformed officer opened the front door, saw Eddie and recognized him. He smiled and started to walk to Eddie's seat, but Eddie glanced at him and made a short shake of his head. The officer looked away and walked to a seat a few feet from Eddie. He was talking to two waitresses who were linked to low level drug dealers, one of them, a teenager.

Waitress: "My ma's been in a car accident," she said. The girl was blond and short and leaned on the counter as she looked at Eddie.

Eddie: "I'll give you a ride to the hospital," he offered.

Waitress: "My sister's coming to get me," she responded. "It's not life threatening. I don't know how bad it is. She'll take me."

The second waitress came over to pat the girl on the shoulder. Eddie noted that she was very pretty, blond, about five feet five and had a heart tattoo on her left hand, about 22 years old. She was identified as Jeannie. There were two initials in the heart that Eddie could not make out.

Eddie: "What's it say?" he asked, pointing to the tattoo.

Jeannie: "It was something stupid I did when I was fifteen."

A tall bearded man came into the diner, shaking the snow off his shoes. He knew the girls and sat down next to Eddie, who recognized him as a hitchhiker he had given rides to on a couple of occasions. The man had said his name was "Bob".

Bob: "What's up?" he asked, looking at the girls.

Eddie: "She's waiting for her sister to take her to the hospital. Her ma's been in an accident, a car accident."

The man turned to Eddie. "You know these girls?"

Eddie: "Just met them."

Bob: "This one's Jeannie. Jeannie, this is Eddie. He's all right." The man introduced Eddie to the waitress with the heart shaped tattoo on her hand.

The girl behind the counter saw her sister pull into the parking lot and grabbed her coat. "See you guys," she said.

"Say hi to your ma," Jeannie said, coming around the counter to sit next to Bob.

"He's ok?" she asked, nodding toward Eddie.

Jeannie: "Yeah, he's good,"

Jeannie: "OK, listen. You guys interested in getting some heroin?"

Eddie: "Yeah, I may be interested depending on the price. How much?" Eddie was interested.

Jeannie: "Thirty dollar bags and fifty dollar bags," she replied.

"I'm in for a fifty dollar bag," Bob said.

"Me too, If it's good, we'll see if I want more," Eddie said.

"You got a car?" she asked, looking at Eddie, who nodded.

Eddie: "Yeah, I have a car, I'll drive you there."

Jeannie: "Pick me up when I get off. Seven o'clock."

Shortly after seven she climbed into Eddie's Thunderbird and gave him an address in Weymouth where they can make the buy.

Jeannie: "So, Eddie, what do you do?"

He reached into his pocket and handed her his card. "I work on cars; do a little carpentry, stuff like that, but what I really do is sell drugs. I buy here and sell in New York."

"No shit. That's cool." She smiled as she looked at Eddie. "My roommate's husband might want a little speed."

Eddie replied: "Geez, I don't know right now. I can barely get enough for my own customers, never mind taking on new ones, maybe I can help out in the future. You never know."

Jeannie: "I can get you some heroin," she said. "I got a source. It's three twenty five for an eighth of an ounce. I can get it in quantity for you." She smiled at Eddie and raised her eyebrows.

Eddie: "You gotta make a few bucks on it if you sell it to me, and I have to be able to make a buck on it, assuming it's good stuff."

Jeannie: "Pull over right there," she said, pointing to a house on Shawmut Street. "I'll get you a taste. I need fifty for the bag."

Eddie gave her sixty dollars, ten of which was for Jeannie. She went into the house and returned almost immediately and handed Ernie his money, saying her roommate had gone to pick up an eighth of an ounce of heroin and would be back soon.

Jeannie: "I'll call you when it's ready, give me your number." she said, and walked back into the house.

Two hours later, Eddie got word to go back to the house. He returned to the house and Jeannie gave him a small bag of heroin.

"I get off at seven tomorrow. Pick me up and we'll have a couple of drinks."

Eddie drove to St. Catherine's to meet Detective Churn to brief him and turn in the heroin. Churn knew all about Jeannie.

Det. Churn: :I know Jeannie, She's a smart girl graduated from Quincy High. She had everything going for her. Now she's a junkie, hangs out with scumbags, too bad."

Eddie told Churn he was meeting Jeannie the following evening and thought she could be a way into a heroin supply chain.

~ ~~

Eddie met Jeannie as agreed and took her for some drinks. He inquired about various drugs and contacting some suppliers to help out his New York people.

Jeannie: "I can get you anything you want. I have great suppliers." Jeannie cocked her head and smiled across table. "I got suppliers all over."

"I have a lot of customers, people I deal with, in New York. I might be interested in some quantity, if it's good shit." Eddie sat back and looked at Jeannie. He saw a troubled young woman who made more trouble for herself every day of her life. She would turn heads when she walked into a room and men wanted to be with her. She obliged, if drugs were part of the deal, gravitating to the low life's who always seemed to have a something she wanted, heroin, mostly, but meth was alright, too. If it would get her high, Jeannie wanted the drugs and didn't care who or where they came from, nor what she may have to do to get them. This is why she tried to stay close with Eddie, he was a source of money for her, and possibly drugs her main concern. On the other hand Eddie looked at her as a source of suppliers and he would use her to get to those suppliers.

As Lt. Lyme once said to Ernie; "I'll work with the devil himself to clean up the streets of drugs which are the source of most robberies and much more."

Her availability had given her a network of dealers and she knew who had what at any given moment. Eddie wanted access to her network. He knew that he had to be part of the junkie world to become one of them. His life in Brooklyn had given him insight into how junkies look and act. He had seen addicts scratch themselves and slowly nod off as they experienced their highs. Eddie began to slowly scratch his shoulders and chest. He mimicked the actions of an addict and watched Jeannie's eyes as she looked at him. He nodded off, faking it and trying to have her believe that he was high, and then slowly opened his eyes.

Jeannie: "I know where you are, Eddie. I'd like to go there with you." She smiled at him.

Eddie: "It's all I got. I ain't got no more," he replied.

Jeannie: "You know, my roommate Betty and her husband have a good source, too. Guy her husband has always got what you need. You know what I mean? I can introduce you. He likes me and wants me. For you I'll take care of him."

Eddie: "I'm always looking for good stuff, but don't do anything like that for me. I'm not in the pimping business and I refuse to get into it. If you want him, that's your business." Eddie got a slight bit upset with her.

Jeannie: "OK, OK. I understand, but I do it all the time, it's OK."

Eddie: "Not for me."

She seemed to lose interest in the conversation. She looked around and then stood up. There would be no heroin from Eddie tonight, so she decided to look for another source.

Jeannie: "Give me a ride?" she asked.

Eddie: "Yeah, sure, where to?"

Jeannie: "You know Waylen Beyer? You know where he lives, right?"

Eddie: "You know he got busted."

Jeannie: "He's always getting busted, but he always comes back." She climbed into the Thunderbird and closed the door. Eddie started the car and drove her where she wanted to go.

He did not go into Waylon's apartment. Jeannie got out and walked through a side door of the apartment house and up the stairs. Eddie could not determine whether a line had formed outside Waylen's door, but he noticed an unmarked police car a half block away and knew that the place was being watched.

He drove to St. Catherine's to meet Detective Churn and discuss Jeannie and the network she was opening to him. Churn said he would pass the information on to the Lieutenant.

"I got too many shit-bags to deal with," Eddie said, laughing. "They call me at all hours. I'm never home anymore."

"We got a lot of shit-bags around here," Churn said. "Maybe you can clean 'em up."

Eddie: "I'll do my best to get the suppliers."

Churn: "You hearing anything about any guns?"

Eddie: "A little here and there. Why? Do you know something that I should know?"

Churn: "No, nothing special at all."

Edie left the meeting and headed back home. When he got in the door the red phone rang, he answered it. It was Sergio a Mafioso informant from the north end.

Sergio: "Hey man did you hear about what Whitey is doing?"

Eddie: "No, tell me about it."

Sergio: "Talk on the street. Some rumors about a big drug shipment being swapped for some guns for the IRA. Guns will go to Ireland. The drugs will stay here in New England, nothing solid. Keep your eyes open."

Eddie: "What's the name of the ship or boat they are using?"

Sergio: "They call it The Valhalla."

Eddie thought about the rumor as he drove home. There was always talk of guns on the street. There was always a market for handguns and rifles. There was sympathy for the Irish Republican Army in the Irish neighborhoods, especially in South Boston where the "Southies" saw themselves as an Irish bastion and where Irish flags and tattoos were common. They still had to answer to the Italians in Boston and in Rhode Island; the chain of command, so to speak. He thought of his own tattoo, the "W" on his ankle, the pride of Washington Avenue in Brooklyn, and he understood the tribal mood in South Boston.

Guns for the IRA. Jesus! he thought.

Having this information, Ernie telephoned Detective Churn who in turn contacted the boat men on the job and informed them. The Valhalla escaped, but a couple of weeks later Ernie received some additional information.

Sergio: Hey remember the ship of guns I told you about?"

Eddie: "Yes, I remember."

Sergio: "Guess what? Whitey is being paid with drugs, a ship full of drugs."

Eddie; "Do you know the name of the ship?"

Sergio: "No, but I can tell you that they plan on unloading the ship in Quincy."

Eddie; "Thanks, Sergio, for letting me know."

Chapter Eleven

Cocaine Delivery

Thursday, February 23

The days had been above freezing, which allowed much of the snow to melt, and the sunshine seemed warmer, even though spring was weeks away. Ernie joked with the boys as they left for school, handing them their lunch bags as they walked out the door for the walk to school.

Teresa poured herself a cup of coffee and sat at the kitchen table, looking at Ernie.

Teresa: "I understand what you are doing, but I don't like this Ernie. I don't like who you hang around with. I don't like the drug dealers and the gun sellers, any of it."

Ernie: "It's just a temporary job and after it's over there's no way they can turn me down for a job in Quincy. No way. It's what we want and it will be a big step up for all of us. Quincy is the top department in the state and they have the best people. I can learn a lot from them."

Teresa: "It was supposed to be a thirty-day job, Ernie. It's been almost two months."

Ernie: "This investigation will be over in a few weeks. I started this job. I have to finish it. No one expected me to get into the people that I have and to move up the ladder within the drug world the way that I did. I certainly didn't expect it. I guess my childhood experiences have helped. This will be over very soon."

Teresa: "Yeah, I know." She wrapped her hands around the warm mug. "I understand. It's hard not to worry."

Ernie: "Honey, once I get the transfer and its official, we'll have a lot better life going for all of us, you, me and the kids, things that I don't have with the transit police."

Teresa: "Ernie, I'm still worried. I don't like those kinds of people. I know what you've been doing. I type your reports. I know, Ernie. I'm afraid that you will come home with a bullet or not at all."

Ernie: "Look at the bright side. What about the kids? I show them the drugs and show them what they look like. They know how this stuff is packaged. That knowledge is keeping drugs out of their hands too. You know they liked me telling them that stuff."

Teresa: "Okay, there is an upside, but Ernie, don't lie to me and say there's no danger. I'm not stupid."

Ernie sat down next to Teresa and placed his arm around her shoulders.

Ernie: "I won't tell you that." His voice was soft. "But I will tell you that I seem to get along very well with these people. I know they're always calling here and I wish I could get that phone in another place so it doesn't bother you, but that's impossible right now. This will all be over in time and we'll laugh about this later."

Teresa looked at her husband. His Afro enlarged his head and his thick, black beard gave him a sinister look that was enhanced by the scar across his face. He wore dungarees, a t-shirt and a denim vest. He was not a man she would want to meet in an alley late at night.

Teresa: "Okay," she said, as she watched him place the .38 into the waistband of his dungarees.

Ernie: "I gotta run into Quincy," he said. "I'll see you later."

He kissed her, as he always did when he left the house, and she heard the Thunderbird starting and Ernie pulling away.

Little did either of them know that this investigation would last close to a year.

~ ~ ~

Teresa sat alone in the empty kitchen. Her boys were gone for the day and, in many ways, gone into their lives. They no longer needed her as they once did. They went to school and played sports and spent time with their friends. Ernie was never home and when he was away, he was with drug dealers, whores and even killers. She stared at the kitchen table and began to cry. She tried very hard to see the upside of what was happening to her family. Benefits and a pension seemed far away.

~ ~ ~

Ernie, as Eddie Pannoni, was back on the street. He pulled into the parking lot of the diner on Sea Street where he met his contacts. He wanted a moment to think about his day but his muse was cut short by the arrival of Wise Johnny, a street character who had a reputation for knowing what was happening. People told him things, confidential and personal information, for reasons no one really understood. He also had a reputation for passing this information around. With Wise Johnny, information was like trading cards, give me something and I've got something for you.

Wise Johnny: "Hey, Eddie. Mind if I sit down?"

"Take a load off." Eddie folded his newspaper and placed it next to him.

"Anything new going on?" Wise Johnny was looking to trade.

Eddie: "Nah, nothin'. You?"

Johnny: "Remember Pauly from Southie?"

Eddie: "Yeah, I know Pauly. He hooked with up Whitey Badger in Southie. Irish gang called The Winter - Hill Gang."

Johnny:"Yeah, him. He's doing a run this afternoon for three kilos."

Eddie: "Coke or heroin?" Eddie was interested in this bit of news from Wise Johnny.

Johnny: "Coke. He don't do heroin."

Eddie: "Well, I wish him luck. Let me ask you, what the fuck are you telling me for? I don't wanna know this shit. What if something goes wrong?"

Johnny: "Yeah, you're right. But I can trust you. Everybody does."

Eddie looked across the table at Wise Johnny. "I really don't want to know, but you're right, you can trust me. When's he leaving?"

Johnny: "Two. Around two this afternoon, it should be an easy trip."

Eddie: "He alone? No, don't tell me. I'm better off not knowin'".

Johnny: "By the way, I heard Jeannie has a large supply of DLs." Dilaudid Hydrochloride is a powerful pain killer in the category of morphine. It is highly addictive.

Eddie: "I'll give her a call."

"Pauly's going alone to his deal. He asked me to ride along but I told him I was busy." Wise Johnny had a grin on his face. "I have a date. I'm going to be paid, laid and par-laid." He laughed at his little joke.

Eddie smiled. "Have a good time."

Johnny: "Oh yeah. I will. Believe me. I will." He sat up straight and wagged his head.

Ernie stood up and pulled a dollar out of his pocket and left it on the table.

Eddie; "I gotta meet some guys down at the beach," he said.

Johnny: "That's where Pauly's goin', down to Hull to make the pickup."

Eddie: "I told you. No speakie!"

Johnny: "Okay, forget it. I never saw you."

Ernie drove to a pay telephone two blocks from the diner and called Detective Churn. He explained what Wise Johnny had told him about Pauly's pickup of three kilos of cocaine at Hull that afternoon.

Churn: "You clear on this?" Churn asked "You gonna be okay if we move in?"

Eddie: "If Wise Johnny told me, he told a dozen people. I'm okay."

Churn: "We'll take it from here."

~ ~ ~

Churn called Boston police narcotics detectives and a surveillance team was sent to Pauly's house. Within an hour a radio call announced that "The bird is out of the nest and flying."

Pauly was driving a Cadillac. Four police cars were behind him, all hauling undercover cops. He kept to the far left lane as he drove to Hull. Suddenly, he crossed all lanes to the right and shot off the exit, leaving two police cars to continue to the next exit. One of the remaining cars picked him up at a convenience store, talking on a pay phone. The detective that was watching him picked up his radio to let the other men know where he was.

Detective: "I got him on the phone. He's probably setting the deal up or confirming this deal right now."

Pauly bought a pack of cigarettes and went back to the Cadillac and headed south to Hull, a beautiful hamlet on the Atlantic Ocean. The town enjoys a large beach that draws crowds from Boston on hot summer days. The beach was almost deserted when Pauly pulled into the parking lot near a bar. He parked the car and went in.

Detective Churn followed him and watched as Pauly ordered a drink and sat back to watch a basketball game on the television over the bar. A few minutes later Detective Rule joined Churn, and the two of them quietly ordered drinks and watched television. They were not noticed by other bar patrons.

The other officers remained outside along the beach wall to observe everyone entering or leaving the bar. They were looking for known drug dealers or anyone known to be one of Pauly's friends.

Half an hour later a man walked in and sat next to Pauly. They shook hands and talked, but neither Churn nor Rule could hear the conversation. Churn went outside to brief the other officers about what was happening in the bar and learned that Pauly's friend's car had already been identified. As they were talking, Pauly and the other man emerged from the bar. Pauly went to the Cadillac and drove it alongside the other man's car so that the driver's windows were next to each other. Pauly handed the man a paper bag. The man passed a package to Pauly.

This was the deal going down and the Police Detectives moved in immediately.

"Police! Do not move! Police!" Churn and Rule moved toward the two cars, holding their badges out, as the other officers covered them. The man who had passed the drugs to Pauly got out of his car holding a 9 millimeter handgun and lifted it to point at Churn.

The detective pointed his .38 at the man and shouted, "Don't! If you do, I will end it all right now, right here for you!"

The man dropped the weapon and the officers took him into custody. They confiscated three kilos of cocaine and one hundred thousand dollars in cash in a large paper bag. There was a discussion over who had jurisdiction over the suspects. The case had gone from Quincy to Boston to Hull.

~ ~ ~

Detective Rule contacted Ernie via telephone and advised him of the case and the arrests. He also told him about the dilemma of jurisdiction; "This could get them off," he told Ernie.

Ernie suggested that he tell the District Attorney that it was a form of hot and continuous pursuit that began in Quincy with a deep cover operative. The district attorney agreed and the men were taken to Quincy.

That night when Eddie met with Churn and Rule at St. Catherine's, Churn thanked him for the tip. "Nice job," he said. "We got a lead on some pills. Could be big. Maybe even tie in the Mob in Rhode Island. We'll talk more to-morrow."

~ ~ ~

Eddie got home at one o'clock in the morning. Teresa was in bed, waiting.

"How'd it go today?" she asked.

"Good," he responded, turning out the light.

The telephone rang at 3am.

Jeannie: "Hey, Eddie. It's Jeannie. Did I call too late?"

He paused, trying to collect his thoughts.

Eddie: "Nah, that's all right. What's up?"

Jeannie: "I got a little something, some DLs. You in-terested?"

Eddie: "Yeah. I heard."

Jeannie: "You did? From who?"

Eddie: "Johnny. Wise Johnny mentioned something about it."

Jeannie: "How the fuck did he know?"

Eddie: "I don't know. People talk."

Jeannie: "You want some?"

Eddie: "Yeah, why don't I call you in the morning, maybe around noon, lunch time. We can get together."

Jeannie: "Call me at work. You got the number?"

Eddie; "Yeah, I'll call you."

He hung up the telephone and rolled over. Teresa was staring at him in the dark.

Teresa: "Does it ever end?" she asked.

Ernie: "Yeah, soon," he said, adding, "I love you."

Teresa: "I love you, too, Ernie." It was dawn before she fell asleep.

***

Friday, February 24

"You need to fix this sink," Teresa said. "The trap, the bent part underneath leaks. That towel you taped there isn't working."

He looked at her. She seemed tired.

Ernie: "I'll take off over the weekend and fix up some things around here. I've got some things I need to do today, but I'm home for the entire weekend."

She studied him over her coffee. "That would be nice."

~ ~ ~

He went to the red telephone and called the diner where Jeannie worked. Her boss answered and offered a terse, "She's working" and hung up the phone. He drove to the diner and saw her behind the counter, flirting with a scruffy-looking young man, who to Eddie looked like someone who should be taken outside and hosed off. She saw Eddie walk to a stool at the counter and came over with a cup of coffee.

Jeannie: "Hey, stranger," she winked at him.

Eddie: "I tried to call but guess who hung up on me."

Jeannie: "Fuck him. We're having a little gathering at my place tonight. C'mon over. I got something for ya. Maybe you want a lot."

Eddie: "If it's good, yeah."

~ ~ ~

The winter sun was setting later in the evening and it was still light when Eddie knocked on the door. A man answered and stared at Eddie as he walked in. There were five people sitting at the kitchen table watching Jeannie open a plastic bag.

Jeannie: "Eddie. C'mon in," she said. "We got some fixin's." She laughed as she opened a packet of heroin.

Eddie sat at the kitchen table and watched Jeannie skin pop the heroin by placing the needle just under her skin, not injecting it into her veins. The man who had answered the door picked up a packet, cooked it, and injected it. A needle was passed around the table and then to Eddie. It was his turn to shoot the heroin.

Eddie: "I don't put that shit in my body. I put the money in my pocket, not up my nose or in my veins. If I did that I would never make any money, " he laughed and put the needle on the table. Jeannie paid no attention and the others were happy to have the heroin for themselves. Eddies statement bothered no one. Not one person, of the six people sitting there, doing the heroin, argued with him. he was accepted into the group, without question.

He spent the next hour trying to make conversation with people who were not really there; whose minds were bathed in artificial fantasies. He managed to purchase a small quantity of heroin and one hundred tablets of dilaudid.

He said he had to use the bathroom. He closed the door and reached into his pocket to remove several plain matchbooks and a small pencil. He made notes of everything that had taken place and the names of those at the table. He closed the matchbooks, put them in his pocket, and flushed the toilet.

He told Jeannie he wanted some serious quantities of heroin for his customers in New York and wanted to meet her suppliers. She said she knew some good people that would sell through her and eventually directly to Eddie.

Jeannie: "I'll call you," she said.

Eddie: "I'm goin' to New York for a few days. I got some business to do. I'll be back next week." He felt sorry for her. She was lost. He knew that she had a mother and a father and that at one time she had been a beautiful little girl with blond hair and a big smile. That little girl was gone and replaced by a beautiful junky whose only goal every day was to flood her brain with drugs; no matter what the end cost would be in money or mortality. Her goal was to escape the life outside her skin.

He met Detective Churn at St. Catherine's, gave him the drugs and told him about Jeannie's promise to introduce him to a bulk supplier of heroin.

Eddie; "I need a couple of days at home," he said. "I need to spend time with my family."

Churn nodded. "See you Monday."

~ ~ ~

The weekend was a family time. Ernie Lijoi Sr. was home and he fixed the pipe, cleaned the basement, and spent time with Teresa and the boys. The red phone rang at all hours but it was not answered. Ernie put a pillow over it. He watched movies with the boys and told Teresa how much he loved her. In the back of his mind he knew that the street business continued and that junkies and dealers were exchanging money and that lives were being flushed away. Even so, for two days, it was someone else's problem.

Chapter Twelve

Rt. 128 Raid

Wednesday, March 1

Jeannie looked like hell, "I'm sick," she said. "I need something. It's fucking cold."

"Call your contacts," Eddie said.

"I ain't got no money. Maybe we can work something out. I can get you something and you can take care of me. What do you say?"

Eddie: "Yeah, good, you will buy it and then sell it to me. We can do that. Who do you know who has something right now?"

Jeannie: "I know this guy. Rinaldi, Sammy Rinaldi. He's got everything. You got any money?"

Eddie gave Jeannie ten dollars for herself and then said, "You take me there and I will make my own deal, agreed?"

Jeannie agreed and Eddie drove Jeannie to a house in Braintree where he met Sammy Rinaldi and his girlfriend, a thin, blond woman whom he judged to be about twenty years old. Rinaldi was a sharp dresser who wore clipped hair and sported a neat mustache. He knew Jeannie and treated her like a friend and welcomed Eddie into his house. Jeannie used the ten dollars Eddie had given her to obtain a packet from Sammy and then she disappeared into a bathroom. Eddie purchased a packet of heroin and asked Sammy if he had anything else.

"Whatever you need," Sammy responded.

Eddie: "I got some people I take care of in New York. I'm always looking to invest. Know what I mean?"

Sammy: "Yeah, I know. I got Crystal, you into that?" He nodded toward his girlfriend. "She's gonna take care of some girls from Wellesley. They're on their way over now."

Rinaldi's telephone rang. The caller wanted some crystal and he told the man to come over. Another caller wanted cocaine. The same answer. Eddie thought Rinaldi's operation was like a take-out chicken stand, with customers calling to place their orders and coming by to hand over their money to take home their drugs.

Rinaldi hung up the phone, Eddie asked him how the supply of cocaine was.

Rinaldi: "I don't have any right now," he said. "My brother is coming up from Florida and he's bringing me a couple of kilos." Eddie did the math and decided that Rinaldi was a major supplier.

Rinaldi: "I don't keep stuff in the house, not quantity," he explained to Eddie. "I got busted by the Feds. I have a place in South Boston where I leave most of my stock and do some cutting. Let me know if you want to do some business. I'm always ready for new business."

Eddie: "I will do that. I'll be in touch." Eddie left the house with Jeannie.

He dropped Jeannie at her home and went to the diner in Dedham to get a cup of coffee and write his notes before he went home. He had written Rinaldi's name and address and information about his girlfriend on some matchbooks, but he wanted some time to collect his thoughts about Rinaldi and what he was doing.

Two Dedham detectives walked into the coffee shop and signaled Eddie that they wanted to talk. One of them looked at Eddie and raised his eyebrows, asking if it was okay to sit down. They knew him as both Ernie Lijoi and Eddie Pannoni. He had worked with them on several cases and they were the only members of the Dedham department who knew who he was. He knew them as Detective Murray and his partner Detective Osborn, both good cops and good guys to work with.

One of them, a thin, dark-complexioned man named Murray, leaned forward.

Murray: "We got a bad situation in the school system," he said in a low voice.

Ernie Lijoi's boys were in Dedham schools.

Ernie; "What's going on?" he asked.

"We got a dealer with no conscience," Murray said.

Eddie: "That's an oxymoron, ain't it?"

Murray: "Yeah, it is, but we still got the problem."

Eddie; "My kids go to these schools. What can I do?"

Murray: "Would you help us out?"

Eddie: "Whatever I can do."

Murray: "We got a guy down at the station. Would you talk to him, Ernie?"

Eddie: "I can't be seen near the station. Give me another spot. And don't call me Ernie. It's Eddie, Eddie from now on. It's safer for my family."

Murray: "How about my house? I live alone and in the woods. Let's do it tomorrow about noon. Okay with you?"

Eddie; "I'll call Quincy to make sure it's okay. That way I'll let Lieutenant Lynch knows what I'll be doing." Eddie said.

Quincy had no problem with the plan. They had a plentiful stack of reports from Eddie to catch up on and names and places to put together. He was told to take the time he needed to help Dedham.

~ ~ ~

It was cold, but sunny when Eddie met Murray and his partner at Murray's house in the woods. They introduced him to a skinny white man with dirty blond hair and gray/blue eyes whom they identified as "Joe Amadeus".

Joe told Eddie he could introduce him to a guy in Dedham who sold cocaine and marijuana. "I need a break on my charges," he said.

Eddie: "We can help you out, but there's no guarantee that the District Attorney will go along with the deal unless we can bring in a much larger fish," Eddie said.

Joe: "I'm just a little guy. All I know is this guy. I'm gonna cut you into him, he is much bigger than me. He supplies a lot of people in this town and he don't care who it is as long as they have the money."

Eddie looked at the man. "Okay, make your call and we'll go from there. One more thing, look at me."

The young man looked at Eddie with fear in his eyes.

Eddie: "If I ever hear that you are pointing me out to anyone, I mean anyone; you will spend the next twenty years of your life in jail. Understand? And don't think I won't find out. I have more people on the street than you will ever know. You got that?"

The man, Joe, stared at Eddie; "Yeah. After we're done, I never saw or heard of you."

Eddie: "That a boy. My name is Eddie. Here's my card. You can call me as soon as you set something up. Make it fast."

Joe: "I'll call you tonight."

Murray pulled Eddie aside. "Thanks. If you need anything, let us know."

"I need a couple hundred dollars to start out," Eddie replied.

Murray: "Meet me in an hour down town."

~ ~ ~

Eddie received three hundred dollars in cash from the Dedham police department and was ready to deal when Joe called that night. He picked him up at East and High Streets and Joe directed him to small Cape Cod-style house, where he parked the Thunderbird and walked with Joe up the driveway. There were no lookouts. The house was within a hundred feet of the Boston/Dedham line and police departments from both jurisdictions ignored the area thinking that it was in the others jurisdiction.

Joe introduced Eddie to a man who had a double heart tattoo on his right forearm. Eddie made a mental note, White male, about 5' 9", two hundred pounds by the name of Jerome White.

Jerome accepted the short introduction without question, which surprised Eddie.

Jerome: "What do you do, Eddie?"

Eddie; "I work on cars, here is one of my cards."

Jerome took the card and laid it on the table. "You're from New York. I can tell by the accent."

Eddie: "Brooklyn born and raised."

Jerome: "What do you need?"

Eddie: "I need something to take back to New York with me. I have plenty of customers there. Things are getting a little tight in the big city."

Jerome: "Things are not slow here. I got coke and grass. My grass connection can get you all you want."

Eddie: "Listen, Jerome. How good is the coke? I need good stuff. My guys do not want any garbage. I get good money for top shelf blow."

Jerome: "Yeah, I bet. Everything in New York is big money. How much coke you want?"

Eddie: "I'll take a taste. I'm going to New York tonight. I'll try it once. If it's good, I'll be back."

Jerome: "Quarter ok?"

Jerome went to the basement of the house and came back with a large bag of cocaine that Eddie estimated was a half-pound. The street value was ten thousand dollars per ounce, so Eddie guessed that Jerome was holding eighty thousand dollars worth of cocaine. He also noticed two handguns, a nine-millimeter and a .38. Jerome took out approximately an eighth ounce of cocaine and handed it to Eddie. "This should take care of what you need."

"How can I get a hold of you?" Eddie asked.

Jerome gave Eddie his phone number and Eddie told him that his number was on the card that Eddie just gave him.

Eddie drove Joe to a drop off point and pulled to the curb. He wanted to be sure that he didn't have to worry about Joe talking.

Eddie: "Do not forget this. You do not know me. You do not know me. Say it."

Joe shaking: "I do not know you."

Eddie: "Remember what I said. If you ever identify me you will spend a miserable twenty years in prison as a woman. Believe me I'll make it happen! You understand don't you? You can go. I don't need you anymore."

Joe: "I understand. Will you take care of my case?"

Eddie: "It will be taken care of once the DA sees what you've done."

Eddie drove off, leaving Joe at the curb. He met Detective Murray the next morning and gave him the quarter ounce of cocaine and a briefing on Jerome. Murray said he would obtain a warrant on the house, but he agreed to Eddie's request that the warrant not be served until Eddie had obtained more evidence.

Jerome had not called, so Eddie picked up the red phone and called the number Jerome had given him. Jerome answered.

Jerome: "Hey, Eddie. What's up? Can we make money together?"

Eddie: "You tell me."

Jerome; "Listen, Eddie, I may be a little hot."

Eddie: "What's that mean?"

Jerome: "A girl I know works at the DA's office. She's a customer, and she heard my name mentioned. I don't know what's going on yet."

Eddie; "Maybe I should stay clear of you, Jerome. I don't need that kind of heat."

Jerome: "It's probably just an investigation. If you know this area, you know that it will be just an investigation for years."

Eddie laughed to himself and thought Jerome had an awakening coming.

Eddie: "Listen, you said that you have a major supplier of grass. How much can you get?"

Jerome: "All you can handle."

Eddie: "Two thousand pounds?"

Jerome: "Wow! That's a lot of grass. It's more than I was thinking."

Eddie: "Talk to your guy. Tell him I have to set up transportation to New York, so that will be an added expense."

Jerome: "I think he can help you with that. Can you drive a truck?"

Eddie: "Yes, I can."

Jerome: "Call me tomorrow night."

Eddie called Detective Murray and briefed him on the marijuana deal and the rat in the DA's office.

Murray: "We'll pick her up after we arrest Jerome. I'll let the DA know."

Eddie called his boss, briefed him about the deal and said he needed a few days.

Lt. Lyme: "Ernie, be careful, anyone selling that kind of quantity will have plenty of guns around and some good coverage. Make sure you're covered and let us know if you need us. See if you can get that girl's name."

~ ~ ~

The phone rang late the next day, Tuesday morning.

Jerome: "My guy can do two thousand pounds, but he wants to talk to you himself. Eddie, I'm cut into this deal or no deal."

Eddie agreed to cut Jerome into the one ton marijuana sale, agreeing that he should get something for setting it up. Twenty-four hours later, the phone rang again.

Jerome: "Tonight at eight, Rossi's on Washington Street. He'll buy dinner."

Eddie: "Tell him exactly what I say: Word for word, say this: I appreciate his respect and I look forward to an enjoyable and profitable dinner with him."

Jerome: "What the fuck! I'll just say we have a meet."

Eddie; "No, say it exactly like this. I appreciate his respect and would enjoy dinner with him."

Jerome was puzzled but he did not feel like arguing. *What the hell,* he thought. *This guy Eddie must know what he's doing.*

~ ~ ~

Eddie went home and shined his wingtip shoes. He put on the same suit he wore for the meeting with the Mafia men who had the stolen bonds. Teresa had pressed a white shirt. He wanted to look good. Jerome was waiting in the lobby of Rossi's. Outside, Dedham police had noted the make of his car and his license plate number.

Jerome: "I told him what you said. He wants to meet you alone." Jerome looked nervous. He pointed to a table where two men in suits were sitting. Eddie walked across the restaurant, to the table.

"Eddie Pannoni," he said, offering his hand.

"Buona sera," said the man on the right. Good evening.

"Buono," Eddie sat down.

"I'm Phil. He's Carl."

The three men measured each other and made small talk. The weather was changing; lots of snow melting, spring will be nice. Phil complained about noisy kids in his neighborhood, but said it was better than New York with its fire engines and the sirens late at night.

They ordered calamari with a hot marinara sauce and a bottle of red wine. They ate silently, eyeing each other and listening to the music that came out of the ceiling. After dinner Phil asked Carl to leave him alone with Eddie. The waiter brought them cappuccino (coffee). Eddie had seen this scene a thousand times in Brooklyn. He knew how to let it play out and be respectful.

Phil turned to Eddie. "Erba, volete (two thousand) Stagni?" Grass, you want two thousand pounds?

Eddie: "Yes."

Phil: "A lot of money."

Eddie: "How much are we talking?"

Phil: "With a respectful guy like yourself, eight thousand per bale."

Eddie thought for a moment. "I have to unload from you and then load my truck to take them to New York."

Phil: "Not my problem, but I can help with some of it, maybe all of it."

Eddie; "The price is high for this large a purchase. Much more then I am used to paying."

Phil: "Tell you what. I like you. Here's what I'm willing to do. I will have my guys do the transfer for you. Better yet, you take the truck and we will set up times for you to call me. If you do not call, I will report the truck stolen."

Eddie agreed. "Now we have to set a better price."

Phil laughed. "Are you crazy? I'm giving you Carolina prices."

Eddie; "I can go to Carolina and get one bale. We're talking here about forty bales."

Phil: "I can go to seventy five hundred, take it or leave it, your decision."

Eddie: "Deal, where and when can we close this?"

Phil told him he liked to do business at the train station on Route 128, where trucks rolled in twenty four hours a day and one more would not draw any attention. He asked if Eddie could drive a truck and Eddie said it would not be a problem, but he acknowledged to himself that he could not handle a tractor-trailer. They agreed on a delivery of forty bales of marijuana Friday night at nine. Eddie assured Phil that he had the cash and said the marijuana bales had to be available for a count before the money was handed over.

Phil told Eddie that would not be a problem and that the bales would be covered by bags of dog food. The men shook hands and Eddie left. He was watched by Dedham detectives as he opened the door of the Thunderbird, started it, and left the parking lot at Rossi's.

~ ~ ~

Eddie went home and called Detective Murray, who wondered where Dedham police were going to get the three hundred thousand dollars needed for the buy. "You won't need it, Eddie told him. A small empty suitcase will do.

Eddie: "Get ten guys you can trust," he said. "Then, get a truck and put two guys in it. Move in when you see me take my hat off and wipe my brow. That's your signal. We're all set for Friday night at 9PM at the 128 Train Station."

***

Friday Night 9 PM:

Eddie drove into the parking lot of the Route 128 train station and saw Phil sitting in a large blue van. Carl was behind the wheel. Eddie parked about thirty feet away and walked to the van.

Eddie: "You got my grass?"

Phil: "It's in the back." Phil looked around to see if anyone was watching. Eddie stepped onto the running board and looked into the rear of the van and saw bags of dog food stacked on what appeared to be bails of green hay. He took off his hat and wiped his brow. Eddie had made a serious mistake. He forgot to have Murray tell the uniformed officers who were making the arrest what he looked like. They had no idea who the undercover officer was. They moved in, shouting and waving their guns.

Eddie looked at Phil. "I think we're going to be arrested," he said. "Are you a cop?"

Phil yelled, "Motherfucker!" as Carl put the van in gear and tried to take off. Eddie grabbed him around the neck, but he had him with his left arm, leaving him unable to grab the steering wheel. Eddie twisted himself in a move to grab the keys and turnoff the engine, but Phil pounded his arm and gunned the van, and drove toward a tractor trailer that was moving through the truck lot, trying to wipe Eddie off of his van against the tractor trailer. Eddie's back was scraped against the rig, but he managed to hold on.

Dedham police opened fire, shooting through the walls of the van as Eddie held on to Phil's throat and tried to reach his .38 with his right hand. He would shoot Phil if he had to. Police bullets bounced around the cargo area of the van, ricocheting in a whining noise that came close to Eddie's ear. Phil jerked the steering wheel, trying to shake Eddie off. He drove the van to a small guard building that served as a check-in station at the entrance to the lot, hoping to wipe Eddie off against the building. As the van swerved, Eddie managed to grab his .38 and fire two rounds into the rear tire of the vehicle, causing the tire to blow. The van veered into a ditch and stopped.

Eddie jumped from the van just as it went into a ditch. Phil, still in the van, grabbed a pair of long tailor's scissors from the seat and jumped from the van to attack Eddie, shouting that he would kill him. His face was filled with rage as he attacked Eddie, jamming one of the sharp, pointed ends into his shoulder. The undercover officer grabbed Phil's arm and tried to pin it behind his back, but the two men fell into the dirt in the ditch. Eddie was fighting for his life with the enraged Phil, who spewed spit as he grunted and screamed, trying to stab Eddie. Eddie was still trying to maintain his cover and screamed, "What are you, a fucking cop?" Detective Murray ran up and hit Phil across the back of the head with the butt of his pistol, knocking him out.

Carl ran away during the fight, but was collared by the Dedham sheriff who was driving his family home from a hockey game. He was traveling on Rt. 128, listening to the frantic chatter on his police radio. The sheriff's wife was in the front seat and his two sons were in the back as he stepped hard on the vehicle's brakes to a screeching stop, pushed open the door of his cruiser, pulled his service revolver and forced Carl to the ground, handcuffing him. Two Massachusetts state troopers saw the sheriff's police lights and sped to the scene. They took Carl into custody and the sheriff drove his family home, then went to the Dedham police station to make a report on arrest of Carl.

In the Van there were forty bales of marijuana, two tons of grass and four hundred pounds of dog food. Police raided Jerome's quaint Cape Cod style house and found a kilo of cocaine and forty pounds of marijuana.

Saturday's papers were screaming the story. Ernie Lijoi, known on the street as Eddie Pannoni, was not mentioned in the newspaper accounts. The arrests and the shootout were said to have been the result of a drug deal arranged by an undercover Quincy police officer. The news paper description spoke of the attempted murder of a deep cover operator, no names were given.

12/24/80 Pg 1

4 arrested at Rte. 128 depot drug bust

Patriot Ledger Staff

DEDHAM – Police shot out three of the four tires on a fleeing van in the Route 128 railroad station parking lot last night and then arrested four men who allegedly were trying to sell 12 pounds of marijuana to an undercover agent for $5,000.

One of the men, his hands cuffed, tried to escape on foot but was recaptured after a chase along the highway.

During a struggle in the lot, one man allegedly pulled long bladed scissors on police, but was disarmed without injury.

Another reportedly had a gun, but did not use it. No one was injured in the scuffle, police said.

One of the men, David J. Hynes, 22, of 83 Hollis St., Weymouth, who was handcuffed, jumped from a police cruiser and tried to escape by running south on Route 128 toward Route 95.

Two state policemen, Daniel J. Duffy and Thomas Curran, who were patrolling the area, along with Sheriff Clifford Marshall, who was returning from a hockey game, spotted Hynes and chased him in their cars.

Marshall and the troopers pinned Hynes between their cars and the guardrail.

Officials said the four men were trying to sell the marijuana to an undercover policeman from Quincy in the parking lot of the Route 128 railroad station when five detectives swooped down to arrest them.

Also arrested besides Hynes were Stephen R. Racotelli, 26, of 11 Thompson St., Hyde Park, on a charge of conspiring to violate the controlled substance act; William J. Dorash, 36, of 194 Bonham Road, Dedham, conspiring to violate the controlled substance act and unlawful

possession of a handgun ; and Anthony J. Izpolito III, 22, of 172 Milton St., Dedham, possession of marijuana.

Hynes was charged with assault with intent to murder and unauthorized distribution of marijuana.

The four were to be arraigned later today in Dedham District Court.

The suspects were in two vans, officials said. As police converged on them, someone in one of the vans pulled a handgun. The other van, driven by Hynes, took off, they said.

Dedham detectives opened fire and shot out three of the van's tires in the parking lot. The van slowed down momentarily and Det. Robert Scheffler and the Quincy undercover officer jumped into the van. Scheffler pulled the keys out of the ignition.

The two officers dragged Hynes from the van and wrestled him to the ground.

am men arrested
chase by police. Arrested in Dedham

Teresa read about it and hurried to the bedroom, where she sat on the bed and cried. *Dear God*, she prayed. *Protect him and our family.*

~ ~ ~

He had come home shortly before dawn and she watched him sleep. There was a bandage on his shoulder and blood leaked through to his t-shirt. She swallowed as she tried to control her emotions. Her hand moved to his bloody t-shirt, but she did not touch him. She wanted him to sleep. Even more, she wanted him to give up this life he had taken on. Teresa stopped for a second and questioned herself; did she really want him back on the busses and trains? No, she thought, that was not safe, either. He had come home with bloody bandages before. This was not the first time and it probably would not be the last, she prayed; "God, Please, keep him safe." In a quiet voice as he lay there sleeping.

~ ~ ~

Six years earlier, Officer Lijoi was a novice transit cop, riding busses at night, protecting the drivers from gang bangers. One summer night he sat behind a driver he knew, a man who had once been a boxer. Midway through the route five young men seventeen to twenty years of age got on the bus. The first one went to the back and sat down. The other four were searching for the money to pay the driver until the man that went to the back was seated, then one of them pulled out a dollar bill and threw it at the driver, the bill fell to the floor.

The driver turned and looked at the kid. "Would you pick that up, please?"

"Pick it up yourself." The kid's friends began to laugh and shout at the driver. "Yeah, motherfucka! Pick it up yourself!"

Officer Lijoi could not reach the dollar because the four kids were between him and the driver. He stood up.

Ernie: "Please, pick up the dollar," he said.

Young Man: "Fuck you," was the response.

Ernie: "Let me by and I'll pick it up myself," he said.

He barely finished his sentence before he felt a sharp pain in his head. One of the men in the back reached to the front, armed with a slap jack, a section of lead pipe wrapped in leather. A slap jack was considered a dangerous weapon and possession carried a five year prison sentence. Ernie was hit on the head and went down and felt boots stomping him. He had fallen through the young men and into the door opening area near the driver, preventing the driver from reaching the young men who were stomping the officer. Ernie managed to get to his knees to reach for his service revolver to defend himself. It was gone. His holster was empty. The man that entered before the group and walked to the back of the bus to take a seat had snuck up as the fight was going on and took Ernie's gun out of his holster. Ernie was unarmed. His gun was gone.

Young man: "Get out of my way!" he shouted. "I'll kill this motherfucking white pig."

Ernie looked up as the other four teenagers stepped aside. He looked at the young man who held the gun and realized the whole thing had been a setup. The kid had gone to the back as part of a plan. Dropping the dollar was the diversion. Ernie looked up from his position on one knee at a young man standing in front of him with a large afro and big eyes, wide eyes holding Ernie's missing gun on Ernie.

Young Man: "I'm gonna kill you, you motherfucka."

Ernie remembered an instructor at the police academy who had outlined this very situation. Try to grab the barrel of the gun to stop the shooter from turning it. Place a finger or thumb behind the trigger or hammer to stop it from firing. The words came to him and he moved. Ernie grabbed the gun and fought with the young man, trying to get his gun back. The other four teenagers ran off the bus and into the night. The gun went off. The bullet grazed Ernie's right temple, cutting open his scalp. The bullet then went through the windshield of the bus and into a nearby building. Ernie reeled from the shot and tried to move toward the teenager, but the kid was fast and ran off the bus with Ernie's gun.

Ernie stood up, blood running down his face and onto his uniform. Calmly, he looked at the passengers on the bus.

Ernie: "You'll all have to come to the police station to make statements. You are all witnesses to what just happened."

MBTA police carried no radios in 1972, so the driver took the bus back to the terminal, where a bloody police officer, a shaken driver and a dozen or so nearly hysterical passengers got off.

Ernie was treated at Boston City Hospital and sent home. Neither the teenager who shot him nor his gun was ever found. In the aftermath of the shooting, MBTA officers were issued radios and new holsters with locking systems, replacing the flimsy holsters that they carried until then..

Teresa had blocked the incident from her mind until she saw her husband asleep with blood leaking through another bandage. Her hands trembled. She smiled. Asleep, he was still her handsome New York boy. His thick, curly hair and his rough beard made him even more handsome, in her eyes. His hands were thick and strong and as she examined them, she saw the scars that calmed her. He could take care of himself. He could fight if he had to and would survive. She felt another emotion, one that she did not share with her husband or her sons. She was lonely and she felt adrift. It was a feeling that was very strong at times and when it was strong it scared her in its intensity. She stared at the man who had swept her off her feet and hoped she would find her way back to the ground. *What's happening to me?* she wondered.

Chapter Thirteen

Heroin

Wednesday, March 15, 1978

The bitter cold had been replaced by rain and fog, and most of the snow had melted in the dampness of the late winter. It was raw. Spring was still a rumor in New England as the people of Quincy went about their business, watching the news on television and dreaming about the coming days at the beach.

Eddie's shoulder was sore, but the bleeding had stopped and the doctor told him it was a superficial wound and would not cause any permanent impairment. He had been home these past few days, spending time with Teresa and the boys and answering the red telephone. Lieutenant Lyme had sent word that he wanted Eddie Pannoni to lie low while the Dedham drug bust fiasco was being cleaned up and prepared for the courts..

Tony had called to talk about the newspaper stories, wondering who the unnamed undercover Quincy police detective might be. Eddie suggested it was someone in the supply chain. Tony agreed and stated that rats are everywhere and Eddie agreed. They both promised to get together in a few days to work out a deal for a kilo or two of cocaine. Jeannie called looking for heroin and Eddie told her he was working on a new source and was looking for quantity for his customers in New York.

He was going stir crazy hanging around the house waiting for the street business to start up again. He fixed a few things in the kitchen and tried to clean up the winter mess in the yard, but his shoulder was not cooperating. Teresa seemed happy to have him around, but she was aware that he was not really there, that his mind was out with the drug dealers on the streets.

The red telephone rang in late afternoon. Eddie picked it up.

Ernie: "Yeah," was his greeting.

Churn: "Tonight at ten o'clock, we'll meet at the same place." He recognized the voice of Abe Churn.

Ernie: "I'll be there." He hung up.

~ ~ ~

It was foggy when he pulled into St. Catherine's parking lot and the glow from the street lights hung in blurry visions above the invisible lampposts. Eddie had to roll down his window to make out the detectives' car. He could see a trail of exhaust coming from the rear of the vehicle as he backed into the spot next to Churn's window so both men could remain in their cars and speak to each other from the driver's seats.

"How's the shoulder?" Churn asked, exhaling a plume of smoke from his cigarette.

"It's good. I'm ready to go." Eddie lit a cigarette of his own with the Zippo lighter he had purchased while in the Air Force and assigned to Rhine Maine Air Base in Germany.

"Lieutenant Lyme wants to talk to you about something. Follow me." Churn backed his unmarked police car out of the parking space and slowly moved to the street with Eddie following him in the Thunderbird. Ten minutes later Churn pulled into a driveway between two houses and proceeded to a small parking area in the rear, where his vehicle could not be seen from the street. Eddie parked next to him. The two men walked up the stairs to a small porch and Churn knocked on the door. Lieutenant Lyme opened it and motioned the men inside.

"You guys look like you could use some coffee," he said. "C'mon in." He motioned to the kitchen table, where a plate of cookies was set beside a small pitcher of milk and a sugar bowl. The lieutenant poured coffee into three mugs and set them down on the table.

Lt. Lyme: "Ernie, how are you?"

Ernie: "Good. I'm good, thanks."

Lt. Lyme: "Hell of a job in Dedham. In fact, you're doing a hell of a job all over. That's what I want to talk to you about. Some of the stuff you're bringing in is almost fifty per cent pure. You're moving up the chain, Ernie, and everybody's interested in where you're going with this, even the mayor."

Churn took one of the cookies and dipped it into his coffee, then took a bite of the soaked cookie.

The lieutenant watched Churn eat the cookie and turned back to Ernie. "We can tell where you are in the chain of dealers and suppliers by the percentage of purity in the drugs that you bring in. Fifteen per cent pure is regular street stuff. Twenty five per cent is a guy selling to the street dealer. Fifty per cent is the guy who knows the guy who's bringing it in from Columbia. We think you're there or almost there."

"Which buys are you talking about?" Ernie asked.

Lt. Lyme: "Stuff from Tony and his friends. We think he's got big time friends."

Ernie: "He hangs out with all kinds of people. Sometimes it seems like he's just bullshitting. He's always talking about big deals. He called me today to talk about the Dedham shootout."

Lt. Lyme: "Did I see a report from you about some guns in his house?"

Ernie: "Yeah, .44 magnum. I think he has other guns, too, and maybe rents them out."

Lt. Lyme: "We need to watch him and get to know his friends."

Lieutenant Lyme reached for a legal pad and took a pen out of his pocket. He drew a chart on the paper and began to write notes on it.

Lt. Lyme: "The stuff comes in around ninety per cent pure from Colombia. It comes in bulk and is weighed in kilograms, two point two pounds. The guy who brings it in can double the weight by cutting it to, say, seventy per cent by adding lidocaine powder, which he can buy cheap. It looks like coke and even numbs skin and sinuses, so the user thinks its coke. The importer turns one kilo into two, sometimes three, and sells both of them for double the price he paid for one. He sells to the next level down and that guy does the same thing, maybe cutting it to fifty per cent and doubling his quantity. The next guy cuts it to twenty five per cent. By the time it goes up somebody's nose, it's down to ten per cent coke and ninety per cent something else and the profits are huge. We are talking about a lot of money. You are at the fifty per cent level. I'm betting that the guy he buys from is bringing it in."

Ernie: "You think Tony is the key?" Ernie looked at the chart Lyme had drawn of the buys and the cutting process.

Lt. Lyme: "I think Tony knows the guy who is the key. Tony's your man. He knows you. He trusts you. And this guy Rinaldi. Sammy. He's got some heroin connections that are pretty good. You've got a hell of an investigation going here, Ernie. Or should I call you Eddie?" He laughed.

"Call me what you want, Lieutenant. I'm still looking to get on with the Quincy department as Ernie Lijoi."

"Don't worry about it. We'll take care of you." Lyme stood up and put the coffee mugs into the sink.

Churn and Eddie went to the door and shook the lieutenant's hand, then they walked into the foggy night and got into their cars. Churn left first. Eddie waited five minutes and drove home.

He was elated to be back on the job, even if his rest had only been five days. It was time to take a break from the street scum to work the case to a close. Tony Cole and Sammy Rinaldi. They were the targets, or at least they would lead him to the targets. Cole and Rinaldi would go down, there was no doubt, but who were they buying from?

The fog was clearing and it began to snow, wet and heavy. The telephone poles and electrical wires became thick, white outlines against the black sky as MBTA Officer Ernie Lijoi Sr. drove the Quincy Police Department's white Thunderbird home to Dedham. Teresa was waiting up knowing that her husband was about to go back into the streets and the meanness that lurked beyond the safety of their home. He pulled into the driveway and turned off the engine. She heard the car door slam and his footsteps on the porch. His eyes were glowing and there was wet snow on his hair as he stepped into the kitchen.

Ernie: "I'm going back to work," he said, smiling.

"I know," she said, sadly.

***

Tony Cole woke up late and wandered into his kitchen around noon. He stood at the window over the sink and watched the ice melt from the roof of the house next door. His wife was not home but he smelled cigarette smoke and knew someone had been by to pick up some cocaine. He had to mix up some smaller batches of blow.

His source in New Hampshire had offered him ten kilos of eighty per cent pure cocaine. He could cut it and make a fortune, but he would have to find buyers, and that was dangerous. He could either keep it around, sell it off in grams to the users and small time dealers he knew, or he could try to sell it in bulk to someone else.

There were only a couple of people that he knew who could deal in kilos and come up with cash, but not enough to cover the cost of several kilos. One man who might be able to do it was Eddie Pannoni, who had bought from him in the past and said he had customers in New York, but he had not dealt in quantity with Eddie. Tony went to a drawer and took out Eddie's card. Picked up the phone and dialed Eddie's number.

"Eddie, its Tony." The tape recorder under the red telephone was turning.

"What's up?"

Tony: "I think I may have something you'd be interested in, quantity, very good stuff, high grade."

Eddie: "How much quantity?"

Tony: "Come by and we can talk."

Eddie went to the closet and took his .38 snub nose revolver down from the shelf, removed the trigger guard, and placed the weapon in his waistband at the small of his back. He grabbed a denim vest and a leather jacket, and left his house.

The air was wet and smelled like melting slush as he opened the trunk of the Thunderbird and placed the gun into his toolbox, next to two other handguns he kept there. He slammed the trunk, looked to see if anyone was watching him, and drove to Tony's house.

~ ~ ~

Pauly was sitting in the living room, smoking a joint, and trying to look normal, despite his red, unfocused eyes. Tony was toying with his large snake pipe, but there was no smoke in it. Tony seemed nervous.

Tony: "You ever go up to New Hampshire?" he asked, looking at Eddie.

Eddie: "Yeah, sure, now and then. I like Maine better, though."

Tony: "What if I told you I got a really good source and I can get you some real quantity, like maybe a few kilos and good stuff?"

Eddie: "From New Hampshire?"

Tony: "I didn't say that, exactly. Maybe a trip up there is all."

Eddie: "If the stuff is that good, we can deal. I would need a taste?"

Tony: "I can do that. But this deal is gonna take some real cash, Thirty thousand per kilo."

Eddie: "If it's good, I can do it, no problem. I got a partner with plenty of cash and I got customers. It has to be good shit, we'll deal, I don't want any of the cut crap. My customers in New York won't take that crap, high quality only."

Tony went to his kitchen and came back with a small bag of white powder. He handed it to Eddie and motioned for him to try it.

Eddie: "I got an appointment. I can't do this blow right now. I'll try it later and call you, how much for this?"

Tony: "A hundred, pay me later."

Eddie left Tony's house with the cocaine in his pocket and went to a coffee shop to meet Jeannie. He wanted to arrange a meeting with Sammy Rinaldi, the sharp-dressing car salesman who claimed he could deliver anything Eddie wanted. Rinaldi had access to heroin, he said, lots of it.

Jeannie was working behind the counter, talking to a customer, when Eddie walked in. She looked tired and her skin was mottled. She scratched at her scalp with a pencil as she listened to the customer's order. She noticed Eddie and winked at him. He went to the far end of the lunch counter and sat on a stool, picking up a menu to look it over. She placed her customer's order at the kitchen window and came down to talk to Eddie.

Jeannie: "How you doin'?" she asked. "What can I get you?" she winked again.

Eddie: "Coffee," he said. "Anything going on?"

Jeannie: "I need a little something, you know. I'm getting kinda sick. Think you can help me out with a couple of bucks?"

Eddie: "Yeah, sure, have you seen Rinaldi lately?"

Jeannie: "I talked to him yesterday. Why? Do you need something?"

Eddie: "I got a customer in New York who is always looking for something, you know, in quantity. Maybe we can hook up with him later."

Jeannie's boss came out of the kitchen to glare at her, and waved her back to work. "I get off at seven, pick me up." she said.

Eddie drank his coffee and looked over the customers who were sulking on stools or in booths. Most of the men had not shaved recently and the women had the look of sadness that accompanies a lifetime of disappointment. They were resigned to being with these men, or men like them. Guys who thought they were doing well if they had the cash to buy some marijuana and a six-pack. They wore hooded sweatshirts that fell out of the collars of their jackets and ankle boots that were water stained by the snow. Eddie knew these people, especially the men. He had grown up with the same low expectations in Brooklyn. The only difference between Quincy and Brooklyn was the accent. These guys don't know there's a life outside of this place, he thought.

At seven, Jeannie grabbed her coat and walked out the front door and waited for Eddie in the parking lot. She got into the Thunderbird and he drove to the house where she was staying.

Jeannie: "I got a surprise for you," she said, getting out of the car.

He followed her inside and saw three people sitting at the kitchen table; the man and woman who lived with Jeannie and Sammy Rindaldi, who was wearing a suit, tie and shined shoes. He looked like the salesman he was, complete with a big smile to show off his white teeth.

Sammy: "How are you, Eddie?"

Jeannie: "I called him and told him you might want something," Jeannie said. "Maybe I can get something too." She looked at Eddie and motioned him to follow her into the living room. "Can you let me have twenty dollars?" He gave her two tens.

Rinaldi sat at the table and pulled several small packets out of the inside pocket of his suit coat. He smiled as Jeannie and her housemates cooked the heroin and shot it up, leaning back in their chairs as they went to wherever junkies go in moments like this. Rinaldi and Eddie watched. Rinaldi tossed a packet to Eddie and smiled. "Need a little something?"

"Not like them," Eddie said. "But I got customers who can use lots of this." Eddie took the packet of heroin, I'll give this a try and see how they like it.

"I can take care of you," Rinaldi said. "Not just this stuff; do you ever need speed? I got it, or can get it. Try what you got there for twenty bucks; if you like it, we can do business for whatever you need."

Eddie: "I have people in New York that can use some speed."

Sammy: "I know a guy who's connected, you know what I mean? He's got very good connections. He can get all you want, pills of any kind."

"Can I meet this guy?"

"I can introduce you. He's over the line in New Hampshire. I'll call him and we can go together. You get yours and I'll get mine."

"Tomorrow morning?" Eddie pressed Rinaldi to set up a meeting quickly.

"I'll make a call." Rinaldi rolled a joint and passed it around. Jeannie and her housemates were nodding off and were barely aware of the marijuana that they were inhaling. Eddie faked a hit on the joint and handed it back to Rinaldi, who took a deep drag on the joint and tried to stifle a cough as he held the smoke in his lungs.

Eddie met Detective Churn at St. Catherine's parking lot and told him about Tony and Rinaldi and the deals that were pending, and said he would be traveling to New Hampshire to make a meet with some top dealer and talk large quantities.

"There's a lot going on up there," Churn said. "I think New Hampshire state police have somebody working undercover. I'll pass this on to Lieutenant Lyme. If there's a problem, we'll call you on the red phone."

Chapter 14

The big buy

Friday, March 17, 1978

It was cold and gray; there was light snow in the air as Eddie Pannoni met Sammy Rinaldi at the coffee shop in Quincy. Rinaldi was wearing a bright green tie and had a green carnation pinned to the lapel of his suit. He was sitting next to a street bum Eddie recognized as a shit bag, a neighborhood leach who always had his hand out for a few dollars in exchange for useless information.

Sammy: "I can't go to New Hampshire today. It's St. Patrick's Day. I gotta sell some cars." Rinaldi's smile was broad. "I should have remembered last night. It's a big day."

St. Patrick's Day is a major event in Boston and the surrounding communities. The large Irish population fills the bars where green beer lubricates the parades in the streets, and politicians of every ethnic background claim to be Irish and cheer the marching Catholic school students who proudly wear their green sashes before hundreds of thousands of people who jam the streets of Southie for an all day drunk. Bands, floats, speeches and tales of Ireland last well into the night.

Furniture stores and car dealers celebrate the day with sales and, before it was outlawed, free beer. More than a few drunks have driven away in new cars, flush with the pride of the Irish and a gallon or two alcoholic beverages in their stomachs.

Rinaldi was going to see what kind of money he could make from the holiday, even though it was apparent to anyone that he had not one drop of Irish blood in him.

Sammy: "Little Paul here knows where to go. He can ride with you. You make your own deal and we can talk about other things later." Rinaldi patted Little Paul on the back and got up from the booth.

Sammy turned to Paul and ordered: "Help my friend out, Paul," smiling.

Eddie watched him leave and turned to the man across the table, who was grinning like an idiot.

"I can help you out," Little Paul said. "I know this guy. I can introduce you. He's a good supplier. Fifty bucks for the introduction and you can buy in bulk."

Eddie: "What the fuck are you, a complete ass hole? I don't need you for an introduction. I already have one. You're along for the ride, but I'll give you ten bucks so you can get something for yourself."

Little Paul was not in a position to bargain and he knew it. In a apologetic voice he said: "Okay."

~ ~ ~

The two men climbed into the Thunderbird and drove to southern New Hampshire through Dracut, a small town between Lowell and the state line. Little Paul directed Eddie down a blacktop road where a small sign welcomed them to New Hampshire and a package store invited them to purchase cheap cigarettes. Several miles later, Little Paul told Eddie to pull into the driveway of a small Cape Cod-style house set back from the road and surrounded by a row of tall trees. An ancient stone fence ran along one side of the house and into the woods. A small, leaning garage that Eddie assumed had once been a barn was at the back of the driveway. The door to the garage was rolled back, revealing a large pile of junk.

Little Paul got out first and went to the front door and knocked. Eddie followed him inside, where five other people were sitting or standing, some drinking beer. Nearly everyone was smoking and the air was thick and it was difficult for Eddie to make out the people on the other side of the room.

A man walked up to Eddie and looked at him. Eddie made a mental note of a white male, about 30 years of age, 6 feet, dark hair, mustache, brown eyes, wearing as set of eye glasses that appeared to swell the size of his eyes.

The man put out his hand to shake. "Jim Depaccio," he said, by way of introduction.

"Eddie Pannoni." The two men shook hands while Little Paul looked around the room.

Depaccio motioned for Eddie to follow him into the kitchen, where he sat at the table and offered Eddie a beer, which he declined. Two other men joined them and passed a joint around, then another. A third man walked into the kitchen and looked at Eddie, who was faking smoking the joint. The man watched him and, when he took the joint, also faked it. Eddie and the man looked at each other and Eddie thought he had seen him before.

The conversation was about pills. What kind? How many? How much? Depaccio knew his products and he was ready to deal, he said, but he did not have as many pills as Eddie was ready to buy. Joints were passed around, beer was drunk, and the day was slipping away. Eddie looked for Jimmy, he needed to talk.

Eddie: "Look, Jim, I came a long way. I'm going to New York tonight and I would love to have a trunk full. I got a few thousand to spend. I need to make a deal."

Depaccio's eyes lit up. He thought he had a chance to make some real money, not the chump change that most of his customers spent on a few pills now and then. Eddie was enjoying the new energy in the room and noticed that the others were fidgeting and were standing and sitting, like they could not remain still. The man Eddie thought he recognized was also smiling, but he was not moving around.

Depaccio leaned forward. "Sorry, I'm all out. But I have a load coming in later today. Tell you what, Eddie. Since you got so much to invest, I'll take you with me as long as we agree that you go through me. Besides, I need a ride." He smiled.

"Where to?" Eddie asked.

Jim: "Rhode Island. Providence. My connection is a connection, if you know what I mean."

Eddie: "Patriakas' group?"

Jim: "Close, not the old man, but his son, Junior. He has four of his guys and they formed a little conglomerate. It's under a real estate thing. They've got a great situation going for them."

Eddie: "Under real estate? Interesting idea. I gotta see this one maybe I can use it in New York?"

Jim: "Yeah. They have these houses that are empty and they're all real estate salesmen, but they use empty houses or apartments as supply spots. It's great. They've been doin' it for five years, maybe longer. What an operation!"

Eddie: "Well, let's go if we're going." Eddie stood up. Everyone else stood up. "Is everybody goin?" asked Eddie.

Jim: "Yeah, these guys are suppliers from New Hampshire and Massachusetts and they all have to resupply. All except Pete here, he's just a good friend." Depaccio pointed to the man Eddie thought he had seen before.

"There's too many for one car," Pete said. "I'll follow you guys."

Outside, in the daylight, Eddie remembered where he had seen Pete before. They had met at skid school, a course on high speed police driving. Pete was an undercover New Hampshire state police officer. Eddie watched him climb into his car and walked over to talk to him privately.

Pete rolled down his window and whispered, "I recognized you. I'll cover your run. I got a radio and I'll let them know who you are. I'll stay with you. You're coming up with some great shit. Keep it going."

Eddie laughed. "Thanks. Listen, I'm gonna get rid of the kid Paul before we leave. He's okay, just a little stupid."

Eddie's car was full. He told Little Paul it was too crowded, dropped him off at the train station in Lowell, gave him twenty dollars, and told him to go home. Paul was disappointed that he was not going on a trip to Rhode Island, but he was happy to have the twenty dollars.

~ ~ ~

Eddie and his Thunderbird full of stoned druggies, followed by Pete in his undercover police car, headed for Interstate 95 and Rhode Island. Pete used his radio to alert the state police that a drug operation was underway. Eddie's passengers were in their own worlds, unaware of much of anything, other than they were in a car going somewhere. Eddie pushed the speed of the Thunderbird to seventy, then eighty, then ninety and a hundred miles per hour. Pete was about a quarter mile back, keeping up. A state police car came up behind Eddie and remained on his bumper, but no lights were on and the siren was silent. Pete was talking to the trooper, who pulled back and then disappeared. Another trooper pulled up behind Eddie and remained there for several miles, and pulled back. Eddie's passengers were half in the bag and did not notice anything.

They passed through Massachusetts at high speed, being tracked by state troopers, who would take positions ahead of Eddie, using their rooftop lights to clear traffic from the speed lane so Eddie and Pete could move through. The Rhode Island state line came within sight, then Eddie saw a Rhode Island trooper pick up the movement of the undercover cars and clear a speed lane. Eddie was amazed and proud that four police agencies were working together spontaneously and nothing had gone wrong.

Eddie pulled off Interstate 95 and followed Depaccio's directions to a small apartment building. Pete was one car back as Eddie pulled up and parked the Thunderbird in front of a sign in the yard that read, "For Sale". Three very large Italian-looking men were standing outside the door to the building. They were wearing suits and ties and had name tags on their jackets. Pete pulled up beside Eddie and parked his car. He looked over at Eddie and winked.

Jim Depaccio walked up to the men, shook hands, and introduced Eddie and Pete. "Go on in," one of the men said, motioning toward a concrete stoop. Pete got out of his car and joined the group as they walked into the lobby of a three family house. Eddie noticed that the place had been fixed up and thought it would be a good investment for someone who had the money, which he did not.

Eddie and Pete pulled back to allow the others to go ahead of them. The group was directed into a first-floor, left=side apartment and into what was an old fashioned empty living room that was quite large. The room was edged with tables and then two rows of tables ran down the middle. They were, each, about ten feet long and there had to be ten or more tables that could be reached from both sides. Each table was piled with hundreds of bags, each bag containing one thousand tablets of various kinds of drugs. It was like looking at a rainbow of pills, every color, every size and thousands of bags of each. Eddie was stunned. He quickly estimated the street value at well over several million dollars.

Pete motioned for Eddie to step out of the room and at that instant a group of Rhode Island state troopers rushed into the room. Pete's communication with the troopers had produced a quick task force of officers who filled the room.

"Son of a bitch!" One of the Mafia men shouted as bedlam broke out. The troopers pushed everyone to the floor and handcuffed them. One by one, the Mafia men, Depaccio, his dealers, Eddie and Pete were led to waiting police cars. The total value of the drugs was estimated at over three million dollars. A mob drug ring and real estate scam were broken up in what amounted to a spur of the moment operation put into play by Depaccio's failure to have enough pills on hand to satisfy a drug buy from an undercover cop he had just met, and another undercover cop who was fast on his feet. A long ago police emergency driving course had been the link between the two men, who now sat handcuffed and still undercover in the backseats of Rhode Island State Police cars.

The two men looked at each other as the drug dealers were being led away. Pete looked down and laughed. Eddie watched Depaccio being placed into a cruiser, his hands behind his back, gazing at a small crowd that had gathered to watch the police raid.

About an hour later, in the basement of a police station in Providence, Eddie and Pete were given beers and congratulated. They drove their undercover cars to their respective homes, at legal speeds, and Eddie sat in his chair and reflected on his day. Teresa watched him and wondered why he was quiet. The boys watched television.

~ ~ ~

Late that night, as Eddie slept and Teresa stared at the ceiling, the red telephone rang. Eddie picked it up.

Tony: "Eddie, its Tony. I got a great deal for you."

Eddie: "Your asshole friend got me arrested."

Tony: "He's not my friend, just an acquaintance."

Eddie: "We'll have to keep an eye on him—I don't trust him anymore."

Tony: "You're right, sorry about the problem, sorry I introduced y ou guys."

Eddie: "That's OK, they didn't get me with anything serious. I can handle it. Call me in the morning."

Eddie hung up the telephone and did not notice as the tape recorder stopped. He turned to Teresa and kissed her goodnight for the second time then he fell into a deep sleep.

He dreamed of a speeding car filled with people who stared into space, unaware of anything happening around them, and of police officers wearing campaign hats and thick leather gloves, and piles of pills so high he could not see the top.

The red telephone rang at noon. It was Tony.

Eddie: "Great to hear from you, where the fuck you been? I tried to call you all weekend."

Tony: "We took the camper out to my sister's place in Orange, New Jersey. Then up to New Hampshire where I picked up something for you."

Eddie: "What we talked about?"

Tony: "Yeah, a taste. I can get quantity, all you can handle with twenty-four hours notice."

Eddie: "You home now?"

Tony: "C'mon by. I'll be here all afternoon."

Eddie slipped on a dungaree vest that came down over his belt, placed his feet into his zip-up black boots, grabbed his jacket at the door and went to the Thunderbird. It was warm and there was a hint of spring in the air. The last of the snow and ice was melting in the dark, shaded places near the house.

He picked up a hitchhiker as he drove to Tony's house. The young man was in his late teens, slight beard, sunglasses, long filthy hair. Eddie recognized him as a pothead who shot pool at local bars. He bought and sold small amounts of marijuana. He asked the kid if he had anything to sell or knew of anyone who had something in quantity and kid shook his head and asked Eddie if he had some spare marijuana. Eddie shook his head and let the kid off at a corner near a pool hall. He gave the kid his card and told him to call if he heard of anything he could buy in quantity, promising to give the kid a piece of the action.

Tony was standing on his porch when Eddie pulled into the driveway.

Tony: "Great fucking day, huh," he said, waving at the sky. "I can't wait to get the camper out in the woods." He appeared to be in a great mood. "C'mon in."

No one else was there. Tony walked inside the living room and lit a joint, taking a deep drag and holding it in until he began to cough, then he handed it to Eddie, who sucked on the joint to create a cloud of smoke, then he made sucking sounds as he handed the joint back to Tony, who grabbed it and took another deep drag.

Tony: "I got something to show ya," Tony said, moving into the kitchen, where he opened the door to the cellar and motioned Eddie to follow him down the stairs. It smelled wet and moldy as they descended and Eddie could make out old paint cans and tools stacked against the stone walls. Tony stooped as he walked to a small closet that was closed off with an old shower curtain. He pulled it back and picked up a large cardboard box and placed it on an old linoleum-topped kitchen table. "Take a look," he said.

Eddie opened the box and saw what appeared to be a pile of oily rags in the shape of handguns. He picked up one of the rags and felt the shape of a revolver.

Tony: "You know anybody who might need one of these for a day or two?" Tony asked.

Eddie: "You rent these out?"

"Yeah," Tony said. "I get a hundred a day."

Eddie: "I don't need one. I got my own. But I may have some friends in New York who would be interested. You got any for sale?"

Tony: "Most of my customers don't want to buy; they just use them once and bring 'em back. If they don't bring 'em back in a week, I call the cops and report the gun stolen. These are all legal. I can get the other kind for sales, but I don't rent those out. You know what I mean?"

Eddie: "What you got here?"

Tony: "What do you need? I got .44s, .38s, couple .357 magnums and a couple of .22s."

Eddie looked through the box, picking up weapons and noting their caliber and make. Some were revolvers and a few were semiautomatics. One appeared to be an army .45, but the light was bad and Eddie couldn't quite make out the numbers or details.

Eddie: "You got a supplier for these guns?"

Tony: "Billy Stine. Remember him? He's got contacts for anything you want and he get make some of it legal. He's connected, if you know what I mean. He can get AK47s, machine guns, probably fuckin' hand grenades, who knows? I don't get into that kind of shit so I stick with small rentals. I just wanted to show you this stuff in case you know somebody who needs somethin' like this." Tony motioned Eddie toward the stairs. "I got something else for you."

He went up the cellar stairs with Eddie following him and he closed the door when he and Eddie were back in the kitchen, which was blindingly bright from the sunshine coming through the window over the sink. He opened a cabinet and handed Eddie a small package.

Tony: "Taste it," he said, "this shit is fuckin' pure."

Eddie opened the small package, looked at the white powder and said: "I don't have to taste it. I know you well enough to have trust in what you tell me. Eddie placed a small amount o his fingers and rubbed them back and forth to feel the fine grit of the powder. "Jesus! This is great stuff a great feel to it as well very fine." he said. "Where'd you get this?"

Tony: "I told you I got a good source. I can get you two kilos by tomorrow."

Eddie: "I'm in for two kilos."

Tony: "I don't want to meet here. How about the parking lot at the coffee shop on Sea Street? Two o'clock in the afternoon. Don't forget to bring the cash, Sixty thousand."

Eddie left Tony's house and drove to a pancake place where the public pay phone was in the back and tucked into a booth that offered privacy from patrons and waiters. He dialed a private line to Detective Churn and told him about his visit to Tony's house. He described the guns in the cellar and Tony's offer to rent them out for robberies and other jobs, and he briefed Churn on the cocaine buy set for the next day.

"Good work," Churn said." You may have found a way into the gun traffic we've been worried about as well as one of the top people in drugs. I'll pass this on to Lieutenant Lyme. He may call you. You need to call the Feds on this one. No way Quincy can come up with sixty thousand, even show money. You got the number?"

Ernie: "Yeah, I'll call Bud Steele at the DEA. I've worked with him in the past. I'll call him."

Churn: "Keep your head down and keep us advised."

Eddie went to the diner and telephoned Steele at the Boston DEA and explained the deal.

"We can cover you," Steele said. "You probably won't need it, but we'll have it there. Take your hat off when you see the dope and we'll move in. We'll take you down with him then we'll see how it goes."

Eddie hung up the phone and went over to the counter where he sat down and ordered some coffee. At the counter, smoking and sipping his coffee, He thought he recognized two or three of the patrons from the bars and pool halls in Quincy and he nodded to them. He could not tell if they recognized him.

Later, Eddie went to Pete's to shoot a few games of pool and troll for drug contacts. He saw some bikers he knew and had a beer with Jeannie, who was waiting for a heroin contact. She said she might have some quantity for him in a day or two, but he noted that she seemed out of it and on the verge of withdrawal. She was in no shape to make any promises about heroin deals or anything else. She scratched her face, her neck and looked at the door as Eddie waved at a low level dealer who was shooting pool with two other men Eddie recognized as street rabble. He spent two hours at Pete's, being seen and passing out his cards. Then he went home.

~ ~ ~

The next morning he got up with the boys and helped Teresa fix their lunches and sat in the kitchen after they left, talking with Teresa about the oldest boy, who was studying for his Confirmation in the Catholic Church. There was an issue about classes he had missed and whether he would be allowed to take part in Confirmation ceremonies with the Bishop. Teresa told Ernie that he might have to visit the monsignor to straighten it out. He took note of it, but his mind was on the cocaine deal with Tony and the DEA's promise to provide sixty thousand dollars in show money.

He stayed at home all morning, taking calls on the red telephone from potheads looking for small quantities of marijuana. One man who wanted some cocaine for a party that night and, "By the way, my car won't start so can you take care of it when you bring the coke?"

Eddie: "Sorry. All my stuff is going to my customer's in New York and I can't take care of you right now," was his answer to all of them. To the last man he added, "I can't get to your car for a few days. You might want to call somebody else."

Tony called at one o'clock to say the deal was on. He sounded nervous and excited. "You got the money?" he asked.

Tony: "Yeah, I got it. You got your end?"

Eddie: "I'm getting it right now. I'll see you there," Eddie replied.

He pulled into the parking lot at one forty five that afternoon. He backed the Thunderbird into a spot under a streetlight in case he did not get back from his arrest by the DEA before dark. He wanted it to be safe. His guns were at home and the only identification he carried was the Massachusetts driver's license under the name Eddie Pannoni. He sat in the car and watched for Tony, who drove into the parking lot in his camper. He drove past Eddie's car and waved, then drove to an open area in the back where he could park the truck.

Eddie got out of the car and walked to where Tony was idling the camper. It was warm and a light rain was falling. People were coming and going from the coffee shop but there was no obvious sign of the DEA. He saw several men in cars, but they appeared to be occupied with maps or stirring sugar into their coffee. Tony waved to him again and got out of the camper, signaling for him to hurry.

Tony: "You got the money? Let me see the money."

Eddie: "Yeah, it's here, but I'm not carrying it around. It's not that I don't trust you, Tony, but I have to see the goods first. I'm sure you understand."

Tony: "Don't make an asshole out of me, Eddie." Tony motioned for Eddie to get into the back of the camper. He closed the door and went to a cushioned bench built into the camper's wall where there was no window. He lifted the cushion and pointed to two bags. "There it is two keys."

Eddie: "I trust you, but I have to check," Eddie said, opening one of the bags and squeezing the drug between his fingers, to tell how fine it was. He was satisfied that it was high grade cocaine.

Eddie: "I'll get the money, it's in my car," he said. "You stay here."

Eddie opened the rear door of the camper, stepped down, and signaled by removing his hat. Three cars sped to the camper and stopped in front and both sides as men in civilian clothes spilled out, guns drawn, yelling at Eddie to get down. Two men rushed into the camper and he could hear them yelling at Tony to lie on the floor.

Tony: "What the fuck!" Tony screamed, as a DEA agent placed him in handcuffs.

Two more agents went in the camper and Eddie could hear one of them whistling as he opened the bench and saw the cocaine. "You are one bad motherfucker," the agent said, turning to Tony. "Who's your friend?"

"I don't know who the fuck he is," Tony said.

The agent came to the door of the camper and looked down at Eddie, who was lying on the ground with his hands cuffed behind his back.

Agent: "Hey, you, who's your friend in here?"

Eddie: "I don't know who he is, some guy I just met."

The DEA agents put Tony and Eddie in separate cars and took them to the federal lockup in Boston. The two DEA agents in the front seat did not speak to Eddie on the drive. They whispered to each other and one of them used a police radio to notify his office that there had been two arrests and the seizure of what appeared to be two kilos of cocaine. The man then turned on the radio to listen to WBZ, where a disc jockey was talking about flesh eating plants between popular tunes.

The cars pulled into the police underground garage where Eddie and Tony were kept apart and taken upstairs to the booking desk, in separate elevators. Eddie was still in handcuffs as the door opened into a booking area. Tony was standing in front of a desk, rubbing his wrists and talking to someone who was going through Tony's wallet. Agent Steele was waiting for Eddie and grabbed his arm.

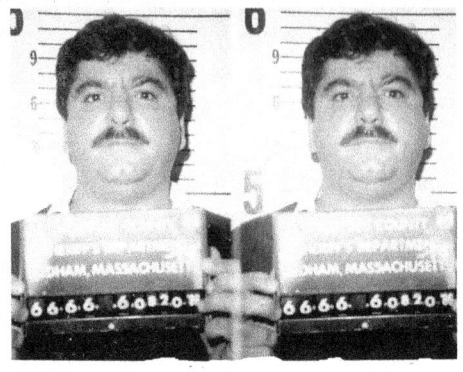

Agent Steel: "We got too much going on out here. I'll take this one to the back and take care of booking him there," he said, leading Eddie to a hallway off the booking area. Tony looked up at him as Eddie was being taken away and mouthed, "Are you a rat?" Tony looked scared and shook his head. Eddie looked at him as if to say: "Are you crazy?"

Steele led Eddie past a dozen offices and then into a small kitchen area that smelled of coffee and disinfectant. He removed the handcuffs and said, "Hell of a job, Detective, have a cup of coffee?"

Eddie could see the amazement on the faces of the young uniformed officers standing in the room. They did not understand what was going on. And one of them asked.

Agent Steel replied: "This man is one of the best deep cover operatives available today. You guys never saw him or met him, right?"

Officer: "Yeah, Yeah, we don't know who he is."

Eddie rubbed his wrists and accepted a mug of black coffee.

Ernie: "Did you guys show up with sixty grand?" he asked.

Steel: "Yes, we did. You never know if you'll need it, but we had it."

Ernie: "That's a lot of money."

Steel: "You wouldn't believe the cash some of these guys flash around. We have to play in their league."

Ernie: "How long do I have to hang around?"

Steel: "Enjoy your coffee. Your guy will be out on bail in a couple of hours. Maybe you can work another deal."

Ernie: "He's got somebody in New Hampshire. He says it's a very good source. He mentioned a name inadvertently one day; I think it was something like McQuethy. He also mentioned that this McQuethy had a partner. That's all I have right now."

"Good info. We'll test what we got today. We may be near the top. This guy McQuethy may be his main source and an importer, a good catch for us."

Eddie: "He also talked about a guy he works with, a car salesmen and I got some information about a jeweler."

Steel: "Keep in touch." Agent Steele went into the hall and motioned for another man to come into the kitchen. "This is Agent Ed Meyer. He knows what's going on and he can help you if you can't get to me."

Meyer was a thin man with a gray mustache. His hair was long for a government agent and almost covered his ears. He had a friendly smile as he offered his card. "Nice job today," he said. The two men sipped coffee and talked about drug dealers, and an hour later Agent Meyer motioned for Eddie to follow him.

It was still raining as Eddie went out a back door into the alley behind the federal lockup. An undercover DEA agent was waiting in a plain, dented two-door sport coupe whose vinyl roof was peeling off. The passenger seat was torn and stained. Eddie climbed inside and shook hands with the agent, who looked as grubby and street-worn as Eddie. Both men wore dungarees, ankle boots and they both needed a shave and a haircut. Another federal agent was black and didn't say much, he wore sunglasses, even though it was getting dark and the sky was cloudy. Then he reached his hand out to Ernie.

"George O'Brien," he said, offering his hand.

"Irish kid, huh," Eddie said. Both men laughed.

"I know where your car is," the agent said. "I'll drop you off a block away and you can walk the rest of the way."

"Thanks. that'll be good," Eddie said. "Do you know any of these guys I'm working on?"

Agent O'Brien: "We've been watching Tony and his friend Billy. Billy's got connections and may be tied to some weapons dealers. Tony is also bad guy. His shit's pretty good, almost pure Colombian. He may know the guy who's bringing it in. Are you working Goldstein, the jeweler? He seems to travel in the same circles as Tony Cole and Jimmy Rinaldi, may be a connection."

Eddie: "I know Rinaldi. He claims he has good heroin connections. I'm just starting to work on Goldstein. I've seen him a couple of times but he doesn't hang out with street people. Tony's mentioned him as a guy I should know, but he hasn't gone into detail. I spoke with Goldstein, the Jeweler,, but he's cute. He wants to speak in codes and he wants to meet your family before he decides to deal with you. It will take some time, but I'll work things out with him. I can guess. What do you guys know?"

O'Brien: "We know he's somebody to watch, but he's careful. He doesn't like to do business with people he doesn't know. You're in a good spot now. Your being busted with Tony makes you look great. That's money in the bank with these guys."

Eddie laughed. "I've been busted with everybody lately."

The agent pulled over two blocks from the coffee shop on Sea Street and handed Eddie his card. There was no name, only a telephone number and an image of what appeared to be an eagle or a large bird. "Call me if you need anything," he said.

Eddie got out and walked back to his car, noting who was watching him from a nearby coffee shop. He drove home by way of Boston, driving through the neighborhood that was listed as his address on the undercover driver's license. If anyone was following him, he wanted them to see him going there, not to Dedham and his family. It took him two hours to get home and when he pulled into his driveway he was confident no one was trailing him.

Chapter Fifteen

The Monsignor

Teresa and the boys were sitting at the kitchen table. The boys were doing their homework and Teresa was helping and watching. Eddie kissed her on the forehead and hugged the boys, then he took off his jacket. Teresa saw the red marks on his wrists and looked at him with worry.

Her voice wavered as she asked, "So, how was your day?"

Ernie: "Good. How was yours?"

Teresa: "Joey has a problem with his Catechism class teacher. You might have to pay a visit to the Monsignor."

Ernie: "What's the problem?"

Joey spoke up. "I missed over three classes last season and the priest told me I would have to do the year over unless I did a three page report on Jesus. If I don't get the credit I can't be confirmed this year."

Ernie: "Okay, that sounds reasonable. Did you do the report on Jesus?"

Joey: "Yes and he said I could move forward with the other kids."

Ernie: "So what's the problem?"

Joey: "He left the parish and Monsignor replaced him and the new priest. The new priest says that I can't move ahead. I told him about my agreement with the priest and he refuses to let me go forward."

"Let me call up there and I'll go see someone and find out if there's any way we can work this out." Ernie looked at Teresa and his eyes betrayed his own problems with the church as a boy.

He called the parish office and the monsignor's housekeeper answered. She also kept his appointment book and told Ernie that he could see him in an hour or it would be a few days before the monsignor was available. "I'll be right over," Ernie said. He grabbed his coat and told Joey he was going to the rectory to see what he could do. Teresa sat at the kitchen table and looked at Eddie as he left. He seemed unaware of his appearance. He looked like a thug.

An hour later Ernie was standing in the vestibule of the rectory, ringing the doorbell. A small curtain covered the window on the door and it moved as an elderly woman peaked out. She looked at Ernie and appeared apprehensive. The door opened slightly.

Maid: "What do you want?" she asked, in a sarcastic manner.

Ernie: "I have an appointment with Monsignor."

Maid: "Why would he want to speak with the likes of you?" She looked at his unshaved face and his street clothes. Her gaze paused on the scar across his face.

Eddie: "It's about my son and his catechism classes."

Maid: "Wait here." She closed the door and left Ernie standing outside. She obviously was afraid of him because of his street look. She was like most and pre-judged him.

~ ~ ~

Five minutes later the door opened again and this time the Monsignor was standing in the doorway, looking at Ernie as though something disgusting had been left on his stoop. Another judgment easily observed in the look on the priests face.

Monsignor: "What can I do for you?"

Ernie: "I want to talk to you about my son's catechism classes."

Monsignor: "Come in, but wipe your shoes."

Ernie stepped inside and wiped his feet on a mat near the door. He looked at the monsignor, but did not identify himself as a police officer. He wanted to see how the priest would conduct himself with someone he thought was street scum. The two men went into a formal living room and the priest motioned for Eddie to sit in one of the wing-back chairs near the fireplace.

He told the priest about Joey's agreement with the previous priest and how the boy had worked hard to write the paper about the life of Jesus and what it meant to him to be confirmed in the church with the other boys his age.

The monsignor waited a moment and said, "There is nothing I can do."

Ernie: "You can check the records. Maybe Father left a note about my son Joey."

Monsignor: "There's no need for that. I told you there's nothing I can do."

Ernie: "You're in charge here, aren't you?"

Monsignor: "You could say that."

At that moment, he looked like Eddie Pannoni, but he was facing the priest as Ernie Lijoi Sr., husband and father. "Look, you're supposed to represent truth and honesty. You're telling me that you are going to let this go as what my son will look at as a lie? A lie from the church?"

The monsignor was unmoved. "There is nothing that I can do. The old priest is no longer here. He is no longer in the area."

Ernie: "Then I guess a phone call is too much to ask."

Monsignor: "It's not that. It's just that I cannot interfere in his work."

Ernie: "This is not interfering, Father. It's being honest with my boy. I tell you I know my son and if I give him the option he will walk away from Catechism classes."

The monsignor sighed and looked at the scruffy man across from him. Monsignor: "There's no need to walk away over a small thing like that."

Ernie: "Father, don't let this Afro and beard fool you. I'm a police officer. I've been a police officer for a long time and if I did my business the way you seem to do yours the public would not stand for it or trust me."

Monsignor: "You're a police officer?"

Ernie: "I work narcotics. That's why I dress this way. This is strictly confidential information; if you say anything to anyone you could cost me my life."

Monsignor: "Oh, I'm sorry. We are somewhat in the same business, as it turns out."

Ernie: "No. When I say something, my word is good."

Monsignor: "Give me a minute."

The priest left the room and was gone for about fifteen minutes. He came back with a file in his hand and sat down opposed Eddie and looked through it. He looked up and shook his head; he could not find any notes.

Monsignor: "There's nothing I can do," he said.

Ernie looked at the man and felt a well of frustration and anger. It was the same feeling he had when the Monsignor in Brooklyn had called him a "little Guinea" years ago, when he was ten years old. Now he had to tell his son that the church would not keep a promise.

~ ~ ~

Joey was waiting when he got home. He and Teresa were watching television and she saw from her husband's face that the monsignor had said no. He explained it to the boy, who looked at his father and mother.

"How can they lie like that?" Joey asked.

Ernie: "You're gonna get lied to a lot in life, but don't let that cloud your thinking."

Joey: "It's not fair." The boy's eyes pleaded with his parents for an answer to one of life's unanswerable challenges.

Ernie: "What do you want to do?"

"Drop the classes," he boy said.

Ernie: "It's okay with me. You just have to convince your mother."

Teresa wanted her boys to be good Catholics. She had her own issues with the church, but she also took some comfort from her faith. But she acknowledged that Joey had a point, so she agreed to allow him to drop out of Catechism classes. He was never confirmed.

Chapter Sixteen
The Jeweler

Wednesday, March 22nd

Spring along the New England coast can be gloomy and damp. The bitter winter gave way to rain and fog softened only by the balmy sixty degrees that took away the last of the filthy slush that lingered against the sides of buildings. The day reflected the mood.

Joey sat at the kitchen table and stared at his bowl, slowing the moving the cereal from one side to the other, lost in disappointment. Teresa watched him and tried not to show her anger at the church that would deny the boy his Confirmation. Ernie Junior, three years younger, happily slurped his breakfast.

Ernie Senior, wearing dungarees and an undershirt, had yet to begin another day as Eddie Pannoni. Right now he was a husband and father who sipped his coffee and worried about his family. Teresa was losing weight and she seemed lost in thought most of the time. She looked at him with concern and hurt, and he wondered what she was really thinking.

Teresa: "You got a busy day?" she asked.

Ernie; "Yeah, I gotta make some calls and maybe meet somebody."

"Okay," she said, turning back to Joey; "Time to get your things together for school."

The boys gathered their things and packed the lunches that Teresa had made. Ernie turned back into Eddie and went to the red telephone to dial Tony's number. It rang six times and Eddie was about to hang up when he heard Tony's voice.

Tony: "Yeah," he said, weakly.

Ernie: "Tony?"

Tony: "Eddie! What the fuck!" Tony's breathing got rapid, as though he had been running.

Eddie: "Yeah, what the fuck!" Eddie responded. "What the hell happened over there?"

Tony: "I don't know, for awhile, I thought it was you. Maybe you told somebody."

Eddie: "Listen, you know me. You know I don't talk to anybody. Who did you talk to?"

There was a pause., Tony got very quiet, then he replied: "I might have told Billy and maybe another guy. I don't know. I got pretty wrecked the night before and some guys came over. How would I fuckin' know they would spread it around?"

Eddie: "Jesus, Tony. You fucked me up pretty good. I could have been locked up. I told them I didn't know you very well and I didn't know what you had in the fuckin' camper. I don't know if they bought it. I got out, but this shit can't happen again, you know that, Tony."

Tony: "It won't happen again. I gotta go see my source and explain everything. I think we're still good, but it might be a couple of days before I'm back in business. I think the feds are watching me."

Eddie: "When you get going again I want some quantity. I'm kind of fucked right now because my people in New York think I have two kilos for them and I ain't got shit. You gonna be able to take care of me?"

Tony: "Yeah. Give me a couple of days. Call me. By the way, Goldstein, the jeweler? I hear he's got some stuff. He can get the same stuff I get but he doesn't do business with people he don't know."

Eddie: "He knows you, right?"

Tony: "Yeah but, right now, it's not a good time for me. Besides, you already bought some of his shit. You got a couple of grams last month and he's the guy who I got it from. You've seen him around."

Eddie; "Yeah, I've talked to him but I've never done business with him. Will you talk to him for me?"

Tony: "Yeah, sure. I'll call him. I'll tell him you're a solid guy he can do business with."

Eddie: "Tell him I'm coming by his store later. We'll see. I gotta go now. You lay low and we'll do that deal."

~ ~~ ~

Goldstein's jewelry store was near the waterfront in what was generally described as a "charming" part of Quincy. Goldstein sold medium to low quality pieces and supplemented his income by selling cocaine to what he believed was a select group of customers. He further believed that by limiting his drug sales to this group he could avoid prison. He was reluctant to take on any new customers for the sale of his cocaine until he got to know them well and sometimes their families as well. He was extremely cautious. Ernie would have to work his charm.

Eddie walked into his store and studied the pieces on display under the glass counters. Goldstein, The Jeweler, had sections for necklaces, rings, watches and specialty items. He recognized Eddie.

Jeweler: "How are you today?" he asked, smiling his salesman's smile.

Eddie: "Good, just looking over your jewelry. You got some nice stuff."

Jeweler: "You have anything in mind?"

Eddie: "Yeah, you know, some of what I got before."

Goldstein didn't bite. "I don't remember what you bought before. A ring?"

Eddie didn't push it. "I'm looking for something special, something for my wife, maybe a necklace." He spent a few minutes looking over the items on display and told

Goldstein he would be back after he thought about what he wanted to purchase. The jeweler would require time and patience before he would deal cocaine to Eddie. The undercover cop would make it a point to visit the store every day and get to know Goldstein. *It may take a week, it may take a month,* Eddie thought, *but I have the time.*

He walked out of the jewelry store and went to the harbor to watch the boats. The air was warm and wet and the boat owners and repair shops were busy preparing the vessels for the summer season. He stood with his foot on a railing, smoking a cigarette, thinking about Goldstein, Tony and their supplier. He resolved to call Bud Steele at the DEA to coordinate a plan. Two men approached him and stood next to him as they lit their cigarettes. He recognized the men as street rabble that turned up at the same dives and pool halls where Eddie Pannoni spent his time.

"I thought I recognized you," one of the men said. "You're Eddie, right?"

Eddie looked at the man and made a mental note. W/m, 5',7", dirty blond hair, mustache, 160 pounds, approximately 18 years old. The other man was noted as White Male about 5 Ft. 10 inches tall, blond hair, 140 pounds, 37 years old.

Eddie: "Whitey, right?" he responded.

Whitey: "Yeah, and this is Moon."

"You guys taking in the sea air?" Eddie asked.

Whitey: "We're doing some business. Maybe we got something you'd be interested in."

The young man Whitey called Moon smiled and leaned into Eddie. "We got a real nice stereo, top of the line, real diamond needle, fuckin' thing is worth a thousand dollars."

"How much you want for it?" Eddie asked.

"Two hundred," Moon replied. Moon was a white male, about 35 years of age, dark hair and complexion, he looked more Italian then he did Irish.

A Quincy police cruiser drove by and Eddie turned his face away, fearing that the officer would recognize him and wave or yell hello. The cruiser stopped a half block away and the officer sat looking at the harbor.

Eddie: "I'm gonna get a cup of coffee. Let me think about the stereo and I'll let you know," as he stepped away from the two young men.

"We can wait. When you come out, let us know," Whitey said, smiling as Eddie walked away.

He went into a coffee shop and ordered a cup to go. Whitey and Moon smoked and watched the boats as the police cruiser drove away. He left the shop and told the two men he wanted to go for a ride with them to talk about the stereo and motioned for them to follow him to his car.

Eddie: "Tell me about this stereo," he said, as the three men drove through the gray, wet streets of Quincy.

Moon: "Whitey and me did about six houses. That's how we got the stereo. We also got four bottles of V.O. and drank them right in the fucking houses." The two men laughed. "You can have the stereo for two hundred. One fifty if you don't sell it to anyone from Adam's Shore."

"You got it where you can get at it easily?" Eddie asked.

"Meet us at five in the parking lot at Quincy station. We'll have it for you and you can give us the money. We got other shit, too, if you want something. We got some jewelry, real silverware, China sets, vases and much more"

Eddie dropped the men off at the harbor and went to a pay phone to talk to Detective Churn about Whitey and Moon and their burglary loot. Churn told him that a stereo matching the one he described was taken in a burglary the day before. Churn told Eddie that Whitey and Moon would be taken care of.

Eddie pulled into the Quincy station parking lot a few minutes before five and saw Moon waiting on the sidewalk.

He was alone. Eddie pulled up to him and rolled down the passenger window.

Eddie: "You got the stereo?"

Moon: "Look, we sold it to somebody else. Some guy gave us twenty five sheets of acid. We couldn't turn it down." Moon gave Eddie the same stupid grin he displayed at the harbor. "We got lots of other stuff. You want some nice jewelry?"

Eddie: "Not today, maybe another time." Eddie drove away.

Two days later Whitey and Moon were arrested and loot from a half dozen burglaries was recovered. Missing was an expensive stereo and several necklaces.

~ ~ ~

The weekend forecast was spring-like, so Detective Lijoi took his wife and boys to Maine to get away from the red telephone. He left the Thunderbird at home, parked in the rear of the driveway, and took the family Chrysler. As the police were rounding up Whitey and Moon, the Lijoi family was driving up I-95, listening to the radio and playing a game of looking for out of state license plates.

"Who can find a plate first?" Teresa began.

The boys looked out the rear windows and shouted their discoveries, excited by the sight of a car from Rhode Island or New York. The game bored the boys after about hour, so Ernie and Teresa pulled into a restaurant just over the Maine line to grab some lunch at a diner that was part of a favorite trading post where Ernie and the boys bought fishing lures.

"What's first, lunch or lures?" Ernie asked.

"I'm hungry," both boys responded.

The diner was busy and the Lijoi family settled at a table to the far left, against a wall, where Ernie sat in a seat that allowed him to view the entire dining room. The boys wanted hot dogs and French fries and ate packets of crackers that were stacked into a square container in the middle of the table. Teresa and Ernie ordered lobster rolls with fries. It was a nice moment, Ernie thought, as he sat back and took a breath, happy to be away from the sleaze of the streets. He looked at Teresa and saw again how thin she was. She looked worried and nervous, but she smiled when she saw him looking at her.

Ernie scanned the restaurant and saw a table of five men in a far corner, leaning into their conversation. Three of them wore leather jackets and did not fit in with the crowd that filled the rest of the tables. Everyone else in the restaurant looked happy and eager to enjoy the weekend. These men looked like the thugs that Ernie played pool and bought drugs from. One of the men turned to look across the dining room and Ernie recognized him as a mid-level drug dealer from Boston, a man he had seen at Tony's house, but had never spoken to. The man turned his attention back to the other men at the table and leaned forward. Another man was seated in the corner and his face was hidden by the others, but when the drug dealer moved his head, Ernie could see the fifth man and he recognized him as a Boston narcotics detective. The man was wearing a suit, laughing and joking with the drug dealers. Maybe he's undercover was Ernie's first thought. His name was Waldo Robinowits.

As Ernie watched the table, each man turned to scan the room and one by one Ernie recognized drug dealers, some of them with reputations for violence. The detective seemed at ease with them and laughed and slapped his companions on the shoulder.

The detective looked up and saw Ernie, his face became white, he was surprised at seeing Ernie. His attitude completely changed, it was obvious. It was also obvious to Ernie that he was not working as a detective. He whispered something to the man next to him, left money on the table, and stood up. Ernie could see the man's badge on his belt.

He was not hiding the fact that he was a detective. The other men watched him stand and then looked over at Ernie.

Jesus! Ernie though. *These guys think I'm Eddie Pannoni. I'm here with my family!*

The detective walked over to Ernie's table and went to Ernie's chair.

Waldo: "How you doin'?" he asked.

Ernie: "Good, good, you?"

Waldo: "Having lunch with some guys, you know how it is."

Ernie: "Yeah, sure. "

The drug dealers at the corner table were glancing at Ernie, and making comments to each other as Ernie and Waldo played the game of chicken.

Waldo: "Gotta run, nice to see ya." The detective smiled at Ernie and his family and left.

One of the drug dealers looked at Ernie and waved. He mouthed the words, "Hi, Eddie," and gave a thumbs up gesture. A few minutes later, the four drug dealers left. Ernie noted the men's faces and the time of the meeting they had had with the detective. He made a note on the inside cover of a matchbook with the time and date

Ernie decided to contact his friends at the DEA and discreetly ask some questions before he decided to write a report. The answers he got were the ones he expected. The DEA had been watching him for a while and asked for a copy of the report if he decided to write one. Ernie later wrote a report to his chief advising him of what he observed because of the reaction that he got from Waldo. This was not a detective dealing with some informants; this was a detective who was and had been suspected of being dirty and this meeting that Ernie witnessed did not mesh in a good way.

After extensive surveillance and investigation, four weeks later the Boston papers headlined a story about a Boston narcotics detective who had been caught working with the dealers and the front page featured a photograph of the detective Ernie had seen at lunch. To the best of Ernie's knowledge, Waldo did not reveal Ernie's cover to the dealers.

Ernie and Teresa spent the weekend with the boys, fishing and hiking and enjoying the crisp early spring weather. They played games and drove to several lakes to scout for property to buy if they ever had the money for a weekend place. A ramshackle cabin on a lakefront lot caught their eye, but it needed work and more money than they had at the time, so they drove home dreaming about fixing the place up and having a retreat from the pressures of their daily lives.

Ernie thought about the investigation and wondered how long it would be before it could be closed. The Quincy Police Department had all but assured him he would have a permanent job when this was over and Teresa was eager for him to get the red telephone out of their bedroom.

Monday morning was chilly and rainy with fog. The Boston area was gloomy as the work week began and commuters were glum as they sat in traffic or rode the trains. Ernie drove the boys to school in the Chrysler and came home to have coffee with Teresa.

Teresa: "You think we'll ever be able to build a new house on the lake?" she asked.

Ernie: "We will," he promised. "Maybe in place of that cabin we looked at."

Teresa: "I hope so, that would be wonderful for all of us, it would save a lot of work. It seems like every time we are there, we have another broken pipe, they are all so old. You are constantly soldering them together."

Ernie: "I don't mind, I actually enjoy doing it."

Ernie showered and dressed and became Eddie again. He made a few calls and told the shit bums he had been in New York for the weekend, delivering drugs and guns to some of his customers and associates.

Chapter Seventeen

The State Charter

Tony called to invite Eddie to a party that night and he promised to have quality and quantity for Eddie.

Tony: "I got what you want," he said, "from last time, the same price."

Eddie: "I gotta see it first," he responded.

Tony: "Yeah, tonight at the party; we'll talk and you can see what I have." He hung up.

Eddie spent the afternoon driving the streets of Quincy picking up hitchhikers, talking to dealers on the CB radio, and shooting pool. Seven people asked him for drugs and he told them all he was looking to buy, not sell. He went to the coffee shop to kill time before Tony's party and saw Jeannie sitting in a booth with one of her customers. She waved at him and pointed to a stool at the counter. He sat down and Jeannie came over to him with a pot of coffee and a mug.

Jeannie: "Hey, stranger. How's it hangin'?" she giggled. Eddie thought she was high, but too wrecked to work.

Eddie: "I'm going over to Tony's later; you going?," he responded.

Jeannie: "Yes, me, too," she said, "gonna maybe get lucky." She giggled again. "I'm off at eleven."

Eddie: "I can't pick you up. I'll be at the party."

Jeannie: "I'm leaving in a couple of minutes. Maybe I'll see you later." She attended to other customers and flirted with most of the men.

Eddie thought she was too smart and too pretty to be so messed up. *Where ever it is that she's going, it isn't good,* he thought, as he paid for the coffee and climbed into the Thunderbird.

~ ~ ~

Tony's place was packed and almost everyone was high by the time Eddie walked in the front door. Marijuana smoke was thick and Eddie thought he would get high just breathing the air in the living room. Men were sitting and standing around with glazed eyes, some having conversations that made no sense. A few women were being hit on and seemed equally dazed and unsure whether they should respond to the men. One of the young women was on her knees, snorting a line of coke off the toe of a cowboy boot worn by a man who was talking to another woman and trying to open her blouse.

Eddie walked through the group and mumbled "shitbags" to himself as he made his way into the kitchen, where Tony was sitting at the table, cutting coke into lines.

Tony: "Eddie, c'mon in; have a toot," he said. He looked as dazed as his customers. "You met Bob? Bob, you know Eddie?"

Bob: "Yeah, hi, Eddie." Bob's was a face Eddie had seen before, one of the street people who are part of the wallpaper of the Quincy drug scene. Bob liked to talk, especially when he was high, and he had given Eddie information in the past. The information had been passed on to Abe Churn and had been used to bring down a few street level drug dealers. Bob was high and gave Eddie a sly grin. He got up from the table and walked Eddie to the kitchen counter near the sink.

Bob: "Listen, Eddie, didn't you say that you buy guns and sell them in New York?"

Eddie: "Yes, that's right. I have people waiting for lots of things."

Bob: "You know Mike O'Reilly? He's a guitar player; He plays in clubs around Boston?"

Eddie: "Yeah, I know Mike, I've heard him play."

Bob: "Eddie, Mike has a shit load of guns for sale."

Eddie looked at Bob and saw his eyes were dilated. He could not tell whether Bob was telling him the truth or just having a grandiose moment on cocaine.

Eddie: "No shit, when can I see them?"

Bob: "He keeps them at his girlfriend's apartment on Beale Street in Boston."

Eddie: "Janis? Her name is Janis, right?" Eddie was fishing.

Bob: "You're thinking about somebody else. Joanne Perry is Mike's girlfriend. You probably met her at a club where he plays."

Eddie; "I'd like to see these guns."

Bob: "I can't guarantee you that, but if I see O'Reilly I'll give him your number and tell him you're interested."

Eddie; "Sounds good. Here's my card, give it to him. I'll be looking forward to a call from him. Nice to see you, Bob."

Bob placed the card in his wallet. Eddie shook Bob's hand and watched as he went to the sofa and sat next to a thin young woman who was wearing a skirt that showed that she had no underpants on, it barely covered her private parts.

Eddie went to the bathroom and wrote notes onto a matchbook cover. He noted the information he had received from Bob and listed everyone he recognized at Tony's house. He lit two matches to leave the scent of phosphorous as though he had been smoking something, and returned to the kitchen.

Eddie: "Tony, I gotta go. Let's talk tomorrow. I really need that stuff we talked about."

Tony: "Stick around, have some fun. Jeannie's coming over later. I think she likes you. I think she wants to climb your vine." Tony was laughing.

Eddie: "She likes everybody, I gotta go. We'll talk tomorrow."

Eddie reeked of marijuana smoke as he drove the Thunderbird to St. Catherine's to meet Detective Churn and his partner Detective Bob Rule. He briefed the men on his conversation with Bob and his pending deal with Tony.

Churn wrote down the information and told Eddie that: "Mike O'Reilly has a reputation and not just for his excellent guitar playing and singing. He was well known as an art thief. We think he is the thief who stole several paintings from the Museum of Art and he's suspected in numerous antique thefts. Doesn't leave any prints. He's a real sharp thief. He knows his stuff. His biggest problem is that he likes antiques better than his singing. He could be a big star if he would only drop the stealing, but I doubt that he will ever do that."

Ernie was amazed. "No shit!"

Churn: "We're gonna have to let the Norfolk County Task Force know about this. They're already working on O'Reilly."

~ ~ ~

Norfolk County is composed of twenty-eight communities in Eastern Massachusetts., beginning with Avon and ending with Wrentham. The county seat is Dedham. Quincy is one of the communities. The task force was formed to coordinate police investigations in the county and work with Boston and other law enforcement agencies in a region where criminals have no concept of political boundaries and would not care even if they did.

The task force had been trying to nab Mike O'Reilly for some time. They knew Joanne Perry was his girlfriend and they knew she lived at 99 Beale Street in a two-bedroom apartment on the second floor. The information that Eddie brought to Detective Church confirmed earlier reports about O'Reilly and Perry, and was enough to obtain a search warrant in Quincy District Court, where the case was considered Quincy's on the strength of the information provided by Ernie Lijoi Sr., undercover, under the guise of

Eddie Pannoni. The task force used the principle that the information of one police officer is the information of all police officers. Probable cause had been met. The warrant was issued without being forced to divulge the identity of the deep cover operative, detective Ernie Lijoi Sr.

~ ~ ~

The task force arrived at Joanne Perry's apartment at two o'clock in the morning. They expected O'Reilly to be there. Joanne Perry answered the door and was shown the warrant. The officers moved passed her after she read the warrant and began to search the apartment. They did not find one gun or any antiques of any kind. One of the detectives moved to a back room where he noticed a door behind a tall chair. He moved the chair and tried the door, but it was locked.

Joanne Perry stood in the doorway to the room and watched. "Get me the key, please" the detective asked.

Joanne: "I don't have a key," she replied.

Detective: "Where does this door go?" he asked.

Joanne: "It's just an old closet. I don't even use it, that's why I put the chair in front of it."

Detective: "I need the key. If you don't give it to me, I'll have to break down the door."

Joanne: "I never had a key."

Detective: "The warrant says we can search all areas. I have to search the closet."

Joanne: "Sorry, I don't have a key."

The detective broke into the closet and opened the door. Inside he saw two large bags and two fifty-gallon drums standing upright. They were filled with guns of all kinds, from very old to newer types all wrapped in oily rags. He also noticed dozens of antique rugs and rifles sticking out of the barrels.

The officers removed the barrels from the closet and pulled out the guns that were wrapped in the oily rags. They discovered two-hundred-fifty antique handguns, rifles and swords, some dating to the early 1800s. They also found stolen paintings that were rolled up and placed in plastic bags. A detective noticed another large plastic bag standing alone in a corner of the closet and opened it. He found a strange looking document written on a different type of paper, it seemed strange, that document had been rolled up and tied with a rubber band.

One of the detectives held the document up. "Does anybody know what this is?" he asked.

"Looks like it may be from a kid's game," an officer responded.

The closet was filthy with animal droppings and garbage piled against the barrels and beneath the plastic bags that held priceless art and collectables. The strange document was taken to a table where it could be examined later, no one could figure it out. The guesses were that it was a kid's game all the way to that it was a very old piece of wallpaper. Officers discovered cocaine and pills in boxes and smaller bags that were hidden on shelves in the back of the closet. Joanne Perry claimed she had no knowledge of anything.

The items were laid out by category, rugs over here, paintings over there; the antique firearms and swords were handled with care and laid out by type. Handguns were lined up together with rifles and swords given their own spot on the floor. The detectives stood back and wondered which robbery it all came from, they would find out. The strange document remained untouched on the table. Everything was taken back to the station after it was all marked as evidence, cauterized and recorded for the courts.

Two hours after the raid began; they laid everything out in the office, on tables, chairs, desks. In the deep darkness before dawn, the district attorney arrived to survey the evidence. He still had sleep in his eyes as he walked around the stacks of paintings and antiques, whistling to himself in wonder. There was no price that could be placed on these items.

He scanned the drugs that had been seized and made a list of what he had seen. He went to the desk in the far corner of the room and looked at the rolled up document. He recognized it as parchment, a thin material made from untanned animal skin. Parchment was used for centuries in the manner paper is used today, and high grade parchment was used for important documents. The district attorney slowly unrolled the document and stared at it.

D.A. Delahunt: "What's this?"

Detective: "We found it in the closet,"

The ADA stared at it again. He bent over and examined it. His eyes grew wide and he scanned the room, looking from officer to officer.

D.A. Delahunt: "If this is what I think it is, it's the biggest find you guys will ever have in your life." He placed the document on the table and spread it out. "Gentlemen, I believe this document is three-hundred and fifty five years old. I think this is the Massachusetts Bay Charter. It was stolen from the State Archives Museum two years ago. The ratification of this document is what gave self-government to what was then the colony of Massachusetts. It was signed in 1629. Look here are the signatories to this document. Just holding it is an honor." He stood back and admired the document. The police officers moved closer and looked at it. They tried to decipher the language and spelling that was used on March 4, 1629:

CHARLES, BY THE GRACE OF GOD, Kinge of England, Scotland, Fraunce, and Ireland, Defendor of the Fayth, &c. To ALL to whome theis Presents shall come Greeting. WHEREAS, our most Deare and Royall Father, Kinge James, of blessed Memory, by his Highnes Letters-patents bearing Date at Westminster the third Day of November, in the eighteenth Yeare of his Raigne, HATH given and graunted vnto the Councell established at Plymouth, in the County of Devon, for the planting, ruling, ordering, and governing of Newe England in America, and to their Successors and Assignes for ever, all that Parte of America, lyeing and being in Bredth, from Forty Degrees of Northerly Latitude from the Equinoctiall Lyne, to forty eight Degrees of the saide Northerly Latitude inclusively, and in Length, of and within all the Breadth aforesaid, throughout the Maine Landes from Sea to Sea; together also with all the Firme Landes, Soyles, Groundes, Havens, Portes, Rivers, Waters, Fishing, Mynes, and Myneralls...

It was the document that gave birth to New England and it had been rolled up by a thief and placed in a filthy closet on Beale Street for months. The ADA made a dawn phone call to the State Archivist and told him what he thought the police had recovered. The archivist hastily dressed and was in the apartment less than an hour later, unable to believe his eyes. He was nearly overcome.

Word of the raid on Beale Street had reached the news media and reporters and television crews were gathered on the sidewalk. They had heard that drugs were seized. They had also heard that paintings had been recovered and there was talk about some antique guns. A police spokesman briefed the reporters and stated what had been recovered. He then introduced the state archivist, who was unknown to most of the reporters. He stepped forward, looking slightly shocked. He explained that officers had found one of the most precious documents in American history and that it was undamaged.

He looked into the cameras that were sending television pictures into thousands of Boston area homes on a crisp and foggy morning and said, "The gods have been good to me and to all of us,"

The Massachusetts Bay Charter was returned to the State Archives Museum and the people of Massachusetts.

~ ~ ~

Ernie climbed into the Thunderbird and went home. He had spent the night roaming the streets and waiting for word on the raid. Teresa was watching television as the boys got ready for school. Ernie walked into the house that morning, happy about what had happened.

Teresa: "Did you hear about the big raid last night?" she asked.

He looked at her and smiled. "Yeah, I heard." He went to bed.

He woke up around noon, feeling groggy. He went into the kitchen where Teresa poured him a cup of coffee and watched as he drank it. He looked tired, she thought, and had lost the spark that was the essence of her New York boy. He was distracted and somber much of the time. She wondered where he was when he was out for hours or even overnight with his drug dealers and their friends and customers.

She still had trouble sleeping and would lie awake for hours, staring at the ceiling and feeling like she was falling through space. Teresa did not type his reports anymore because it was too upsetting to learn what he was doing in those dark hours. She preferred not knowing. It was not knowing that produced new anxieties as her mind wandered over the possibilities.

Teresa: "You have anything to do with the raid in Boston?" she asked.

He looked up from his coffee. "Yeah, I got the original tip."

Teresa walked over to him, kissed him on the cheek and said; "Great job."

They sat in silence for a few minutes before he got up and took a shower, dressed, and became Eddie again. He went to the closet, took down the .38, removed the trigger lock, and went to work. He climbed into the Thunderbird and went to shoot a few games of pool.

Chapter 18

Piper

Teresa went into the bedroom and stared at the red telephone and the tape recorder. Ernie had told her not to listen to the tapes because they would upset her. The calls are from drug dealers and junkies, he said, they say things. She remembered his exact words; *"These tapes are for one thing only, in case I disappear then my guys have a place to start searching."*

She walked to the tape recorder and pressed the "play" switch. The reel's began to turn and she sat on the bed and listened. Teresa listened to several of the tapes when suddenly she heard a female voice:

The female said, "Hey, it's me. Is this you?" the woman laughed.

She heard her husband's voice responded. "Yeah, it's me."

Woman: "What are you doing right now?" The woman's voice was soft.

Eddie: "I'm getting ready to go out. I got some business to take care of."

Woman: "You wanna get together tonight? Maybe fuck around?"

Edie: "Yeah, sure, where are you going?"

Woman: "Maybe go to a bar, have a couple of drinks, maybe get high. Can you bring a set? We don't have any."

It was Jeannie in that conversation and she wanted Eddie to bring her a needle and syringe.

Eddie: "I'll see what I can do," he said.

Woman-Jeannie: "I don't have money," she said. "I can go with you; we can play in the car." She laughed. "I'm gonna take a bath. Nothing like a clean twat for you, you know. I'll see you when you get here." There was the sound of a telephone hanging up.

Teresa stopped the tape recorder and stared at it. She could barely breathe for a moment. She remained absolutely still as though the act of not moving would stop time itself. The room was quiet. There were no sounds from the street. She could not get the words out of her head. *We can play in the car, nothing like a clean twat.*

Her husband spent time with this woman and others like her. They called at all hours and he went out when they called. If he was not with them, he was being shot at or handcuffed. *Where is the bored transit cop who came home every night? Where is Ernie? Who is Eddie and what is he doing right now?*

~ ~ ~

At that moment, Eddie Pannoni was thinking about the same phone call, but he had knowledge Teresa did not have. He knew that, no matter what was said on the phone, the calls were about drugs, not sex.

Jeannie was working a Social Security scam in three states where she had set up phone accounts and needed a ride to Rhode Island to pick up a check there. The call about "getting together" was to arrange a ride to Providence, but sex and drugs were the themes she presented. Jeannie always talked that way, like she was ready for a lay. She talked to her customers at the coffee shop in that manner and to most men who talked to her at parties. Eddie did not know whether she sold herself for drugs and he paid little attention to her sexual innuendo, but Teresa had no way of knowing that and sat devastated in the bedroom she shared with the undercover cop.

Ernie came home late and found her sitting on the sofa, staring at the television but not paying attention.

Ernie: "What's wrong?"

Teresa: "I listened to the tape. I heard that woman."

Ernie: "What woman?

Teresa: "The one who was going to wash herself for you."

He became Ernie again and sat next to her. "She's a junkie and a small time dealer. I use her to get to other people. That's all she is."

Teresa looked at him. "This was going to be a thirty-day job. It's coming up on four months. When is it going to be over, Ernie?"

Ernie: "Soon. We're gonna close them down soon, I'll get the phone moved."

Teresa: "I want you back in our lives where you belong."

Ernie: "I know, believe me, I understand." He put his arm around her and held her and promised himself that this thing would come to an end and his life with his family would be normal again. He would make it up to her.

~ ~ ~

The spring weather was holding. The nights were crisp but the days were warmer and the trees were budding. Daffodils were coming up in the Lijoi yard and neighbors were talking to each across fences again. Some were already in their backyards, planning vegetable gardens and turning the soil. Ernie and his next door neighbor grew tomatoes, squash, lettuce and peppers every year and traded other items such as spinach and Swiss chard with them as his parents and grandparents did before him.

The mid-day sun was warm as Ernie and his neighbor planned the year's crop, walking through each backyard and point to where everything would be planted. Ernie was in a good mood because Teresa seemed happy that morning and he did not have anyone to see until dark.

They heard a noise that sounded like a cat, but neither man could see the animal. Ernie had seen a black female cat a day earlier and had heard sounds in the night, but she was nowhere to be seen. The sound continued as he and his neighbor talked and enjoyed the sunshine. Other neighbors came out to talk and remarked about the cat (crying) noise that they heard all night long.

"I'll find it," Ernie said. "I don't have to be anyplace for a couple of hours."

"See if you can shut it up," one neighbor said.

"Ernie, the cat man," said another, laughing as he got into his car to go to work. "Now you can put your police training to work."

He followed the sound of the cat to a downspout on the house next door and then along the steps of the front stoop to a drain that ran to the storm sewer, which ran to the river. The drainpipe from the roof of the house had long ago been taken down, only the section that went to the storm sewer remained, with about two feet showing above ground with no cap or cover.

Ernie looked down into the pipe and saw a kitten peeking up, hiding in the bend that went to the sewer line. He could not reach the animal, so he went into his kitchen and came back with a bowl of milk, which he placed near the top of the pipe. He went back into the house and watched to see if the kitten came out. When it did, he slowly walked back to the pipe, but the kitten jumped back into the pipe and Ernie could not grab it. He came back with a can of tuna, and the result was the same. The animal came up, showed interest, and ran back down the pipe when Ernie showed up. Several of his neighbors thought it was a good show and watched and laughed as the kitten got away. The animal was filthy from its trips up and down the pipe and was covered in grime that had accumulated in the pipe over many years.

He told Teresa what he was trying to do and she scolded him for giving the tuna to the kitten and suggested that he try using his shop vacuum to suck the animal out of the pipe. He attached a wide nozzle and an eight foot hose, turned it on, and stuck it down the pipe until he felt weight on the tube, as though he was fishing, this time for a cat. The fishing line tenses when a fish is on the hook, only in this case he had a small, furry, filthy animal. The tube that he was holding became much heavier; he slowly raised it out of the hole. He turned off the vacuum and the kitten fell into his hand.

He and Teresa cleaned the kitten and used an eye dropper to feed it. They took it to a veterinarian and learned that it was a girl and it was fine. That night they put the kitten in a box and placed a towel over it as a blanket to keep it warm.

Ernie: "Let's call it Piper," he said.

Teresa: "Yes, that's perfect since you found it in a pipe," smiling.

~ ~ ~

That night Eddie went to the coffee shop in Quincy. Jeannie was trying to flirt with a customer, but she needed a shot of heroin, her nose was running as she scratched her face. She smiled and her smile seemed strained as she waved at Eddie and pointed to a stool at the counter. She came around with a pot of coffee and a mug and leaned forward so he could look down her blouse.

Jeannie: "Your friend Robby is here. He was asking about you."

Eddie looked down the counter and saw Robby looking at him. He had not seen the man in several weeks and had no desire to talk to him now. He had long ago classified Robby as a lowlife who had no value in a drug investigation that went to the highest levels of the game. Robby would always be a low level street bum. Robby got up from his stool and walked over to Eddie.

Robby: "How ya doin' man? I haven't seen you in awhile." He offered his hand.

Eddie: "I'm good. Busy, you know what that's like." Eddie shook Robby's hand but he did not offer him the stool next to him. Robby sat down and turned to Eddie.

Robby: "You interested in a little investment?"

Eddie: "Yes, sure, what do you have?"

Robby: Robby leaned forward and spoke in a low voice. "I know a guy who's looking for backing to do a bank."

Eddie: "That's very interesting, who's the guy? Where is he? Where's the bank?"

Robby: "You interested, I can get you in touch with the guy."

Eddie: "Depends on how much and what the return will be." Eddie looked at Robby for a moment. The man looked around to see if anyone was listening.

Robby: "You have to speak with him, but I want a cut for the connection if you decide to back him."

Eddie: "We can work that out. You know me. I would never leave you out in the cold."

Robby: "Let's take a ride." Robby got up and motioned for Eddie to follow him. "Let's take your car," he said.

Robby directed Eddie to drive to the town of Norwood and told him to stop in front of a curtain and draperies shop.

Robby: "I'll be right back." Robby went inside and came back with a young, muscular man dressed in grey clothing whose face was covered by a thick beard. Eddie noted his height at six feet. Robby and the man climbed into the Thunderbird and all three men sat in silence for several minutes. Eddie waited for someone else to speak.

The young man spoke first. "Do you think you might be able to finance my next venture?"

Eddie: "What's your name, partner?"

"They call me Spaz; my name is Billy Barns.

Eddie stared at the man. "What is your next venture?"

Spaz: "A bank."

Eddie: "Which bank?"

Spaz: "Look across the street, that one," the man said, pointing to a bank across the street. "I've been casing it for a year. I work in the drapery shop. I know what I need."

The man went through a list of items he thought he would need to rob the bank, including a van, a car, and specialty tools that Eddie had never heard of.

"How much money do you need?" Eddie asked.

Spaz: "Twenty-thousand."

Eddie: "You won't need that much. I can get this stuff and have it ready when you need it."

Spaz: "Well, then, I'll need about five thousand."

Eddie: "When do you need it?"

Spaz: "When I'm released," the man said.

Eddie: "Released from what?"

Spaz: "Walpole. I'm doing seven to ten, but I should be out in about a year."

Eddie: "You're on work release at the curtain store?"

Spaz: "That's right. I've been checking out the bank."

Eddie: "Well, maybe we can talk when you get out. I don't think we can do business right now." It was agreed that Spaz would contact Robby who would contact Eddie when the time was right, in a year or so.

Eddie and Robby drove back to Quincy in silence. He pulled into the parking lot of the coffee shop and parked in a spot in the back.

Eddie: "What the fuck was that? You bring me an investment that's a guy on work release who thinks he wants to rob a bank when he gets out. Jesus, Robby. This fuckin' guy probably goes back to his cell every night and bullshits with the other guys about how he's gonna rob a fuckin' bank, naming names like he's a big shot. Don't do this to me again. That guy's got trouble written all over him. I ain't gonna go to jail for bullshit deals."

Robby: "I thought it was worth a shot, Eddie. Maybe we can do business some other time."

Eddie: "Yeah, maybe." Robby got out of the car and went into the coffee shop.

Eddie drove to St. Catherine's to meet with Detective Churn. He told him about the Walpole inmate Spaz who planned to rob the bank across the street from his work release employer. Ernie also gave him an update about his attempts to get into the jeweler Goldstein's drug business. He gave Churn a list of druggies he had been talking to and a summary of drug deals he had in the works.

Ernie: "I need to talk to Lieutenant Lyme," he said. "I need to ask him about getting the red phone removed, or at least moved to some other place in my house. My wife is having problems with the thing ringing at all hours."

Churn: "I'll tell him," Churn said. "How's everything else?"

Eddie: "Good. I got shit-bags calling me and trying to buy and sell drugs all day and all night. Most of them are pretty far down the pipe. I'm gonna work Tony and Goldstein to move up. I've got some gun deals going on, too."

Churn: "You're doing great job, Ernie. This is gonna be big when it goes down."

Eddie: "I gotta wrap this up. My wife is having serious problems with it."

Churn: "I'll talk to the lieutenant about the phone."

Eddie drove home and climbed in beside Teresa. Piper the cat cried out from her box when she saw Ernie and went to sleep.

Chapter Nineteen

Eddie's Guns

Tony called in the morning to invite Eddie to a small party at his house. He said he was still working on a deal for Eddie but that his source was wary because the arrest during the last deal, but he had some product that Eddie's customers in New York would like.

Tony: "I got somebody who wants to meet you," he added. "Might be something in it for you."

Eddie went to Tony's in the late afternoon and found the place filled with illegal smoke. He made his way through a small crowd in the living room and into the kitchen where Jeannie and two others were shooting heroin at the table. Tony was talking to a man Eddie had seen a few times in bars and dives, but he had never met the man. Tony walked the man over and put his arm around Eddie's shoulders.

Tony: "Harry, this is Eddie. He's a friend and good guy. We've done some business and we're gonna do more business."

Eddie looked at the man and noted a white male about 5' 10", long brown hair, mustache, thin, hook nose, brown eyes, scar on forehead.

Eddie: "Hey, Harry," he said with a smile, offering his hand.

Harry responded by shaking and offering a joint he had been smoking. Eddie faked a hit and handed it back, coughing and trying to hold his breath.

"Good shit, huh," Harry mumbled, handing the joint to Tony.

"Harry's got a deal he wants to talk to you about. I'll be around." Tony wandered to the sofa and packed his snake pipe with a wad of hashish.

"Let's go outside," Harry said, moving to the door and stepping onto the porch.

Eddie followed him. "What's up?" he asked.

"Eddie, do you have a gun?"

"Yeah, several. I buy and sell."

"Can I see them?"

"Yeah, sure."

Eddie took Harry to his car and opened the trunk. He grabbed the tool box, opened it, and removed the trays that held the screw drivers. All three of his guns were wrapped in oily rags, including his .38, a 9 millimeter semiautomatic and a .25 caliber semiautomatic.

Harry looked at the guns but did not try to pick them up.

Harry: "Man, I need a cover man and you're perfect for the job."

Eddie: "Why? Because I have guns?"

Harry: "I need at least one gun. All you have to do is cover the job."

Eddie: "What's the job?"

Harry: "A drug store in Foxborough."

Eddie: "Sounds easy enough. When do you need me?"

Harry: "This weekend. We go in, take what we want, and take off."

Eddie: "You have a driver?"

Harry: "All taken care of."

Eddie looked at Harry. "There's only one problem. I got to be in New York tonight and I won't be back for four days, so I can't help you. It's Easter weekend."

Harry: "Can you rent me a gun?"

Eddie: "Not these. These are sold and promised in New York. I'm gonna make two thousand on these guns."

Harry: "I don't blame you. Listen, I've heard that Tony rents guns. You know about that?"

Eddie: "Look, you do business with me, you talk to me. If you do business with Tony, you talk to Tony, not me. I don't know what Tony does, you should talk to him."

Harry: "Yeah, you're right. Thanks."

The two men walked into Tony's house, where Eddie noted every face he could recognize, what they were doing, and whether they were buying or using. He went into the bathroom and wrote his notes on the inside of three match-books. He lit a match before he left the bathroom and flushed the toilet.

~ ~ ~

Ernie and Teresa spent Easter weekend at home and took the boys to Mass. The oldest boy was still nurturing his resentment toward the Catholic Church and silently endured what many of the faithful see at the most joyous event of the Christian year. They spent Sunday afternoon together and talked about the rundown cabin in Maine and wondered if anyone had made an offer for it.

Monday morning the boys went to school, Teresa made coffee, and Ernie played with Piper. Teresa was relaxed and smiled as she watched the kitten climb up Ernie's pants. The red telephone rang just before lunch. It was Lieutenant Lyme.

Lt. Lyme: "Can you meet me tonight at St. Catherine's around ten?"

Eddie: "Sure, I'll see you there."

Five minutes later the phone rang again. This time it was Harry.

Harry: "We scored this weekend. I got something you might like." He gave the man he believed to be Eddie Pannoni an address in Quincy. "I'm home this afternoon. Bring some beer when you come over."

~ ~ ~

Eddie was on the street again. He picked up three six packs and drove to the address Harry had given him. He knocked on the door of the small Cape Cod style house and Harry quickly opened it.

Harry: "C'mon in," he said. He seemed nervous and excited.

Eddie saw three people sitting at a small table. One he noted as black male, 6', wide brim hat, ¾ length black coat. The man got up from the table and walked past Eddie without speaking, opened the front door and left. Eddie tried to make out his face but the man kept his hat lowered. Eddie noted that he appeared to be in his twenties and wore a Fu Manchu mustache. Two young women remained at the table. Eddie had seen them both before and recognized them as drug users.

Harry motioned Eddie to the bedroom and opened the door. He saw Jeannie ironing a pair of pants and rubbing her side.

Jeannie: "Fuckin' Archie hit me with a baseball bat because I wouldn't fuck him," she said.

"Who's Archie?" Eddie asked.

"You don't know him," she replied.

Harry spoke. "We made a score at the drugstore in Foxborough over the weekend. Fuckin' place doesn't even use alarms. We were inside for half an hour we went in through the roof. We got it all, everything we wanted; percodans, Dilaudid, Dioxin, you name it, we got it. You want some?"

Eddie: "How much are you charging?"

Harry: "I've been getting two dollars for the percodans. I'll let you have them for a dollar if you buy quantity."

Eddie looked at the bed and saw a large black suitcase filled with bottles and jars of drugs of all sizes and colors.

Eddie; "This is all you got out of the drug store?"

Harry: "No, we got a couple of rooms in town where we're keeping it. We're trying to get rid of all of it fast, here's a present." Harry gave Eddie two dioxin tablets.

Eddie: "Give me the address where you keep the stuff and I'll meet you there. I have to talk to some people. We may want it all. We can work a deal."

Harry's face lit up. He took a breath, gave Eddie the name of a motel and the two room numbers.

Jeannie was still rubbing her side. "If you got something to spend I got a diamond ring you can have for five hundred, it's three-quarter carat and real gold."

Eddie: "You have it with you?"

Jeannie: "No, it's at Rita's. Come by later."

Eddie turned back to Harry. "How many of your buyers know about this?"

Harry: "We've talked to a couple of guys. First come, first served. You get there first with the money and you get the stuff. That's how it works."

Eddie: "I understand. I'll talk to my people and come by the hotel later."

Eddie drove to a pay phone and called Detective Churn. He gave him and address of the motel and the room numbers and said he would be in one of the rooms at eight o'clock. Churn said he would call the DEA and they would raid the place while Eddie Pannoni was making his deal.

He drove to Goldstein's and spent half an hour looking over watches and necklaces. The jeweler watched him and asked if there was anything he wanted to buy.

Eddie looked at him and smiled. "I'm interested in some jewelry. You know what I mean by the word 'Jewelry'?"

Jeweler: "I think I know what you have in mind. Come back tomorrow. I close at six. Meet me here then and we can talk about some 'special pieces'."

Goldstein was coming around. Eddie knew that Tony and others had told the jeweler that Eddie was a good guy and he had seen Goldstein with drug dealers, but the man was cautious. So far, he had not said or done anything that would justify suspicion or a warrant.

Eddie went to Ray's to shoot pool and be seen by the street rabble that gathered as the sun went down. The smoke was heavy and the smell of marijuana hung in the air as the sound of pool balls clacking together mixed with the noise of dozens of people talking at the same time. He passed out a few of his cards and listened as several people told him what was wrong with their cars. He told them to give him a call and he would see what he could do. One man wanted Eddie to sell him a bag of marijuana. Another tried to unload a stolen CB radio. He drank half a beer and bought a round for three bikers who told him they could get him all the pills he wanted.

The time was 7:15 PM, it took fifteen minutes for him to drive to the motel and circle the parking lot for a safe place to park the Thunderbird. He backed in under a streetlight and locked the car. His three handguns were safely under the screwdriver tray in the toolbox that was locked in the trunk. He walked around the motel, checking room numbers and noting escape routes and stairwells. He saw three cars parked in dark spots and the silhouettes of men sitting inside. Churn and the DEA agents, he thought. He knew they would be armed with a warrant and had already scanned the building and knew where he was going. He climbed an outside staircase to the second floor balcony and walked down the concrete corridor until he came to the two rooms, side by side. He glanced at the surveillance cars and saw the doors open and plainclothes men slowly getting out of the vehicle.

He knocked on the door of the room on the left and heard a man talking as he walked to the door. Harry smiled and waved him in. There were four men and three women sitting on the two beds. The place was reeking with the smell of weed and alcohol. Eddie entered and saw that a bottle of gin had been spilled on the carpet. He pulled the door so it appeared to be closed, but left it slightly ajar so anyone from outside could walk in by pushing on the door.

"Watch that spot," Harry said, "we had a little accident." He giggled like a small girl.

Jeannie sat next to a man Eddie did not recognize. She was high and her gaze was unsure. She cocked her head as she looked at Eddie.

Jeannie: "I know you," she mumbled.

"So," Harry said. "You here to buy?"

"Where is it?" Eddie asked.

Harry went to the far side of a bed and picked up a suitcase. He took it to a small desk and opened it and showed Eddie the drugs that had been stolen from the Foxborough pharmacy the previous weekend.

Harry: "Everything and anything you want, we got." He grinned and took a long toke from a joint that had been passed to him by one of the men on the bed.

Eddie: "How much?"

Harry: "Ten thousand dollars, cash for everything."

Eddie: "That's a lot of money, Harry. What's the count in the suitcase?"

Eddie moved away from the door and stood next to the wall close to the window that opened onto the balcony. There was a knock on the door and the shout "Police! Open the door! We have a warrant!"

Everyone in the room froze except Jeannie, who looked as though she was trying to remember where she was. Harry moved to close the suitcase as four men rushed into the room, holding badges in one hand and handguns in the other.

Detective: "Everybody down! Now! Get down!"

The men on the bed tried to stand, but Churn and the DEA agents pushed them to the floor. Eddie got down on his knees, then went face down on the carpet next to the spilled gin. He put his hands behind his head and waited for the agents to cuff him.

It was all over in a few minutes. Harry, Jeannie and the others were led to a police van that had been waiting nearby. The agents singled Eddie out for special treatment, yelling," We've been watching you. You sit right here. We got a warrant for your car."

Harry looked scared as he was taken away. Eddie glared at him and shook his head. One of the DEA agents checked the contents of the suitcase and logged the contents, closed it, and sealed it.

The van pulled out of the parking lot and Churn took off Eddie's handcuffs.

Churn: "It didn't take them long to turn this place into a shit hole," he said, looking around the room. "What's next door?"

"I didn't see it," Eddie said. "I'm sure it's a dump like this."

The DEA agents used a master key to open the next room and found a few items of clothing, a small bag of marijuana and a package of tampons.

~ ~ ~

An hour later Eddie pulled the Thunderbird into the parking lot at St. Catherine's and parked next to Lieutenant Lyme's car. There was another man sitting in the passenger's seat. Both men were wearing suits. Eddie looked at the lieutenant and at the other man and wondered why Lyme was not alone as usual. He got out of the Thunderbird and walked to Lyme's car as the lieutenant rolled down his window.

Lt. Lyme: "Get in," he said, motioning to the back seat.

Ernie opened the rear door and climbed inside. The other man smiled.

Lt. Lyme: "Ernie, this is Mayor Tobin. He would like to speak with you."

Ernie offered his hand over the seat and the two men shook as the mayor spoke.

Mayor: "I'll get right to the point. Why do you want to transfer from MBTA to Quincy?"

Ernie: "Well, Sir, I enjoy my job in Quincy. I feel as though I'm doing something for the citizens of this city and the state, as well as the country. It's like when I was in the service when we stood for the flag raising. I would get chills every time as I saluted the flag. It gives me a great feeling, like I'm accomplishing something.

Mayor: "Well said. What about your roots?

Ernie: "My roots, Sir?"

Mayor: "Your family, where's your family?"

Ernie: "My family is in Dedham. I have a wife, two children and a home there."

Mayor: "Then that's your roots."

Ernie: "Yes, Sir. By the way, I brought these for Lieutenant Lyme. Maybe you want to see them."

Ernie handed the mayor a fist full of three by five cards containing all of the names, addresses and information of every drug dealer he had been dealing with and had singled out those who appeared to have high level connections.

The mayor took the cards and looked at them. He saw what they contained and quickly handed the cards back to Ernie.

Mayor: "Don't give me those. I don't want to know the particulars of what you're doing. It's not my business. Not yet, anyway."

Lieutenant Lyme took the cards and examined them for a moment.

Lt. Lyme: "Ernie has been doing a great job, Mr. Mayor. That's why I wanted you to meet him along with what we discussed."

Mayor: "Is there anything else, Lieutenant?"

Lt. Lyme: "No, Sir, not from me."

Mayor: "Ernie, you have any questions?"

Ernie: "No, Sir."

Lt. Lyme: "Ernie, you got anything you need to give to the guys tonight?"

Ernie: "Have you talked to Detective Churn about an operation we had earlier, Sir?

Lt. Lyme: "I didn't get a full briefing. Is that over and done?"

Ernie: "Yes. We got some bad guys and all of the evidence from the drug store robbery was recovered."

Lt. Lyme: "Good work. Go home, Ernie. We'll talk about the telephone thing later."

He climbed into the Thunderbird and sat for a moment as Lieutenant Lyme and the mayor drove away. He knew that Lyme was on his side and the mayor had taken the time to meet him in the parking lot at St. Catherine's. He allowed himself to feel that his transfer to Quincy was a done deal.

~ ~ ~

He walked into his living room with a smile on his face. Teresa looked up from the sofa. "Are you okay?"

Ernie: "You'll never guess what happened tonight. Remember what I've been saying all along, what I really want out of this whole thing besides the job itself?"

Teresa: "You want to transfer to Quincy some day," she replied, staring at him.

Ernie: "I think it's going to happen. Do you know who I just met with? I met with the mayor. I think Lieutenant Lyme arranged the meeting so I can transfer to Quincy."

Teresa smiled and wondered if the transfer meant that Ernie's time as a deep undercover detective was coming to an end. "That's wonderful. How should we celebrate?"

Ernie: "Let's take a trip to the cabin in Maine."

Teresa grabbed his hands and saw the latest handcuff marks on his wrist, indicating that he had been arrested again. She looked into his eyes and saw he was excited and hopeful.

Teresa: "Okay, let's go up again this weekend."

~ ~ ~

Goldstein called shortly after midnight and said he had something to do the next night and Eddie should come by for his special pieces of jewelry early in the week.

Chapter 20

Opium Powder

Monday, April 3

The red telephone rang just as the morning sunshine began to filter through the curtains. It had been cold over-night, and the wind howled, but the days were growing longer.

"Hello," Eddie's voice was thin with sleep.

"Eddie? This Eddie?"

"Yeah, who's this?"

"It's Rita, we met a couple times at Tony's, maybe at Jeannie's, too. I got red hair. You remember?

Eddie: "Okay, sure. What can I do for you at this hour?"

Rita: "I'm looking for Jeannie, is she with you?"

Eddie: "No."

Rita: "We went to Boston last night, the two of us. We spent three hundred on some shit and it was no good. It was my money. You think she's screwing me out of my money? This shit's no good."

Eddie: "First, it's none of my business, why bother me? Second, I don't think she's do that to a friend, even if she's hung up on dope."

Rita: "I know, but she and Jerry tried it and said they got off. I think its shitty stuff."

Eddie: "It's kind of strange, Rita." He looked over at Teresa, who was waking up and looking at him.

Rita: "Yes, it is and I want that bitch to take me back to that motherfucker. I have a .45 in my pocketbook and the Luise brothers to back me up,. You ever heard of them?"

Eddie: "No, Rita, I don't know who they are."

Rita: "You hear from Jeannie you tell her to call me. I gotta talk to her. Listen, as long as I got you on the phone, you interested in some Eskatrol? I'm going to see my contact and we go in together I can get them for six hundred dollars for a thousand pills. We can split them."

Eddie rubbed his face and thought to himself that it was a little early to be making drug deals. Eskatrol is an amphetamine. "Yes, I'm interested. I can't go today because I have some other business."

Rita: "Okay, anytime you want to get some, we'll go. By the way, did Jeannie tell you I got a ring to sell, a real diamond?"

"Yeah, we can talk about it another time." Eddie hung up the phone and rolled over to face Teresa, who sat up and put on her robe.

~ ~ ~

An hour later the phone rang again; it was Jeannie calling: "Hi, Eddie, it's Jeannie."

Eddie: "Hi, you know that Rita's looking for you. She thinks you ripped her off on some dope."

Jeannie: "Fuck her. She did it all and has no bitch now because she can't bring it back and tell the lady we got it from to try it herself to see if it's shitty. If it was that bad, why'd she use it up? You have to save some to show if you don't like it, you know that."

Eddie: "So, what's up, Jeannie?"

Jeannie: "I'm in Weymouth at a motel. Jerry's here. We got something you'll like. I'm high as a fuckin' kite."

Ernie thought to himself, *she's always high*, and at that moment he hated the world she lived in. She was either high and next she would be sick. Her life was spent with men who could alter her state of mind and send away the demons she could not face. She would do anything for that high and Eddie did not want to think about the things she had done. Despite the disaster her life had become, he liked her and thought that there was a decent person inside.

Eddie: "Where are you?"

She gave him the name of the motel and the room number and told him they would be there all morning.

Eddie: "I'll be there later," he said. He heard her mumble something and hang up the phone. He stared at the ceiling for a moment and tried to collect his thoughts. He had been dreaming about the lake house in Maine and in the dream he and Teresa had fixed it up and were on a dock watching the boys paddle a canoe. There were no drug addicts in the dream. In real life, no one had made an offer on the place and, he admitted to himself, it was pretty rundown. He was excited at the prospect of spending weekends far away from the sleazy world of Quincy druggies and thugs and fixing up a cabin for Teresa and the boys.

~ ~ ~

Ernie drove to Weymouth and found the motel where Jeannie and Jerry were staying. He knocked on the door of room 109 and Jerry answered. He was wearing a sweatshirt, briefs and dirty socks. Jeannie and another woman were on the bed, wearing light tops and panties, barely conscious.

Jeannie: "Hey, Eddie. C'mon in. We got something special here."

Eddie walked in and sat at a small table while he watched Jeannie and Jerry who were high as well as the other woman. They were all looking out and staring into the world. Although they could see Ernie, he was not sure that they really saw him there.

"You tell Rita to fuck herself? "Jeannie asked.

Jerry: "Eddie, look at this. This is called opium powder." He held a white plastic bag toward Eddie. Jerry had the dead serious look of a drunken man as he gazed into

Eddie's eyes. "This opium was in an old fashioned container and I wrote down what it said on the outside. It said opium powder fourteen-point-one per cent." He pulled a piece of paper out of his wallet and showed it to Eddie.

"What are you going to do with it?" Eddie asked.

Jerry: "I don't know what it's worth."

Eddie; "I might be interested in buying it."

"I'll talk to the guy who has the other half," Jerry said.

Eddie: "Who's that?"

Jerry: "Pauly, You know Pauly."

Shit, Eddie thought to himself, *a low life shit-bags like that.* "Yeah, I know him."

Jerry: "I'll talk to him to see what he knows about it."

Eddie: "Let me know what you decide."

"Here, I got something for you." Jerry gave him three Percodan tablets. "Free."

Eddie; "I don't need these, but thanks."

Jerry: "No, take them, my treat."

Eddie went to the door and was about to leave when Jeannie tried to stand , but was unsteady, "I need to go with you."

She walked with Eddie to the Thunderbird and asked if he would stay with her.

Jeannie: "I think I'm overdosing, Eddie. I'm scared. I don't want to be left here. I don't know what will happen if I fall asleep. Can I ride with you? Will you talk to me?"

~ ~ ~

Eddie drove to the coffee shop in Quincy and used the pay phone to call Detective Churn's private number.

Eddie explained the situation to Detective Churn and asked, "Should I take her to a hospital, what do you think?"

Churn: "If she's still talking, just keep her at the coffee shop for a couple of hours and see what happens. If she becomes unconscious or incoherent, you can take her to the emergency room."

Two hours later, after getting her to eat and watching her slowly come around, Eddie took her home.

~ ~ ~

The next morning, the red telephone rang and it was Jeannie. "I'm moving in with Jerry. Can you give me a ride to get my stuff? We're at the motel in Weymouth."

Eddie went and picked her up then drove her to the motel.

Jerry answered the door. "I'm still waiting for a call from Pauly about the opium powder."

"Why don't we weigh what you have so we'll know how much you've got here?"

"Yeah, let's do that," Jerry said, as though the idea had never occurred to him.

Eddie went to the Thunderbird and opened the trunk. Next to the tool box that contained his handguns was a small cardboard box that held a sensitive scale that Lieutenant Lyme had obtained and given to him. He took the scale into the motel room, set it on the table, and poured the powder onto the flat surface of the scale.

Eddie: "Seven and a half ounces," he said, pouring the powder back into the white plastic bag.

The telephone in the motel room rang and Jeannie picked it up. She mumbled something and handed the phone to Jerry. He then handed the phone to Eddie.

Eddie: "Who's this?" he asked.

Pauly: "It's Pauly, Eddie, how you doing?"

Eddie: "I'm good, Pauly, how you been?"

Pauly: "Eddie, I gotta get rid of this opium powder. I'll give you a good deal."

Eddie: "I'm interested, Pauly, if the price is right."

Pauly: "How about twelve hundred,? Take it all for twelve hundred."

Eddie: "Too much, I'd be willing to go ($500) five hundred for the lot, no more."

Pauly: "Let me think about that."

Eddie: "We can discuss it, let me know when you're ready to sell."

Pauly: "Put Jerry on."

The two men talked for several minutes, with Jerry holding his hand over the telephone. Jeannie sat on the bed and looked like a child waiting for a school bus. Jerry hung up the phone and took a deep breath.

Eddie looked at him and pointed to the white plastic bag. "I need a sample of this to test. Nothing personal, Jerry, but who knows what this is?"

Jerry gave Eddie a small sample of the powder that was wrapped in foil and Eddie handed him twenty dollars. He asked Eddie to take Jeannie to pick up her clothes and other things and then to his house.

Jerry: "I gotta evict a couple of guys before she moves in. They're doin' some business and attracting too much attention. I don't want her around if there's trouble." Jerry took the plastic bag containing the powder to his car, along with another bag that held some personal items he had needed at the motel.

~ ~ ~

Eddie and Jeannie were walking to the Thunderbird when Detective Churn and three DEA agents pulled in and yelled for everyone to get down. Eddie pulled the foil from his jacket and tossed it into some bushes that were near the parking lot, then he got down in a spread eagle position.

Churn and the agents searched the room and Eddie's car. Jerry was on the floor of the room and was not moving. His car was not searched. One by one, Churn pulled each person aside and asked them if they had any drugs. "Tell me now before I search or it will be worse for you later."

Jeannie looked confused and had to be coaxed into saying she had no drugs. Jerry shook his head and mumbled "no" to Det. Churn's questions. Churn pulled Eddie aside and loudly asked him if he had any drugs on him. Eddie shook his head to the negative as he whispered that there was opium powder in the bushes. Churn let them all go and promised to keep an eye on them.

~ ~ ~

Two hours later all three were at Jerry's house, wondering how they had escaped arrest. "I've been busted three times in the past month", Eddie said. Jerry looked at him like he was a hero. Eddie would meet Detective Churn at St. Catherine's at ten to get the report on what the lab had to say about Jerry's opium powder.

"You think Pauly's gonna rip me off?" Jerry looked like a little boy who thought someone was going to take his candy.

"Why would he do that?" Eddie shook his head.

Jerry: "I don't know. I don't trust him."

Eddie: "We don't know anything right now. The cops know about it, that's why they shook us down. Maybe they're watching Pauly. If the cops know about this stuff, it isn't worth anything. This stuff's been in Jerry's car and it's cold out. It's supposed to be kept a room temperature, according to what Jerry wrote down from the container. If we can get Pauly's half, I might have something I can make a few bucks on. Right now, maybe Pauly's half is the only thing that's still good."

Jeannie became animated. "We have to do the opium deal right now. We can't wait around."

Eddie: "I don't have the money on me, for one. And we don't have Pauly's half, for two."

Jeannie: "You'll get his half and this deal is worth ten times what you're paying for it."

"Sweetheart, it's not worth anything right now." Eddie got up to leave as Pauly knocked on the front door.

He was quiet and looked around as he entered the house. "Anybody else here?" he asked.

"Just us," Jeannie responded, glaring at him.

Pauly: "I think we need to wait a couple of days before we do anything with this stuff. I heard about what happened at the motel. I think the cops are watching us."

Jeannie sat down and looked away, lighting a cigarette. Jerry went into the kitchen and came out with a can of beer. Eddie stood by the door. Jerry lowered his voice.

Pauly: "You can have my half for three hundred. Meet me at the Overview Hotel in Braintree at eight o'clock."

"What are you two whispering about?" Jeannie was watching the conversation, but could not hear what was being said.

Eddie nodded his head, opened the front door, and left. He drove to the coffee shop and ordered a sandwich and a cup of coffee. He smoked a cigarette with a second cup of coffee and nodded to a few of the customers he recognized. No one spoke to him and for that he was grateful.

~ ~ ~

Pauly was waiting in the hotel parking lot when Eddie drove up and he jumped into the Thunderbird before Eddie had finished backing it into a spot in a dark corner in back. He handed Pauly cash and Pauly handed Eddie the container that held his half of the opium powder.

"Where'd you get this?" Eddie asked. "How do I know it's any good?"

"Ask the jeweler," Pauly responded, and quickly climbed back into his truck and drove away.

Ernie sat in his car and promised himself a visit to Goldstein to take the jeweler up on his offer of some special pieces. *Does 'special pieces' mean what I think it means?* Ernie thought Goldstein was referring to drugs, he would find out in time. "Tomorrow night!" he said to himself.

~ ~ ~

He drove to St. Catherine's and met Detective Churn and his partner. The men sat in Churn's unmarked car and smoked for a few minutes, making small talk. The night was cold but it was clear and it had been a long day.

Ernie handed the container to Churn. "It's more of the opium powder. I need to get the other half from Jerry. He thinks Pauly's gonna fuck him, I think that he's right. Was there any word from the lab on this stuff?"

Det. Churn: "As advertised. Opium powder. You get a gold star for this," as he laughed.

Ernie: "Could be Goldstein who has this stuff or it may have come from the drug store robbery, who knows? Pauly is shitting his pants in fear and may not even know, but he did mention, "The Jeweler", so I'll see what I can do with it. I'm pushing Goldstein to sell me some cocaine and I might make a buy tomorrow night if I understood his code correctly. Tony says they both have the same source in New Hampshire. It'll be nice to get this dance done and over. I'm spending my life with shit-bags."

Churn: "This investigation is going on a little longer than we thought that it would. We're getting a lot more than we expected, so it's a good operation. You deserve a lot of credit, Ernie. This is hard work, not just on you; it's hard on your family as well. Believe me, we understand. Quincy will take care of you. Did you talk to the lieutenant about the phone yet?"

Ernie: "He said we'd talk later. This thing is hard on my family. The dam red phone rings all the time. Maybe we can get this done in another month. I need to get Goldstein and Tony moving toward their source so that we can end this and move on to bigger and better things."

The men sat in silence as they finished their smokes. Eddie drove home in the Thunderbird and Churn took the unmarked car to the Quincy detectives office, cleaned out the fast food wrappers, and handed the keys to a young detective who was working the overnight shift.

Chapter 21

The Jeweler

Tuesday morning was clear and cold and Eddie wanted to sleep in, but the boys were noisy as they got ready for school and the smell of Teresa's coffee was too tempting, so he put on a bathrobe and his slippers and sat at the kitchen table. Teresa looked drawn and tense, but she smiled when she saw him looking at her. He felt an intense rush of love for her and saw a goodness that marked her life and her devotion to their family. He looked at the boys and saw them as promises to a new world for the Lijoi family.

At that moment, he felt separated from them. He saw himself as the kid in Brooklyn whose father knocked him around. He saw the mustachios who took out a contract on his life. He saw the shit-bags who at that moment were wondering where their next high would come from. Here he was, in the warm, safe kitchen of his house in Dedham, drinking the coffee that was made by a good woman who loved him.

Teresa; "You have a busy day?"

Ernie: "Just something later on, Maybe meet some people."

Teresa; "I have an appointment later, so I'll be out for awhile."

Ernie; "Who do you have an appointment with?" he asked.

Teresa: "It's not a big deal," she responded.

The boys left for school and Teresa cleaned up the breakfast dishes. Ernie read the paper, took a shower, and became Eddie again. He put on his dungarees, tee shirt, vest and boots and checked the toolbox in the trunk of the Thunderbird. The three handguns were safe under the screwdriver drawer and there was extra ammunition for each of them. He turned the radio on and listened to WBZ. The newscaster led with a local political scandal, then a shooting, then something about President Carter and the economy.

~ ~~ ~

Eddie held onto the steering wheel tightly as he went over in his mind the people he was dealing with on the street. He knew there were only a few people who controlled most of the action, but the network of low level dealers and users made it all work because they took anything they could get and they performed any act they thought would get them some dope or an easy score. The upper level dealers and suppliers used the shit-bags to move product and keep the market alive. It was not difficult to sell drugs to people like Jeannie and Jerry. They were like kids, he thought, who believe anything that they were told by their suppliers, who ever that supplier would be.

Goldstein was another matter. He was smart and shrewd and he knew what he had to lose. He was not the type to accept as a normal cost of doing business the occasional arrest and even incarceration. He wanted to run his jewelry store and he wanted to make easy money selling cocaine, but he was not ready to throw himself into the street life where Jeannie, Jerry and Tony lived. Tony was crazy, but he had good connections and he could lead Eddie Pannoni to his supplier. The same supplier Goldstein used. Ernie's plan was for all of the major dealers and suppliers to be arrested at the same time. They would all go down together.

Eddie stopped by the pool hall and nursed a beer for an hour, then he went to the coffee shop and noted who was there and who was not. Jeannie was not working. He recognized a few shit-bags hunched over their coffee mugs, waiting for connections or just recovering from last night. He sat back and thought about how normal everything looked. A tourist enjoying a day in quaint Quincy would not see anything odd at the coffee shop and would have no way of knowing the street business that defined many of the people who filled the booths. That same tourist walking along the waterfront would not have any way of knowing the thieving, lying and dealing that went on behind the clapboard siding of the picturesque houses. Ernie-Eddie was becoming cynical. Weeks of living with street bums had changed the way he looked at life in this city.

Life as a transit cop was cleaner and the lines were easier to see. He rode busses and trains and nabbed bad guys, then he went home to Teresa and the boys. Now, he drank coffee with shit-bags who could be likeable and easy to be around. but the job went home with him. On the other hand, he thought, some of these people were pathetic. He looked at a young couple sitting in a booth across the room. The young man was skinny and his light brown hair was filthy and matted. The girl was also skinny and pale and had a face like a child. He guessed their ages at late teens. They shared a single cup of coffee. She was pleading with him about something and he could see her earnest eyes staring at the young man. He looked ashamed and overwhelmed. Eddie guessed that they had no money for food because they spent their cash on drugs. He also guessed that the young man pimped out the girl to get drug money. *They're lost,* he thought. *God help them.* He left the coffee shop and drove to the jewelry shop owned by Goldstein who was commonly known on the street as, "The Jeweler."

The parking lot across from the store was almost empty. He saw Tony's camper parked near the back, under a tree that was beginning to bud. He backed the Thunderbird into a spot about twenty feet from Tony's camper and lit a cigarette. About five minutes later, Tony came out of the store, waved to Eddie and walked to Eddie's car.

Tony: "The Jeweler said that he thought you might be coming by, He said that you were looking for a little necklace for your wife?"

Eddie: "You know what I'm looking for, What are you here for?"

Tony: "Same thing you are, the kind of jewelry that affects the head. Roll them tight, as they say. I picked up a half ounce. He's only got two ounces left. He's not sure he wants to sell directly to you right now. You may still have to go through me."

Eddie: "Goldstein sold you a half ounce?" he asked.

"Yes" Tony replied.

Eddie: "Any more then the two ounces in the pipeline or expected down the road?"

Tony: "He says he's getting more tonight," Tony said, shrugging his shoulders. "I don't know for sure. I'm still trying to get some quantity. I may go up to New Hampshire in a few days to see what's up there. If you need some of what I got here, come by later."

Eddie nodded and got out of the Thunderbird as Tony left the area in his camper. He went into the store and saw Goldstein standing behind the counter, writing in a ledger.

Jeweler: "My supply of specialty jewelry is low right now," he said.

Eddie: "I'm still interested in whatever you may have," he replied.

Jeweler: "I'm not sure I want to sell directly to you right now. You may have to go through Tony for awhile."

Eddie; "We've been through this. He's not reliable. I have customers in New York and I need somebody, like you, who's reliable, someone that I can count on."

Jeweler: "Put three hundred on the counter," Goldstein pointed to the glass topped case.

Eddie took out cash and counted it out, placing it on the counter. Goldstein went into the back room and came out with a small one ounce packet and a cheap-looking necklace. He placed the two items on the counter and took the cash.

Jeweler: "I hope your wife likes the necklace," he grinned. "Maybe we can do more business later."

Eddie: as long as my wife likes this jewelry, we can do a lot more business, if you agree."

Jeweler: "Show her the jewelry and get back to me."

Eddie put the packet and the necklace into his coat pocket. "Nice doing business with you," he said, smiling and waving as he left. He sat in the car and looked at the necklace. It was cheap, like a carnival prize. There appeared to be one ounce of cocaine in the packet. Goldstein had provided the necklace in a clumsy attempt to cover himself in the cocaine deal and, Eddie assumed, would claim he had sold the necklace for three hundred dollars and had no idea where the cocaine came from, if the transaction came to the attention of the police. *What a dipshit!*, Eddie thought.

He went to a payphone and called Detective Churn's private number.

Ernie: "Tony and Goldstein may be going to their source in New Hampshire tonight. I just bought an ounce from the jeweler. I'll give it to you at St. Catherine's later."

Det. Churn: "Congratulations, you are the first one to ever get into Goldstein. No one has ever been able to do it. You deserve a lot of credit for this one. I can't wait to tell the lieutenant. I'll notify DEA about Tony and Goldstein. I know that they will want to watch them."

~ ~ ~

He went to Tony's and bought a small quantity of cocaine from the supply Tony had purchased from the jeweler. The lab would match the samples. Tony was stoned and he waved his .44 around and threatened to shoot anyone who smoked from his snake pipe. Three gas company workers Eddie had not seen before were sitting at Tony's kitchen table, shooting up. One of them examined a bag of marijuana he had bought from Tony and was counting the buds. He complained that there were sticks in the bag and Tony waved the .44 in his face and told him to shut up. The man and his friends stood up and quietly left by the back door.

Tony: "I'm going to New Hampshire later. I'll have some good shit this time tomorrow." He seemed better able to focus and looked at Eddie with a steady gaze. "I need to get straight." He shook his head and went back into the living room where he placed the .44 under the sofa cushion. "Leave it fucking alone," he shouted to anyone within hearing distance.

Eddie went into the bathroom and wrote his notes on matchbook covers, lit a match, flushed the toilet, and left. He drove to St. Catherine's and met Detective Churn. He gave Churn the cocaine samples and handwrote his notes on a legal pad, giving them to Churn as well. The two men smoked and talked about police department rumors, then Eddie went home and Churn went to the detective unit, cleaned out the car, and handed the keys to the overnight man.

~ ~ ~

Ernie had gone home to spend some time with his family. The red telephone rang again at nine thirty the next morning. It was Rita.

Rita: "I'm at Quincy Courthouse. I got a possession hearing, me and Pauly. I think he's gonna hurt me. Can you come down?"

Eddie: "What do you mean he's gonna hurt you?"

Rita: "I think he's gonna make trouble. He thinks I'm the reason he got busted."

Eddie: "Okay, I'll be there. Give me half an hour."

~ ~ ~

Ernie Lijoi Sr., husband and father, once again became Eddie, the drug dealer. It took him ten minutes to shower and shave, dress, check the .38, and climb into the Thunderbird. At quarter past ten he walked into Quincy Court-house, having left the .38 in the toolbox in the trunk. Rita was sitting with Jerry on a bench in the hallway outside the courtrooms. There was no sign of Pauly.

The three of them made small talk for several minutes until Rita's name was called and a bailiff motioned her into one of the courtrooms.

Jerry looked uncomfortable. "Can I tell you some-thing?"

Eddie looked at him and nodded.

Jerry: "I got a fuckin' default warrant out on me. I feel weird being in here. I'm thinking of turning myself in."

Eddie: "What's the warrant for?" he asked.

Jerry: "Possession, simple possession, no distribution. I got a lawyer who thinks I'm an asshole for not showing up at the hearing. He says I should get this straightened out and maybe he can get it continued for so long that the DA will want to forget about it or go for probation."

Eddie: "I think you should get this cleaned up. You don't want to get picked up on the warrant. They'll lock you up for months and treat you like a piece of shit."

Jerry: "You're right. I'll call my lawyer and work something out with the court. Can you wait for Rita? She wanted me to come up in case Pauly made trouble but he ain't even here."

Rita came out of the courtroom followed by a middle-aged man in a suit. She tilted her head at the man. "He's my lawyer. I got probation if I behave like a good girl," she giggled.

"Rita, you weren't good when you were a girl and you sure ain't good now," Jerry said, nodding at the lawyer, who glanced at Jerry and Eddie and hurriedly walked away.

Eddie, Jerry and Rita went to the coffee shop and sat in a booth and were joined by Jeannie, who was working.

"Anybody got anything?" Jeannie asked.

"I got probation," Rita responded, laughing.

"I got a line on some Quaaludes," Jeannie said. "Maria somebody, lives in Somerville. She's supposed to have a good supply."

Eddie: "Maria somebody, do you have an address or phone number?" he asked. "I got customers who would like some Quaaludes."

Jeannie: "If you got the money, I got the number." She took a piece of paper out of her pocket and handed it to Eddie. "That's it."

Eddie; "Does she know you? Can I just call this number and say I'm looking for drugs?" Eddie wondered whether Jeannie had even spoken to this woman Maria and if the number was real.

Jeannie: "I met her last night at a party. She gave me her number but I can't remember her last name. Some guys said she was a good source."

Jerry was surprised at Jeannie's statement about , "some guys."

"Some guys?" Jerry asked. "You know anything about these guys? Like if they're cops?"

Jeannie: "They're not cops. They got pretty fucked up. Cops don't do that."

"Why don't you call her?" Eddie asked.

Jeannie: "I ain't got no money to buy anything or I would call her."

Eddie: "You call her and remind her about last night. Tell her you got a guy, me, who wants to buy some Quaaludes. I get on and we make the deal."

Jeannie went to the pay phone in the back and placed a call. She spoke into the phone for several minutes and waved Eddie over. She handed him the phone and whispered, "She's got some stuff for us."

Eddie: "Is this Maria?" he took the phone.

Maria: "Eddie? Is this Eddie?"

Eddie: "Yeah, nice to talk to you, I hear you got something for the head you can sell?"

Maria: "I got thirty 'ludes. It's all I can sell right now, I also have a few percodans."

Eddie; "I'll take the 'ludes, I don't need the percs."

Maria: "You'll take some in front of me, won't you?"

Eddie: "What's the problem?"

Maria: "I want to make sure you're not a cop."

Eddie: "We can discuss whether or not I'm a cop when I get there."

She paused and told him to go to a drugstore on Charles Circle and call her from there. She hung up.

Eddie left Rita, Jerry and Jeannie and drove to Charles Circle where he found the drug store. He called Maria's number and it rang five times before she picked it up. She sounded nervous. She gave him directions that sounded like she was a character in a spy movie, listing a dozen streets and telling him to go left and right and turn down alleys and double back. Eddie thought she was paranoid and, he admitted to himself, she had reason to be. She was giving directions to a deep undercover cop who would add her name to his list of dealers to be rounded up when this operation came to an end.

~ ~ ~

Maria lived under an assumed name in a two-bedroom apartment. Her landlord claimed to know her as Judy Taub and told would-be creditors that she worked for him as his secretary. This allowed her to obtain credit cards under her false name and to open bank accounts as Judy Taub.

As instructed, Eddie turned up at her door with a bottle of Southern Comfort. "It's the only thing I drink," she explained. "Everybody I do business with has to bring me a bottle."

She poured herself four fingers into a water glass and sat down without offering Eddie a drink. He sat on the sofa and made mental notes. White female, late 20s, 110 lbs,5'5" tall, dark brown hair, brown eyes, mole on left side of mouth.

Maria: "Loads of people from Quincy come here to buy drugs, usually younger then you" she said. "I can't sell all of the 'ludes. How about taking only twenty?"

Eddie: "I promised somebody twenty-five. I can do the twenty, but I can't take any now or I'll be too short. I hope you understand."

Maria: "Three dollars apiece," she said.

Eddie: "That's steep, twenty-five for the twenty."

Maria: "Fifty dollars."

Eddie: "I'll give you thirty for the twenty."

She laughed, "You fucker. I'll do thirty five for the twenty 'ludes."

Eddie: "Deal."

Maria: "It's a deal if you do me a favor. I rented a rug cleaning machine to clean this carpet. Can you take it back for me? It's a place in Charles Plaza, on Cambridge Street."

~~ ~

Eddie left Maria's with twenty Quaaludes and a rug cleaning machine. A meter maid was writing a ticket for the Thunderbird because the meter had expired. Eddie walked over to her and gave her a hard time, putting his face close to hers and calling her names. He wanted the meter maid to remember him. She had no way of knowing that this crazy man who was complaining about his ticket would want her testimony that he was here at this address on this day when Maria-also-known-as-Judy went on trial.

He dropped off the rug cleaning machine and returned to the coffee shop, where Jeannie was flirting with a customer and scratching her face. She filled a mug with coffee and came over to Eddie, placing the mug in front of him.

Jeannie: "How'd it go?"

Eddie: "Good. I gotta get some stuff to my customers, you know."

Jeannie: "Anything for me?"

Eddie: "It's all been sold. She didn't have as many as we thought, you know how it goes."

Jeannie's boss glared at her to get back to work, so she winked at Eddie and shook her ass as she walked behind the counter. *What a waste,* Eddie thought, wondering how long it would be before something bad happened to her.

He met Detective Churn at St. Catherine's at eleven o'clock, gave him the Quaaludes, a typed report and went home.

Chapter 22

Murder

The alarm rang at seven o'clock and Ernie Lijoi groaned. He slowly rolled over and stared at the clock, then he pressed the button to turn it off. He was tired and he wanted to stay in his warm bed and snuggle up to Teresa and sleep the morning away. She nudged him.

Teresa; "Mr. Sleepyhead, it's time to get up." She sat on the side of the bed and reached for her robe. "You have a busy day?"

Ernie: "Same as usual." He had an appointment to buy some heroin from Tony and Pauly at nine o'clock. He showered and shaved and sat with the boys as they ate their breakfast and gathered their things for school, then he drove the Thunderbird to Tony's house. The morning was crisp and bright and the daffodils were blooming. He thought about the new house in Maine and considered making an offer, even though he and Teresa had not yet come to a decision about the place. He would be making more money and have better benefits once he was fulltime on the Quincy department and maybe that would be enough.

~ ~ ~

Tony was on his porch wearing a flannel bathrobe and drinking coffee when Eddie Pannoni pulled into the driveway. "You're just in time, come on in."

Pauly was sitting on the sofa, brooding, and talking to Peter and George, two other shit-bags Eddie had seen on the street. The three men looked as though they had been up all night.

"Hey, Eddie, you know these guys; Peter, George?" He did not introduce them.

Eddie: "Seen them around. How you guys doing?"

Pauly: "We might need to ask for a favor, Eddie. Maybe you can give us a ride to check something out."

Eddie: "I got time, sure. Let me do a little business with Tony and we can talk about it." He went into the kitchen and purchased fifty packets of heroin and asked Tony when he could get him a few kilos of cocaine.

Tony: "One week, tops,"

Eddie: "I don't mean to be pushy, but you've been saying that for awhile. I might need to go someplace else."

Tony: "I understand. I can handle it. I've got you covered on this and we won't have to worry about the problem we had before. Everybody's being kind of careful right now."

Eddie: "What's up with Pauly and those guys?"

Tony: "They got a little problem is all. They can tell you about it."

Eddie spoke with Pauly, Peter and George who asked him to drive them somewhere. He agreed and they left the house.

Eddie drove Pauly, Peter and George, the two shit-bags, to a small warehouse district where they told him to pull over next to a phone booth. One of the men got out and went to the phone booth and checked it out, looking at the floor and the glass walls. He came back to the car and got in.

Pauly: "There's a lot of blood on the floor.".

George: "Then you hit him."

Peter: "Fuckin' 'A', I got the bastard."

Eddie listened and remembered a news report he had heard on the radio on his way to Tony's. He asked: "Guys, there was a shooting in this area last night. You involved with that?"

Peter: "We took care of a rat. A number one Rat." he said.

George: "Asshole will think twice before he fucks with us again."

"You did the guy?" Eddie asked.

Peter: "He was calling the fuckin' cops about a job we were gonna do. We were forced to take him out."

Eddie looked at the two men. "I heard a news report that the guy was calling a friend for a ride when the friend heard some shots."

"That's what the cops want you to think," Peter said.

"They're just covering it up, that he was a rat," George said.

"What now?" asked Eddie.

"Let's just go back to Tony's." George replied.

"So what happened?" Eddie asked.

George: "We found this pharmaceutical warehouse in Rhode Island and we're gonna hit it. We got a little high last night and we're talking about it with this asshole, asking him if he wants in. He gets real quiet, kind of on the nod, and then says robbing places is not his bag. We ask him if he wants some of the profits, all he has to do is come along and maybe help out a little. 'I don't think I can handle anything like that', he says. We tell him we can guide him, help him along, and he acts like a pussy and says no thanks. He leaves and goes down the street. Me and Peter are like, do you trust him? We go after him to see where he's going and fuckin' two blocks later, there he is making a call in a phone booth. I grabbed my gun and started firing at the fuckin' guy because I know he's calling the cops. I fuckin' know it."

"Hey! Stop right there," Eddie said. "I don't want to know about this. If you guys get busted for assault or murder or whatever, I don't want to be part of it. It's not my business. If I don't know and you guys get busted, then you can't blame me, so don't tell me anything." He drove them back to Tony's house where he dropped them off.

On his way home he stopped at a phone booth and called Detective Churn. He related what had he had heard and Churn reported that the man who had been shot in the phone booth was hit three times and died in the early hours. Churn said he would call the District Attorney's office and wait to make arrests until Ernie picked up the same information on the street, meaning it would be considered general information. Two days later, a low level heroin dealer told the man he knew as Eddie Pannoni that George and Peter had shot another shit-bag in a telephone booth. They were arrested and charged with murder. George eventually ratted on Peter in exchange for a deal for himself..

Tony was not sympathetic. "Fuck 'em" he said.

Chapter 23

McQuethy & Woodbridge

"So, here's the deal," said the real estate agent. "The seller has two cabins on adjoining lots and he wants to sell both of them for a total of sixty thousand dollars. That's thirty apiece. You've both seen them and know that they need a little work."

"Actually, we've only seen one of them," Teresa corrected. "We only looked at the second one from the outside. It's smaller, as I recall."

Agent: "And it's a little rougher on the inside. The lot on the bigger cabin is slightly larger, but both of them are waterfront." The agent was a middle-aged woman with a stack of red hair, a round Irish face and long red fingernails. She had agreed to meet Teresa and Ernie at a diner near the lake to talk to them about the cabin they had been visiting on their spring weekends. "Do you think you can find somebody to go in with you so you can divide the lots? It's a pretty good deal that way."

"Thirty thousand apiece, that's not bad." Ernie was trying to run numbers in his head and was estimating what it would take on their half of the deal, and how much money would be needed to make the cabin livable.

"Let's talk to my brother, Joey/ Maybe he will take one of the houses?" Teresa said, looking at a survey of the two lake lots.

Ernie: "Maybe you have somebody in your family who'd be interested."

They had talked about a weekend place for years and the undercover assignment had made it more important that their family have a place to go to get away from the world that Ernie submerged himself in as Eddie Pannoni. He liked to take the boys fishing and the Maine place would be ideal for that, their own place on a lake instead of renting a place.

By evening they were home in Dedham and calling family members to see if anyone wanted to go in with them to buy the two cabins. Everyone thought it was a great deal but no one was willing to commit. "Give us a few days," they all said. Teresa and Ernie looked at each other and hoped it would work out.

~ ~ ~

The next morning was a return to the rat hole for Ernie. He drove a woman named Pauline to see a man who was locked up in Dedham. Pauline was the girlfriend of a mid-level dealer who had been picked up on a possession charge and the man she knew as Eddie wanted to be helpful, so he took her to visit Davey Vespusian, whom Eddie had met through Tony. Davey was handsome and popular with the ladies and had once confessed to Eddie that the only reason he sold drugs was to get laid. Pauline was not the only fish in the tank, he had said, but he greeted her like she was the only girl in the world. Visiting rules allowed the inmates to sit at tables with visitors. Physical contact was discouraged, but not banned, and guards roamed the room looking for misconduct. Davey was the model prisoner, smiling and being polite and even greeting the guards by name and asking about their families.

Davey: "Eddie, you doin' all right?" he asked.

Eddie: "Pretty good. How's life for you?"

Davey: "I'm out in a couple of days, probation proba-bly. Once my lawyer gets things worked out. Are we gonna do some business?"

Eddie: "I'm always looking, Davey."

He leaned in and spoke in a low voice, "I got a good connection for some heroin. We can do something when I get out. Pauline will give you a call. You'll like it." Davey leaned back.

The visit lasted half an hour and Eddie and Pauline left the jail. She wanted Eddie to drive her to the waterfront to look at the boats and two of them sat watching the early spring boater's check out their vessels.

Pauline: "I know you deal in quantity, Eddie. I want you to know that Davey and I can take care of you. You've got a good reputation, not like some of these bums we have to deal with. Everybody says you're okay."

Eddie: "Who's everybody?"

She mentioned many of the people he had on his list and there were no new names. They made small talk and exchanged meaningless gossip and he took her home. He went to the coffee shop to see who was there and he dropped by the pool hall to be seen and pass out some of his cards.

~ ~ ~

He met Detective Churn at St. Catherine's at eleven. "DEA says your boys are doing some travelling to New Hampshire. You'll never guess who they're visiting."

Eddie: "Who?"

Detective Churn: "One David Stewart McQuethy, Junior. It seems he's doing business out of daddy's weekend house, the one with ten bathrooms. They also own planes, boats, houses in Florida, Massachusetts, New Hampshire, California and all over the world. They are richer then rich."

Eddie: "No shit. That's the New Hampshire connection? I don't understand this. He has everything he wants and he is still dealing drugs. That's what happens when a kid is spoiled and given everything, I guess."

Churn: "Seems to be, maybe Junior is having trouble making ends meet on his substantial trust fund."

~ ~ ~

David Stewart McQuethy Senior was one of New England's most prominent and wealthiest developers and contractors. He had built landmark properties in Boston, Providence and New Haven and had redeveloped rundown colonial era neighborhoods into fashionable and very expensive housing and shopping for the young and the rich. His name was magic among a certain class of people and his personal houses were shown in the very best magazines. Yet he did not have enough time to teach his son how to work hard for his income.

~ ~ ~

"(DEA) Federal Drug Enforcement Administration has pictures of your friends Tony and the jeweler Goldstein having a little get together on the veranda. Goldstein seems right at home but Tony looks a little uncomfortable. Maybe the bust last month or he's just low class. The U.S. Attorney and the DEA, thinks Junior and his partner Joseph (Arms) Woodbridge may be doing business with some Colombian partners. Our friends the feds would like you to push these guys into making a major deal, as much as you can get, to see what happens in the pipeline. The feds will put up as much money as you need."

"We're talking about big dollars here," Ernie said. "We could be looking at millions of dollars to make the buy. A simple order of four kilos will be around a hundred thousand. I can set up multiple orders. all at the same time when we are ready."

Churn: "The feds are approving it, so go for it. Keep me and Lieutenant Lyme informed all the way and we will pass it on to the feds. We can get you out of this rat hole soon."

Ernie left Detective Churn and went back home for the night.

~ ~ ~

The next morning, the red telephone rang at eight-thirty. It was Pauline with news that Davey was out and ready to do business. He had been released minutes earlier and was already trying to contact his connection and she wanted to know if he was interested.

Eddie: "I'm always looking. I got some things to do this morning but call me later and maybe we can get together. I'm going to New York in a couple of days to make my deliveries; you know what I mean, so if we can make it happen, we can do business. It will be perfect timing for my trip to New York."

Pauline: "I'll tell him. Later, then."

He went to see Goldstein at his store, prepared to push the man on the cocaine buy. The jeweler was behind the counter, as usual, wiping a gold watch with a soft cloth.

Jeweler: "My friend, what can I do for you?"

Eddie: "I really need some of that specialty jeweler we discussed. I need quantity. I've got some customers in New York who are very interested and I'm going down there in a couple of days. Can you help me out?"

Goldstein looked at Eddie over the top of his glasses and nodded his head. "You married?"

Eddie: "Yeah."

Jeweler: "Why don't we get out wives together and have dinner together, get to know each other?"

Eddie: "I try not to mix business with personal matters. I would rather we did our business in private and not get other people involved, if you don't mind."

Jeweler: "How much jewelry do you have in mind?"

Eddie: "All I can get."

Jeweler: "One, two or three kilo's?"

Eddie: "That's right, I can move large quantities."

Jeweler: "That can get expensive, very expensive. It could run you oh, I don't know, forty or fifty thousand dollars, maybe more."

Eddie: "Me and my people can handle it. We're looking for quantity and quality and we're willing to pay for it."

Jeweler: "I can get you a sample by this time tomorrow. If you approve, we can do something in a couple of days."

Eddie: "That sounds good. I'll see you tomorrow about this time."

Eddie left the Jewelry shop and went to the diner where he telephoned Tony from the pay phone and said he needed to see him about the deal they were talking about and Tony told him it would be a couple of days, maybe a week.

Eddie: "I need all you can get as soon as you can get it."

Tony: "Let me check into how much is available, we'll talk later."

~ ~ ~

Jeannie was talking to a man Eddie knew to be a heroin dealer and she was smiling, so Eddie assumed she was going to score. She gave him a small wave and winked, and turned her attention to the man. He saw several people he recognized and stopped to talk to two of them, passing on street gossip and asking them if they knew of anything he might be interested in. They both said they were looking for something for themselves but if they heard of anything they would let him know. It was a typical day on the street, some were scoring and others were looking for that precious high place to put their mind for a while.

Detective Churn was waiting when Eddie pulled the Thunderbird into St. Catherine's parking lot. His window was rolled down and he was smoking into the crisp spring night when Eddie backed in next to him.

"You don't see that many stars these days," Churn said, looking up. "We got too much pollution. But look at that. Just like when we were kids."

Eddie had not noticed the stars. He had been thinking about Goldstein and Tony and David Stewart McQuethy,

Junior. He wondered how long it would be before he could close the net and go back to being Ernie Lijoi Sr.

His thoughts were on Teresa. She was still losing weight and had stopped asking him about his work. She seemed to be somewhere else and had a smaller smile when he looked at her. Something was happening inside her and she was not talking to him about it. He felt an urgency to pay more attention to his family.

He was sitting with Detective Churn discussing the cases when he stuck his head out the car's window and looked up.

Eddie: "Big dipper, right there," he said, pointing to a spot in the night sky.

Churn: "Speaking of big dippers, how're your dealers doing?"

Eddie: "I've told them I need to move some quantity. Same old shit, though. Yeah, yeah, couple of days. If they move on this they should be paying a visit to our friend McQuethy Junior very soon."

Churn: "I'll tell DEA and Lieutenant Lyme let us know how much cash you think that you will need and we will make the arrangements?"

"As much as I can get, Goldstein is saying fifty thousand or so for his deal. We'll be looking at five, ten kilos, maybe more. The cost on them is at thirty thousand per kilo, more or less. We'll have to be ready for whatever they come up with for quantity. Tony's the odd question. Who knows what he can get? He's done some bigger deals but Junior may have a problem with quantity like this with a guy who got busted last month."

Churn: "In my experience, McQuethy Junior wants to make money. He'll go for it. He gets a sniff at the dollars you're talking about; his head will tell him to do it."

Eddie: "The DEA is going to bring down Junior on this. This case will be the beginning of the end of these cases, I hope."

Churn: "It'll be hard to keep this going after the net closes on McQuethy. I wish we knew more about his partner, Joe (Arms) Woodbridge, but we can't have it all. He'll have his day."

The two men smoked and talked about the coming arrests and Churn passed along some police department gossip. Eddie became Ernie again and liked the feeling of being with another police officer and talking about things that were real and mattered in his life, not make-believe conversations with delusional drug addicts and dealers. He pulled out of the parking lot with his window down, breathing the air and he took a look at the starry sky as he pulled onto the highway.

~ ~ ~

Teresa was up and watching Johnny Carson when her husband pulled into the driveway. She sat staring at the television as he walked in the front door, took off his coat, went to the bed room and locked his .38 in a strongbox, and came to sit with her.

Ernie: "How are you doing", he asked, softly.

Teresa: "I'm all right, I guess."

Ernie: "You guess? What is wrong, tell me?"

Teresa: "It's hard, Ernie. It's hard being the wife of an undercover cop. I never know what you're doing or when you will be home. Or even if you'll be home at all, but I try not thinking about that."

Ernie: "We are coming to the end of this case. It'll be over soon, I promise."

Teresa: "When?"

Ernie: "A couple of weeks, maybe a month."

Teresa: "I have to tell you something, something you don't know, Ernie."

He looked at her and his heart sank.

Teresa: "I've been seeing somebody, a therapist, a psychologist, to help me get through this. I think I'm having a nervous breakdown." She looked into his eyes. "I can't eat. I can't sleep. All I can think about is what you're doing, or what I imagine you're doing and the crazy people you're with."

Ernie: "Why didn't you tell me?"

Teresa: "I didn't want to worry you. You have a lot going on and I know it's hard for you too."

He held her and told her it would be all right. "We'll get through this, Teresa, we're gonna be okay."

Chapter 24

The Jeweler

The New Hampshire home of David Stewart McQuethy Senior encompassed a twenty-five thousand square foot dwelling on over one thousand acres of scenic woods. The house was set on a hillside and overlooked a small valley and private lake. There were no leaves to block the view of the house as DEA agents watched Goldstein pull his van into the gravel parking area and step out. The Jeweler looked around and appeared to be scanning the woods for anyone who might be watching him, but he had very little chance of spotting the agents, who took telephoto pictures of him as he walked to a near French door and rapped on the glass. McQuethy Jr. came to the door with a big smile and welcomed Goldstein into the house. The two men could be seen sitting in wingback chairs by a fire, although it was not possible to discern what they were talking about. The agents were constantly taking pictures of all that was going on. Half an hour later McQuethy got up from the chair and was gone from the room for about five minutes. He returned with a black plastic package, which he placed into a shopping bag and handed to Goldstein. The jeweler shook hands with McQuethy and left through the French doors without looking back. He drove away.

Ninety minutes later Tony pulled into the parking area and went to the French doors and left with package that was similar in size to the one Goldstein had carried away.

One of the agents turned to the man with the camera. ""We should be able to get a warrant to search this place. We'll watch these two and see if we can get it through Detective Ernie Lijoi Sr., Quincy's undercover." The agents spent the next five hours observing the Stewart home, saw the lights go out, and left.

Some of the agents followed Goldstein while others followed Tony to watch the packages and see where they went. They had plenty of pictures to identify the drug packages.

~ ~ ~

Ernie was at home. At ten the next morning the red telephone rang and Eddie picked it up.

"It's Tony. I've got what you want, all of it, five kilos. When can you meet me?"

Eddie: "Yes. I can this afternoon. Good for you?"

Tony: "You got the money, right? You're not gonna make me look like a dick on this, are you?"

Eddie: "I never make you look like a dick, Tony. I'll have my end."

Eddie called Lieutenant's Lyme's private number and briefed him. Lyme said he would contact the DEA about the cash required to make the deal and get back to him.

Five minutes later Goldstein called to inform Eddie that his special order jewelry was in and could come by for a sample. "I'd like to get this done as soon as possible," he said.

Eddie; "I've got another appointment this afternoon and I can come by before or after that. If the sample is good, we can take care of everything."

Eddie: "How many kilo's?"

Jeweler: "five at twenty fine thou each."

Eddie: "OK with me."

Goldstein the Jeweler: "Do you have the resources?"

Eddie; "I'll have to see my people, but that will not be a problem."

The Jeweler: "How about six o'clock?"

Eddie: "If there's a problem, I'll call you."

Eddie called Lieutenant Lyme back and told him business was going to be very good that day. "I hope DEA has lots of cash on hand. Are they gonna make the arrests during the buys?"

Lt. Lyme: "They indicated to me that they may let the buy go down, then move in. That means somebody will be making sure the money doesn't disappear. I think they're gonna move on Junior at the same time, just as you suggested."

~ ~ ~

Eddie met DEA agents at a parking lot in the rear of a small warehouse district. Agent Ed Meyer was in the back seat, wearing a windbreaker against the spring chill. He had the window down and was smoking.

Meyer: "How'd you work two big deals like this all in one day?"

Eddie: "I've been pushing both of them for weeks and they have the same source. They gotta know I'm buying big today and so does their supplier. Money talks."

Meyer: "We're talking to Junior right now. The U.S. Attorney called his daddy and told him to get the boy a lawyer. Both of them are pretty shook up, so maybe we can get something out of him. He had product at the house when we served him and he caved without an argument. We're gonna shut down your guys after the deal. You leave, we'll move in. We've got funds for the buy and the bills are marked." Meyer gave two paper bags to Eddie. Both contained large amounts of cash. "We'll be covering you and so will your men from Quincy."

Eddie took the bags to the Thunderbird and placed them under a blanket in the trunk. They were kept separate in case someone, say Tony, watched him get the cash, he would not see the other bag and ask questions. It was the first time Eddie had done two major deals in one day and he was cautious as he drove to Tony's house. He noticed several utility company vans parked on Tony's block and men who wore work clothing acting as though they were preparing for a job. Down the block an older junker car was parked near the curb with its hood up. Three men were peering into the engine compartment.

Eddie knocked on Tony's door and waited as he heard footsteps, then Tony opened the door. "Jesus, c'mon in, let's get this deal done. You got the money?"

Eddie: "Not with me, but I can get my hands on it. You have the blow?"

Tony: "Sure I have it. You sure you go the money? I got a lot riding on this. It's the first time my guy's let me pick up this much since I got busted last time. This has to go down right."

Eddie: "Let's see what you have." Eddie moved into Tony's living room. There was no one else in the house.

Tony: "I told everybody I needed some time alone today. I don't want anybody else around here when we do this. There is too much money and product. You never know what people will do."

Eddie: "Tony, who else knows about this deal?"

Tony: "My supplier, he wanted to know, Goldstein knows I deal with you, but he doesn't know how much this one is. I may have told a couple of people I had something big happening, you know, when I was fucked up but I swear I didn't tell anybody how much is involved. I promise."

Eddie: "Let's see what you got here," he said; satisfied that Tony's arrest would not automatically be traced back to him.

Tony motioned for Eddie to follow him into the basement and the two men climbed down the stairs to the dank area where Tony kept the guns he rented out. He took a cardboard box down from a shelf that was filled with old paint cans and varnish remover and placed it on a small hand-made table that was chipped and cut from use as a utility space. He opened the box and showed Eddie the contents, a plastic bag containing four individually wrapped kilos of cocaine which amounted to 8.8 pounds of blow. He used a screwdriver to punch a small hole in one of the bags and motioned for Eddie to sample what was inside.

Eddie said, "Nno, I trust you after all of this time and I know that you would never try to fuck me."That would be dangerous."

Eddie was satisfied that the bag held high grade cocaine. "I thought we were doing five," Eddie said.

Tony: "I was hoping to keep one for other customers. I got a business to run."

Eddie: "That cuts the price down," Eddie said, watching Tony's reaction.

Tony: "By a kilo, or ($30,000) thirty thousand, yeah."

The men discussed what Eddie would pay for the four kilos Tony had to sell and then the undercover officer went out to his car and removed a bag from the trunk. He went to the driver's seat and climbed in, casually removing cash from the bag to reflect four, rather than five, kilos. He placed the extra cash under the seat and took the bag into Tony's kitchen, where he placed it on the table. Tony removed the money, counted it, and nodded his head. He handed the plastic bag to Eddie and stuck out his hand to shake saying. "Great doing business with you."

Eddie: "You, too, let's do this again. Is your supplier ready to move more product like this?"

Tony: "Not a problem, He's got all you need."

Eddie patted Tony on the shoulder and left with the cocaine. He placed it into the trunk of the Thunderbird and drove away as the men in utility workers clothing and the men who appeared to be fixing an old car moved to Tony's house. The three men who were under the hood of the car moved to the back of the house and the utility workers climbed onto the porch. DEA Agent Ed Meyer pulled a car into Tony's driveway, got out, went to the door, and knocked. A few seconds later, Tony opened the door and

Agent Meyer and two other men produced badges and a warrant and pushed Tony aside as they entered the house. There were no flashing lights and no uniformed officers. It was very quiet and in the three hours the house was searched. Plainclothes officers and federal agents discovered two dozen weapons, a kilo and a half of cocaine and five dozen tablets of controlled substances. Tony was taken to the DEA office in Boston for questioning and spent over an hour offering the names of everyone he knew, including Eddie Pannoni, whom he described as a major drug dealer. The last name he revealed was James Stewart McQuethy, Junior, whom he identified as a source of cocaine.

~ ~ ~

While Tony's house was being searched, Eddie drove the Thunderbird to an alley behind a small warehouse and pulled up behind two nondescript sedans. Detective Churn of the Qunicy department and Agent Bud Steele of the DEA were smoking against a building and talking as Eddie got out of the Thunderbird and opened the trunk. "Who gets the prize?" he asked, holding up the plastic bag containing the cocaine.

"We bought it, it's ours," joked Agent Steele. Eddie handed him the bag and was briefed about what was happening at Tony's house.

Eddie also handed Agent Steele the difference in the money that was left over from the deal and remarked, "We only got four kilo's."

Agent Steele had an update on Goldstein and McQuethy. "There's a tap on the jeweler's phone and we know that he has not been talking to anyone about what's going down. Junior's under wraps and has not made any calls and nobody's called about your man Tony. So, as far as he knows everything's fine and he's about to make some money selling you a few kilos of cocaine."

Eddie took in this information, he was happy to hear that the phone was tapped and wondered how long the tap had been placed on Goldstein's telephone. Detective Churn was silent and glanced from his shoes to Eddie without indicating what, if anything, he knew. "When are you meeting Goldstein?"

Eddie: "I'm going over there now. I don't want to give anyone a chance to let him know what has happened to Tony. He'll get spooked and who knows how long it will be before I can get him ready to do another deal. He's already a little shaky. He's like an animal with its nose in the air, always looking for the scent of danger. He didn't even want to deal with me; I had to waltz him around for a long time."

Churn: "You have got backup in place. Be very careful, this guy is capable of anything" he said.

Eddie drove the Thunderbird to Goldstein's store and parked in the back. As he drove into the area he saw two vans within a block of the store, both with utility workers inside, and several men who appeared to be milling around, smoking. Goldstein came to the front door and motioned for him to go to the back door. He had two Doberman pincher dogs with him. The animals stared at Eddie as he watched Goldstein motioned him to the rear of the store. The back door opened onto a small portion of the lot where the trash cans were kept and there were empty wet boxes collapsed into a pile next to the stairs that led to the building's storage area. Goldstein motioned him up and watched warily as the dogs approached him.

"Meet Hans and Wolfgang," the jeweler said by way of greeting. "They keep things honest around here." Goldstein walked to a small office and offered Eddie a seat. "I'm going to get something. Sit here and don't make any fast moves or try to get up. They're trained and they won't bother you as long as you stay where you are." He looked down at Eddie, who was sitting on a wooden chair, and smiled a thin little smile. Eddie could not tell whether it was friendly or sinister. Goldstein turned and went into the front of the store.

Eddie looked at the dogs. They were well muscled and alert. They were both black with tan markings on their legs and muzzles. Their ears had been trimmed to point straight up in triangles over their pointed heads and both dogs stared at Eddie as he looked from one to the other. He kept his hands on his knees and briefly wondered what would happen if he tried to pet the dogs. He moved his right hand and the dog at his knee issued a low growl, briefly showing his teeth. He moved his left hand and the other dog's hair stood up on his back as he growled and inched toward Eddie. The undercover officer was frozen by the animals and could not move. He wanted to get up and rifle through the papers on Goldstein's desk and look through the drawers to see if there was any evidence that the man was engaging in illegal activities other than drug dealing, but the dogs kept him from doing anything other than sitting and waiting for Goldstein to return. He looked at his watch. Five minutes passed, ten minutes. The dogs did not move. They pinned Eddie to his seat and maintained their stares, never looking at each other or responding to any sound that came from the street.

He heard footsteps and Goldstein appeared in the doorway. The dogs looked at him as he told Eddie to follow him to the basement. "Up!" he commanded and the Dobermans stood up and came to him. Eddie followed the jeweler down crude wooden steps to a cellar that had a damp dirt floor and stone walls. Rough wood shelves had been erected and placed on the dirt and Eddie saw boxes stacked on the un-sanded planks. Goldstein was smiling, almost too friendly, as he turned to look at Eddie. The dogs took up positions on opposite sides of the cellar and watched Eddie, ready to move on Goldstein's command.

The Jeweler: "So, we are in business," he said.

Eddie: "Yes, we are. You have the special items we discussed?"

Jeweler: "Yes, I do. I want to commend you for your discretion on this matter. Some would-be customers throw the word cocaine or drugs around and that makes me uncomfortable. Your use of the word jewelry impressed me as professional. You're not like the usual scum that is looking for a quick drug fix. We can do business together, I hope. I know you've talked to Tony and others about obtaining supplies sufficient to meet the needs of your New York customers, I would not want to interfere in your business with others, but if our arrangement works out, you may not need to deal with others. Do you get my meaning?"

Eddie: "Yes, I do," He responded, wondering where Goldstein was going with this.

Jeweler: "My supplier likes discretion and is a bit concerned about some of the other people with whom he is doing business. In other words, you and I may be partners, in a manner of speaking, and our friend Tony may become a smaller player. This is between the two of us and is not to be passed along to anyone else."

Eddie: "I've been doing business with Tony and I haven't had any problems with him," he offered.

Jeweler: "Except for the arrest that almost landed you in prison a few weeks ago," Goldstein responded.

Eddie: "I don't know what happened there, but it got straightened out."

Jeweler: "Do you know who straightened it out?"

Eddie: "It was a misunderstanding as far as the police were concerned."

Jeweler: "Well, let's get about our business. Do you have the funds?"

Eddie: "Not on me, but yes, I do."

Goldstein went to one of the rough shelves and pulled down a cardboard box, which he took to a small metal table and opened. "I have your specialty jewelry in here," he said, motioning for Eddie to come to the table, He put out his hand to the dogs and they remained where they were.

Eddie saw the same plastic-wrapped bag as he had seen earlier in the day at Tony's house. Goldstein slipped a small silver spoon into a slit in wrapped kilo of cocaine and offered it to Eddie who looked at Goldstein and said; "I believe I can trust that you would not screw me. It would be dangerous for you to do that. I'll accept the delivery based on your word. I am satisfied that you will not mess up a good thing.

Jeweler: "I would never screw any of my customers. I can let you have four. I need some for my other customers, those who don't purchase in such quantities, but who constitute my base business, so to speak."

The two men discussed an adjustment to the price and Eddie said he needed to go to his car to get the cash. He looked at the dogs, then at Goldstein.

"Stay!" Goldstein held his hand out to the dogs. "You can go up. They won't bother you. Meet me in the office upstairs."

Eddie went out to the Thunderbird and repeated the process he had used to make cash adjustments at Tony house, getting the bag out of the trunk, sitting in the front seat and putting aside the difference between five kilo's and four. He placed the extra cash under the driver's seat and walked back up the stairs to Goldstein's office. The dogs were sitting in a corner of the stock room, watching him. Goldstein was in the small office, placing the plastic bag into a shopping bag. He watched Eddie approach and reached for the bag that contained the cash. He asked for a moment to count it, which Eddie found unusual. Goldstein counted the cash with the speed of a man accustomed to handling large sums of cash in short periods of time.

Eddie left the jeweler's shop as the sun was dropping over the horizon. The early spring light was still weak and the air was chilled, but he caught the scent of turned soil and knew that someone had been making preparations for summer flowers. He put the bag into the trunk and started the Thunderbird, backing out of his space and pulling onto the street. He went two blocks and stopped at a red light. He looked into his rear view mirror and saw a group of cars and vans pulling into the jeweler's parking lot. The warrant was being served and around midnight DEA agents would take Goldstein into an interrogation room and inform him that more than a kilo of cocaine had been found in his shop. They would tell him they knew who his supplier was and that the man was cooperating with them. Goldstein remained silent and demanded to speak to his attorney. He was released on bail at nine thirty the next morning and immediately drove to his shop, where he placed a phone call that was picked up on by the State Police who were running a wire tap on him. He telephoned someone that he felt was capable of taking care of this situation for him. Ernie was not aware of this, not yet.

Eddie returned the unused money to the DEA and gave the agents the bag containing the cocaine he had purchased from Goldstein. He knew the time was coming when the investigation would have to be wrapped up. Tony's arrest would not cause much comment because he had been busted before and had a reputation as a guy who could not keep his mouth shut. Goldstein could be another matter and might look for someone to point fingers at and may try to link Eddie to his arrest. McQuethy Junior was in the hands of the U.S. Attorney for the District of Massachusetts and was in the process of being turned into an informant, but Eddie was not completely up to date on that aspect of the case.

Chapter 25

The Contract

It had been a long day and night and Eddie went home to get some sleep. He took a shower, crawled under the sheets and was sinking into a deep sleep when the red telephone rang. He decided to ignore it, but it kept ringing and whoever was calling would not hang up. He gave in, rolled over to answer it.

Eddie: "Yeah."

Lieutenant Lyme: "Ernie?"

He recognized the voice of Lieutenant Lyme.

Ernie: "Yes, sir. What's up?"

Lt. Lyme: "A couple of things. First, great job on these buys, eighty five per cent pure. This stuff is as pure as it gets. We got a big fish and a good case, but we have a small problem. It seems your friend Goldstein has some heavy friends. He put out a contract on your life. He is offering twenty five thousand to see you dead. State police picked it up on a telephone tap they've been running. We're running it down now and putting it together. Stay close to home for awhile and don't go to see any of your street friends until we can get this cleaned up. We're gonna bring him downtown and have a talk with him."

He let the news sink in and told Lyme he would stay at home until he received new instructions. He decided not to tell Teresa about the contract on his life. Instead, he would sleep and spend time at home, explaining that he had been putting in long hours and needed rest, which was, after all, true. He had no trouble falling asleep and woke only when Teresa came to check on him and whispered his name as the boys were coming home from school. He spent the evening with Teresa and the boys, helping with dinner and watching television until the boys went to bed. He and Teresa watched Johnny Carson and went to bed like a normal couple, with no talk about shit-bags and fear and contracts on his life.

~ ~ ~

McQuethy Junior was an easy nut to crack. The DEA agents who questioned him laid out their case and Junior's lawyer advised his client that things did not look good. The attorney was L. Patrick Finnegan, routinely described as Boston's best and most well-known defense lawyer. Finnegan had been a legal star since the days when he defended a serial rapist and sadist and got him off with a twenty year sentence by proving that the district attorney's office had attempted to pad the charges with non-related crimes. Well-heeled criminals had flocked to his door ever since and not one of them had ever received the maximum sentence and many cases were either dropped or the charges were reduced to misdemeanors and sentences to probation. Finnegan listened to what the DEA had to say and asked to consult with his client, meaning McQuethy Senior. The case was straight forward. The U.S. Attorney was offering a deal. Junior would become an informant and his cooperation would be the basis of whatever charges and punishment might be in the works down the road. Finnegan took this to mean Junior might not face any jail time and, in fact, might not face serious charges at all, depending upon his cooperation. In other words, Junior could save himself by ratting out everyone higher in the drug chain, mainly the Columbian drug lords and a common strategy in the world of drug investigations.

After a lot of discussion and bickering, McQuethy Junior agreed and spoke of many things and people including his partner Joseph (Arms) Woodbridge. Junior indicated that he would not tell his partner, Arms, anything about what he was about to do. The DEA agreed with his decision.

He was allowed to go home under his father's supervision and would be given random drug tests over coming weeks. On his way to the elevator, in the company of Finnegan and his father, Junior brushed up against a man he had seen before. The man was accompanied by an attorney known to Finnegan but not to Junior and Senior. In the elevator Finnegan said to no one in particular, "I know that lawyer. He represents drug dealers." Junior remembered where he had seen the man. It had been in Colombia on one of his drug missions and the man had been at the house of Junior's supplier. He assumed that the man had been busted just as he had and let the matter go.

Goldstein was another matter. DEA agents and Quincy detectives found him to be arrogant and uncooperative. His lawyer was a small time defense attorney whose clients came from the ranks of street scum. The attorney advised his client to shut up about everything and not admit to anything, even the cocaine found in his shop. "Make them work for it," was the lawyer's advice. "They don't have anything if you don't give it to them." When told that state police had a recording of his client ordering a hit on a known drug dealer named Eddie Pannoni, the lawyer asked what else was known about Pannoni, only to be told that they were holding warrant for him and that they would like to catch up with him. The attorney was also told that the issue at hand was the attempted murder, not the background of the individual Goldstein wanted killed. Goldstein was not released on bond.

Eddie did not leave the house in Dedham for three days. State Police picked up two men who had been linked to the Winter Hill gang in Somerville, a notorious bunch of street thugs who were best known for beating up jockeys to fix horse races, and both admitted that Goldstein had offered them money to kill Eddie Pannoni, whom Goldstein claimed was a rat. State Police interrogators told the men that Pannoni was a suspected drug and weapons dealer and that his 'day in court was coming', but if anything happened to him before police could arrest him, the two men from Somerville would be the first to be suspected. Besides, they said, Goldstein had his own problems and would not be in a position to pay anyone for anything.

"Leave Pannoni to us," said a police sergeant, "we'll know what to do with him."

One of the men, a short, red-haired Irish thug, said Goldstein was a "fuckin' dick" and he'd like to get his hands on him.

"We've got him covered," said the sergeant.

~ ~ ~

Tony's arrest was news on the street because he had more contacts and customers than Goldstein, who was not well known to the shit-bags. The primary effect of his arrest was a sudden shortage of drugs for the people who bought from him. He had promised about a dozen of his customers that high grade cocaine would be available and his arrest dried up that source, along with pills and marijuana.

That night Eddie met Lieutenant Lyme and Detective Church at St. Catherine's and was told that the operation was in its final phase. Lyme offered Eddie a cigarette.

Lt. Lyme told Eddie, "There's a guy in the department—you don't know him—but he's a lawyer working with the detectives. He has all of your reports. He's working with the DA's office, building a list of people we're gonna pick up. He's working up names, charges, warrants and property we'll seize. We're working with other departments in the area and the feds. This entire operation will go down in one day."

The lieutenant continued, "Ernie, your investigation will go down in police history as one of the largest in the

United States, between you and the federal agencies involved. You should be proud."

Lt. Lyme: "We'll have a meeting with everyone involved one week from today. I'll give you the details in a couple of days. So far, we've got over a hundred names to take down in our area alone. The feds have about a hundred additional people spread out all over the east coast associated with McQuethy, Woodbridge, The Jeweler and Tony and I believe they also have a bank in South Carolina that's laundering money from one of your guys. McQuethy Junior has property in Florida we think has been used to stash his cocaine and money and the feds will take that down, too. Good work."

The next day, Eddie drove to the coffee shop to look around and check the attitude on the street. It was the same crowd with the same attitude and no one seemed to notice that anything had changed. Jeannie was behind the counter, flirting and scratching her neck and Eddie knew she was looking for some heroin. A young man in a leather jacket invited himself into Eddie's booth and asked if he had anything to sell.

Eddie: "I'm looking myself," he said.

Young Man: "Things are tight," the man said, "I hear somebody got busted."

"Yeah, me too," said Eddie. He left the coffee shop and went to the pool hall where he played a few games of pool and bought a few rounds of beer for patrons who appeared to have no idea that anything had happened. No one looked at him differently and everyone seemed happy to see him, mostly to ask if he had any drugs to sell or share.

David Stewart McQuethy, Junior returned with his father to the family's weekend home in New Hampshire in the company of their attorney and a senior DEA agent. The government wanted Junior to use his plane and return to Colombia to purchase a quantity of high grade cocaine and to provide a list of names of those with whom he was doing business, along with descriptions of their homes, vehicles and associates. McQuethy Senior was silent as he watched his son agree to work with federal agents. He had provided his son with every advantage that money could buy including an exclusive education, trips abroad and access to the finer things in life. He stared at his son and wondered what would drive a privileged young man to import cocaine from international murderers and sell it to street thugs. He could not tell whether he was angry or disappointed. He could barely look at the young man he had raised.

Mr. McQuethy Sr.: "Junior, please be certain of what you decide to do. Those people are dangerous; you'll be on your own. I don't want to lose you."

McQuethy Jr.: "Dad, don't worry, I go back and forth all the time. I never have any problems with my connections."

Junior had explained to the agents how he had used his father's private plane to fly to the Caribbean, then to Colombia, to pick up and transport up to one hundred kilos of cocaine at a time. "I usually take my partner, Arms, with me. We would then sell the drugs to dealers up and down the East Coast." He acknowledged ties to figures linked to organized crime, including the Winter Hill gang and the Rhode Island Mafia. He took the agents, his father and attorney Finnegan to a small storage shed on the property where he had stashed duffel bags stuffed with cash. His father went behind the shed and threw up.

McQuethy Sr.: "Why? What did you need the money for?"

Junior: "I didn't need the money; it was just something to do."

McQuethy Sr.: "Maybe you can help make this right and save the family name."

Jr.: "The family name, that's all you think about."

Sr.: "You know better than that. You're upset, I'll be quiet."

Chapter 26

Shutting Down

The meeting was scheduled for four o'clock in the morning at the Quincy Department of Civil Defense, the largest available room in the city. Every police department in the Boston area where Eddie Pannoni had made contacts or met drug dealers was asked to send two representatives to a top secret meeting. Newly promoted detective Ernie Lijoi Sr. arrived at 3:30 wearing his dungarees, boots and jacket. His .38 was tucked into the back of his pants. Lieutenant Lyme and Detective Churn were there, along with a half dozen other Quincy officers, setting up chairs. There was a long table at the head of the room where large cardboard boxes were placed. Inside the boxes were warrants. Ernie looked around and thought to himself that the room could accommodate at least 300 people and still have plenty of room to spare at the same time. He helped place the chairs and watched as the room slowly filled with over two hundred law enforcement officers from local and federal agencies. Lieutenant Lyme went to the table at the head of the room and held up his hands.

"Can we come to order, please? Please take your seats." The room quieted and all eyes were on Lyme and the scruffy man standing next to him. "We all have a long day ahead of us and I want to get started. I want to introduce the members of my team." He asked Quincy's detectives to stand as he read their names. "We have body warrants, search warrants and confiscation orders to be served today. All of the teams will move in at the same time. Most of the people named on these warrants will be asleep; some will be stoned or still drunk from whatever they drank last night." There was a chuckle from the room. "You know why you're here but very few of you know who is responsible for all of these warrants." Lyme pointed to Ernie. "This man has been working deep undercover since the first of the year. For the time being I want his name to be kept confidential, but by the end of the day he'll be known to everyone on these warrants. Some of you know his real name and have worked with him on federal and local cases. Some of you have seen him on the street and know him as Eddie Pannoni, drug dealer and would-be weapons dealer. His deep undercover work will make a major dent in drug trafficking in New England and as far south as Florida. We have combed his reports from months of undercover work and have targeted individuals who we believe are or have engaged in illegal drug distribution or weapons violations. These warrants represent the work of this man. It is my honor to introduce Detective Ernie Lijoi Sr." The officers and agents left their seats and stood applauding as Ernie looked back at them. Some of them cheered, others looked surprised Ernie. "I thought you were a drug dealer from New York," said one man, offering his hand. Another related a story he had heard from his own street sources about Eddie Pannoni the drug dealer.

Lt. Lyme stepped up and shook Ernie's hand. He told the teams to step forward and pick up their assigned warrants. It took about a half hour to distribute the warrants. The various teams began pulling together and in about forty five minutes they were ready to start out on their quest. The action was set to begin at six sharp in the morning, It was now five a.m..

Before the men left the building, Lt. Lyme advised them that all evidence would be brought back to the station after marking it appropriately and that the evidence should be turned into the evidence department. "All arrests will be booked through the garage where we have everything set up. All confiscated items that are too large, like a car, will be left in the area until a tow truck can pick it up. We will have a man available to make those arrangements for you."

As the officers filed out of the room, they stopped by Ernie to congratulate him on a great job. Several had stories about Ernie, things that they had heard, times that they watched him and one guy simply said, "Wow, man; you had everyone fooled, including me."

~ ~ ~

Unmarked police cars and vans drove away into the predawn darkness as those named on the warrants slept. Federal officers called colleagues in Maine, New Hampshire, Rhode Island, South Carolina and Florida to issue the order to move in. Detectives from Quincy, Boston, Braintree, Brockton, Marshfield, Dorchester and Jamaica Plain drove to the addresses on the warrants and were in place shortly before six. More than fifty addresses were targeted. Federal agents from DEA and ATF accompanied half of the teams. Agent Bud Steele was with a group in Boston and expressed the feelings of the law enforcement teams when he stood outside the home of a man who sold cocaine and stolen pills. "In a drug search, you just go through the door."

Doors crashed at over four dozen addresses at precisely the same moment. "Police! We have a warrant! Stay down!" Some officers had their weapons in hand, others carried identification and warrants. Sammy Rinaldi was snuggling against a young woman he had met the previous night, an Irish girl from Southie, who had taken a liking to him when he offered her a few lines of cocaine. He was hoping to get some affection from the girl before he got up to go to work at the car dealership where the spring weather was bringing out the customers. He was nuzzling the girl's neck when he heard his door crash open and the shouts of "Police!" came up the stairs. He was still staring at the bedroom door when a detective pushed it open and held a badge to his face.

"Samuel Rinaldi?" the detective asked.

"Yes," he replied.

"We have a warrant, you are under arrest on narcotics charges."

The girl sat up, covering herself, as Rinaldi put on his pants. Police discovered three ounces of cocaine, two ounces of marijuana, six Quaaludes and some pornography.

~ ~ ~

Jeannie was in bed with Harry when police burst into the apartment they shared. She was semi-conscious from a heroin dose she had injected an hour earlier. Harry was hung over from a night of booze and drugs.

So it went, as officers confiscated cocaine, heroin, pills, marijuana, guns, stolen jewelry, cash, cars, trucks and houses and made numerous arrests.

Lieutenant Lyme had told Ernie his work was finished and he could go home to his wife and sons to a well-earned rest.

"I think I'll stick around," he said. "I want to see these people face to face." And so he went to the garage to wait for the shit-bags to be brought in for processing. Lyme, Churn and two federal agents had stationed themselves at a series of tables on the right side of the garage where they could watch detectives entering with suspects and property.

The tables were arranged to quickly book the incoming suspects. Officers at the first table took names and logged in the prisoners. The second table was for prints, the third held booking sheets which had been made out in advance, the forth was for pictures. Ernie stood near the last table and faced the suspects as they were led up the stairs to holding cells.

The doors to the garage bays were opened, ready for the seized vehicles to be inspected and tagged. The first familiar face to appear in the doorway was Sammy Rinaldi, followed by the freckle-faced Irish girl he had picked up the night before. She looked bewildered and scared. Her hands were shaking and she was crying. Rinaldi did not look his normal dapper self. His pants were wrinkled and his shoes were untied. He wore a cotton sweater that was stained with what appeared to be vomit. When Rinaldi first noticed Ernie his face brightened. He briefly believed that Ernie as Eddie Pannoni had been arrested, too, and was about to shout to him, but his face dropped when he saw Ernie with the other officers, looking at him. He knew then that Eddie was a cop and that this arrest was not a trivial matter of a roundup of street people.

Rinaldi: "What the fuck?"

Ernie: "You're under arrest,"

Rinaldi: "You motherfucker!"

Ernie: "Tell it to the judge."

The girl looked from Sammy to Ernie and cried loudly, she became hysterical. A female officer took charge of her and handled the situation..

Pauly was next to be escorted into the garage. A detective drove Pauly's Mustang convertible into the bay and gunned the engine before shutting it down. Pauly looked sick as he stared at Ernie, who smiled at him. "Hey, Eddie," he said, looking confused.

Ernie: "It's Ernie. Call me Detective Lijoi."

Pauly: "Ah, Jesus! No shit! I can't believe it, you fucken piece of shit!"

Lieutenant Lyme pulled Ernie aside. "You don't have to stay. There's no use letting these guys be abusive."

Ernie: "Lieutenant, I'm the reason these guys are being arrested and I want to face them and if they have something to say, so be it. Let them say it now and get it off of their chest."

"You do what you feel that you have to do," Lyme said. "You don't have to stick around and take the abuse, but I do understand your logic."

~ ~ ~

Several men who had played pool with the man they believed to be Eddie Pannoni were brought in and looked in disbelief at Detective Lijoi. They had not combed their hair and some were wearing pajama bottoms. One man had trouble focusing and appeared to be stoned and did not realize that what he was experiencing was not a drug dream, so he cocked his head to one side and said, "Wow! This is real." as he was led upstairs.

News of the raids had reached newspapers and radio and television newsrooms and reporters and photographers gathered outside the garage, capturing the images of dozens of drug dealers being unloaded from police cruisers and vans, and unmarked cars. Ernie stood where he could not be seen by the photographers. He was not ready for the spotlight. A television station carried a live report calling the operation the biggest drug bust in New England history. A police source was quoted as saying the arrests were the work of a single undercover officer who had been working the streets for months. This officer had worked with the FBI, DEA and ATF to accomplish this feat that will go down as one of the largest operations in history stretching from Canada to Florida and beyond.

~ ~ ~

Two federal agents brought Billy Stine to the table. He had been picked up on local drug charges and federal fire-arms violations. The local charges were logged and Stine was led away to be processed by the U.S. Attorney on the more serious gun charges. He glared at Ernie and spat on the floor. Six hours later he would agree to cooperate with federal agents and his testimony would be used to shut down a gun smuggling operation that funneled firearms to the Irish Republican Army from the Boston Winter Hill Gang.

~ ~ ~

Hour after hour, the shit-bags and dealers that Eddie Pannoni had come to know were led by the tables, pro-cessed, fingerprinted and photographed, and Detective Lijoi stood and looked each man and woman in the eye.

Jeannie looked like hell when she was brought in. She was high on something and smiled when she saw Ernie, shouting, "I fuckin know you!" and laughed. Harry was downcast and looked embarrassed. He offered his hand when he walked by Ernie but did not say anything. Two Mafia men who had sold Ernie cocaine and pills were es-corted to the table by uniformed officers. Both men wore suits and dress shirts without ties and they stared at Ernie as they were fingerprinted and photographed. One of the men, a chubby, dark skinned fellow with a scar across his fore-head named Jerry, laughed out loud and offered his hand to Ernie.

Jerry: "You got me fair. No planted evidence. No bull-shit. Maybe we can have a beer someday." Ernie shook his hand and said, "Sure."

Maria, the woman who had sold Quaaludes to the man she thought was Eddie, shouted at the officers who brought her in and yelled, "You son of a bitch!" at Ernie. "I knew you were a fuckin' cop!"

~ ~ ~

Rita, Pauline, Jerry and Davey Vespusian were led to the tables and booked. Davey, who had confided in Eddie Pannoni that he only sold drugs because it helped him get women, cast an eye over the females who were being pro-cessed and tried to get a telephone number from Rita, who threw back her red-haired head and whispered, "You gotta be kidding me!"

Davey: "We're not gonna be in forever."

Rita: "This is no place to pick up women/"

Davey: "I'm just being sociable."

Rita: "Try it with somebody else."

~ ~ ~

The arresting officers and agents seized the vehicles that had been involved in the trafficking, the cars and vans began to fill the parking lot near the police garage. Detec-tives inspected the vehicles and took photographs. Identifi-cation numbers were matched against state motor vehicle records and addresses and owners were noted.

Television crews packed the parking lot and reporters shouted questions at detectives and suspects. The story dominated the news. Every television and radio station led with it and some provided special reports that interrupted normal programs. Community newspapers in the towns where the raids occurred screamed headlines the next morning proclaiming "Biggest Drugs Raid Ever!" and dis-played photographs of suspects hiding their faces. The po-lice and agents had seized drugs, weapons, cash and stolen merchandise. One newspaper said it was the beginning of an all-out war on illegal drug dealing in the Boston area and reported that a small regiment of lawmen had fanned out to conduct the raids.

The news was good for the citizens of Eastern Massachusetts who had endured the sight of drug dealers and users on street corners and in parks. Thousands of good citizens sat in their living rooms and cheered as suspects were paraded in front of cameras and police spokesman announced that the raids were the work of months of undercover work.

~ ~ ~

Teresa sat in her living room while the boys did their homework. She watched the television and dabbed her eyes as the work her husband had done came to its end. Her hands shook as she looked at the men and women who were trying to hide their faces from the cameras and she knew that Ernie had come into contact with every one of them and had probably bought drugs from them. Reporters said some of the suspects were gun dealers and others had long criminal records and were thought to be violent members of organized crime. She was emotionally drained from the months that her husband had spent on the streets with these people. She thought about the nights when she had asked him about his day and he had replied, "It was okay." Her therapist had told her it was all right to feel anxious and upset, but she had tried to hide it from Ernie. She looked at the news coverage of the raids and saw dozens of police officers, but she did not see her husband, and she wondered if that was a good or bad sign.

~ ~ ~

The television was on over the bar in a small Colombian restaurant just off Harvard Square. The place was known for its free coffee and it was popular with students who used it for late-night study sessions after the restaurant patrons had eaten and left. A few students were reading and paying little attention to the news, but three Columbian men were standing behind the bar and watching every face that was being paraded before the cameras. Their faces became tight as the meaning of the raids came to them. It was a major blow to their business, which was cocaine. There was no mention of the man they did business with, nor were two of his biggest customers named, but the men knew that all three had been picked up days earlier and that their primary contact had been seen at the U.S. Attorney's office in the company of a well-known defense lawyer. It did not take a great deal of intelligence to deduce that the man had been turned and that someone with knowledge of the Boston area drug and weapons business had been telling everything to the police.

Their contacts had informed them about raids as far south as Florida and that a South Carolina bank they used to launder money had been seized. They watched until the newscast was over and then they closed the restaurant early, telling the students that there had been a family emergency and they had to leave, apologizing for the inconvenience. The men talked and smoked in a small back room, making a telephone call to Medellin at two o'clock in the morning. At dawn one of the men went to the newsstand on Harvard Square and purchased copies of every local newspaper. He went to Logan Airport and boarded a flight to Bogota, then a connecting flight to Medellin, where he gave the newspapers to a man who analyzed the accounts of the raids.

There was a meeting that night in Columbia and it was agreed that someone in New England had become an informer.

Their biggest worry was McQuethy and his partner Arms or Woodbridge which ever name he as using at the time. They would have to be found.

Chapter 27

Deaths

The Cessna flew from Boston to Miami, where John Stewart McQuethy, Junior and his partner Woodbridge met with a man who was an agent for men in Colombia, representing the Saldado Family. He informed the man that he wanted to purchase one hundred fifty kilos of cocaine to bring to New England and the man had told him that such a purchase would be no problem. A phone call was made and Junior was told to fly to Colombia. The man stated that he would accompany Junior to Bogota.

The weather was clear and Junior could see the blue-green water beneath him as the small plane flew over the islands and reefs, catching sight of sailboats, yachts and powerboats maneuvering between the cargo ships and tankers. It was beautiful and his thoughts turned to his current problem with the government. The feds had offered him a measure of immunity and even transfer to the witness protection program if he helped them get to the top drug lords in Medellin and the others with whom they dealt in New England. His father had made him promise to cooperate, but he knew the risks. He was not dealing with men who were stupid or forgiving. The man in the Cessna with him betrayed no knowledge of the raids in New England and showed no emotion. The man sat silently, looking out at the water below, no expression on his face. Junior could not read the situation and it made him nervous. Did they know he had been arrested? Did they know about the raids? Almost certainly they knew about the raids because it had been in the news all over the country, but his arrest had not been announced.

The plane landed in Bogota and he refueled as his companion watched and then announced that he would accompany him to Medellin. There was no conversation on the flight and they were met by the same goons who had driven him to and from the compound on earlier trips. No smiles, no handshakes, just an open car door and a ride.

The representative for the Soldado family met him at the door of the house and welcomed him as usual. The two men sat on the patio and Junior admired the mountains as he drank a rum and Coke. So far, nothing was different.

"So, my friend, how are things?" Soldado asked.

"Things are good. The market is good." Junior took a sip of his coke.

Soldado: "What can I do for you today?"

Arms: "One hundred fifty kilos will do us fine."

"Are you certain that you and Arms can move that amount, my friend?" Soldado smiled at Junior, but his eyes were steady.

McQuethy: "Yes, you know our experience from past deals, I have a network that can move it."

Soldado called one of his lieutenants over and whispered something into his ear. The man nodded, looked at Junior, and went into the house.

"Finish your drink. When you are ready, you will be driven back to the airport and your plane will be loaded with everything you need. Do you have the cash?"

Junior handed Soldado a large duffel bag containing several million dollars. The Colombian opened it and handed it to another man. "I need a small favor," he said.

McQuethy: "What do you need?" Junior was showing his nervousness and wanted to get back to his plane and fly home.

Soldado "I need you to make a little delivery for me, nothing special, just a stop to drop something off in Miami, a package. It is important to me that you do this."

"Of course I will handle it for you." Junior knew better than to ask what was in the package. He had been asked on earlier trips to make such deliveries and they had caused no problems. Florida authorities were unable to monitor what was taking place on the countless islands in the chain. It would not be difficult to land on a smooth, flat beach, drop off a package in Miami, and fly north to Boston.

He was driven back to the airport and the Cessna was fueled and ready to leave. He saw packages stacked in the small rear cargo area, covered with canvas and tied down. A smaller package, which he estimated to be about ten kilos, was separated from the rest of the cargo and was not tied down. His companion Arms, had returned to the plane with him and, without speaking, climbed into the passenger's seat. Junior flew out of Medellin and headed for Florida on a bright afternoon with few clouds and unlimited visibility. He sat in silence, scanning the sea below, and wondering where all of this would end. The feds had offered to place a special tracking device on the plane, but worried that it would be discovered by the men who loaded the cocaine into the cargo area. He had been assured that the device was not obvious and would be difficult to find, even by men who knew where to look, but he had balked and so he now flew without an electronic signal to tell others where he was. So far, he thought, things were going well.

The blue green water was interrupted by islands whose shorelines were difficult to define from the air. The land was brown and dark green. The water was clear and he thought he saw a submarine moving in a deep blue area of the sea. The sand on many beaches was bright white and blinding to anyone not wearing dark glasses. His companion stared out the window and said nothing. Junior had his nautical map that pinpointed the islands where he was able to land if he wished, but he continued to Florida where he would drop off the package. He lowered the nose of the aircraft and brought it down to two hundred feet as he approached the area where he searched for the island. There were hundreds of possible landing sites and he planned to fly over the area where he was to land to check the beach for tourists, debris and police. To his right he saw another small plane approaching from the east and circle as though the pilot were watching him. The plane came alongside about a hundred yards off to his left and he saw two men inside, both wearing sunglasses and glancing his way. The plane was outfitted with pontoons to allow it to land on the water.

He veered away from the plane and flew over a small island and decided that it was not the one where he would want to land, so he flew low over the water to neighboring island that he determined was his destination. He was low and could see fish and a small boat whose occupants looked up at him as he flew over. The beach was about three quarters of a mile long, flat and smooth and there were no tourists sunning themselves. He could see the shores of Florida and was very close. He prepared to land and allowed the plane to drop slowly; he was no more than 75 feet above the water. Suddenly, an explosion in the rear of the plane blew off most of the tail and the aircraft's nose dropped and the propeller spun into the water a hundred yards from the beach, causing the plane to flip over on its back. For a moment there was silence, then the sound of the surf hitting the beach sand.

Junior was dead, he had a piece e of the plane sticking out of his head. His companion, Arms was thrown from the aircraft. He observed McQuethy as he was thrown out of the door by the explosion. The second plane landed nearby and approached the wreckage and one of the men jumped into the water to help Arms escape and then helped him climb aboard the seaplane. Junior was left to drown as the sunset over the island. The plane sank in fifteen feet of water. A small group of men walked to the edge of the beach to see where it sank and witnesses later told the Florida authorities that they heard several vehicles noises and an explosion just before the plane went down..

Police boats arrived several hours later and it was decided to wait until dawn to recover the wreckage. A salvage craft was brought to the scene and by late afternoon the body of John Stewart McQuethy, Junior was recovered, along with four hundred pounds of marijuana wrapped to look like cocaine on the wholesale market. No cocaine was aboard the plane.

The U.S. Attorney in Boston was called and informed of what happened and he personally called John Stewart McQuethy, Senior to relay the information.

"He was killed by the drug lords," he said.

Senior was silent for several minutes. "He was trying to make it right," he said. "He was a real man. I know that more than anyone."

Agent: "He was working for us and we'll tell that to the world.

The next morning federal prosecutors announced that Junior had died while working undercover for the United States Government as part of the war on drugs. His body was brought back to Boston and he was buried in honor.

~ ~ ~

Soldado held an emergency meeting with the men who had helped him build his cocaine business. The subject was what to do about business in New England in the wake of the drug arrests and the loss, as he saw it, of one of his major buyers. The key question was who was responsible? Neither Soldado nor anyone else in Colombia had ever heard of Ernie Lijoi Sr. or Eddie Pannoni, who would have melted into the woodwork in a world of street level dealers and hustlers.

The men discussed everyone they knew in the Boston area and drew up a list of potential informants or contacts who might have been turned by the police or other law enforcement agencies. They drank and talked and smoked cigars far into the night five days after Junior died. They reviewed their New England operation and went over the men they dealt with and the process that was used to select Junior and his partner as primary buyers of their product. Who knew about their operation? Who introduced them to Junior? Who were his friends?

Soldado stated, "Arms is still alive; we will have to eliminate him. I'll contact the org Family in New York City. They will handle it for the right price."

After a night of drinking and arguing their list contained several names. Names that they decided were all informants. No one knew for certain or even had a strong suspicion, but they were all in agreement that Arms was the number one suspect working against the Soldado Family. He was the key man. The good news, as they saw it, was that the five were known to be friends and socialize together, even play cards together on Tuesday nights in a Boston pub. A decision was made.

~ ~ ~

The men arrived one by one at the pub on a rainy Tuesday night in June. The place was used as a disco on weekends and the manager had installed a large mirror ball on the ceiling and cages where female dancers would gyrate while the pulsing music pounded the floor from large high quality speakers stacked against the walls. But on this night, the mirror ball was still and the disco music was silent, replaced by Frank Sinatra and Ella Fitzgerald. The pub's second floor room was set aside on Tuesdays for a special group of investors who played poker and smoked Cuban cigars. It was rumored on the street that the five were "connected" and had ties to very powerful, if not violent, friends. Not one of the five ever confirmed or denied the reports and all had legitimate jobs. One of the five was the manager of the pub and another turned out to be Arms, who enjoyed playing cards.

The game began a little after nine o'clock and continued well past midnight, when a bartender told the men to help themselves to anything they wanted. He counted the cash and locked the register and then he grabbed an umbrella and opened the door to the alley, got into his car and drove home.

~ ~ ~

The next morning was foggy and heavy traffic delayed a floor cleaner named Benji Booker, who mopped the pub before it opened for lunch business. Benji arrived a few minutes after ten and was in a hurry to get to work to make up for the half hour he lost on his way in from Lowell, where he lived with his sister. He parked his ten year old van in the alley and used his key to open the steel door that led to the small office and a hallway where he stored mops, a bucket and cleaning supplies. He stepped into the hallway and noticed a strong odor, something like vomit and shit. His first thought was that someone drank too much the night before and was sick on the floor. "Damn!" he said out loud, knowing that no one else was within hearing. He grabbed the bucket that had wheels attached at the bottom, placed a large ringer over the bucket, filled it with warm water, grabbed a mop, and pushed the bucket down the hall into the basement room where he expected to find a place where someone had been sick. What he saw caused him to vomit into the bucket.

Five men were dead. Three were at the poker table, their heads and upper bodies unrecognizable. Two others were on the floor, their heads gone in a mass of gore, their torsos torn open by shotgun blasts. Benji shook as he was sick and he fled the room, running into the alley and then into the street, shouting, "Call the police! Call the police!"

A Boston police cruiser was parked at the end of the block and two officers were talking to a man who appeared to be drunk. They heard the shouting and turned on their siren and lights as they drove to where Benji was screaming into a crowd that was gathering. He took the officers into the pub where the officers stared at the carnage and called for backup.

~ ~ ~

The papers screamed the story that five men had been gunned in a pub, but police had no motive and suspected robbery. In Colombia, Soldado considered the matter closed, assuming that Arms was one of the five that had been the informant responsible for bringing down his New England operation. He set about rebuilding the operation by making discreet inquiries with Italians who were known to be ruthless but reliable.

Soldado was satisfied that Arms was dead and he would be able to rebuild the organization. There was just one aspect that he needed to take care of so that he would not have any interference in the future.

Soldado looked at his men, "We will have to eliminate this Detective Ernie Lijoi Sr. as soon as possible."

~ ~ ~

Back in the states, Ernie was meeting with Agent Steele.

"I have a ton of calls from informants, people looking to get a break on this case what the hell do I do with them all?" Ernie asked.

"Guess," Steele replied. "Some made guys are already sniffing around looking to talk with you. How would you like a job?"

"Doing what?" Ernie replied.

Steele: "This; working here at the DEA. You've got the smarts and the balls for it, Ernie. We can use you."

Ernie: "I have a job."

Steele: "Not this job. We need guys like you."

Ernie thought about what it would mean for his family, the endless undercover work and the nights away from home, the toll it would take on Teresa and the boys.

Ernie: "No thanks. I'm a Quincy detective now. That's where I belong."

Steele: "Call me if you need anything. We'll be working together again."

Ernie walked into the sunlight of a bright summer day and unlocked the Thunderbird. He removed the top and enjoyed the sunshine, sitting back and allowing himself a laugh. Ernie wondered, he never thought that it would turn out like this? He picked up his CB microphone, keyed the transmitter, and announced to the world, "Mr. Blue signing off."

Epilogue

The lake house was tilted to the left as he and Teresa looked at it from the shore. "Can you fix that?" she asked.

Ernie: "Sure. I'll stand on that side and push until you tell me it's straight."

She laughed. "I'm serious. Can that be fixed?"

Ernie: "Who knows? We can try."

~ ~ ~

Detective and Mrs. Ernie Lijoi and their boys owned the lake house and spent their summer weekends there. Ernie worked on the place and fished with the boys and the family cooked bass and ate home grown tomatoes. Teresa smiled a lot and would find herself touching Ernie, as if to confirm he was really there. The place was a mess and they spent the first half of the summer cleaning out the trash and years of neglect. Ernie built shelves and painted walls while Teresa planted a garden and organized the kitchen. By fall she was making mouth watering Italian dishes as Ernie and the boys made fishing lures. They would own the lake house for twenty years and spend weekends alone when the boys were grown and gone to their own lives.

~ ~ ~

Soldado and his Italian friends would rebuild his New England cocaine operation and again face Ernie Lijoi Sr. when he learned that a schooner filled with cocaine was arriving at the Quincy docks. Ernie would be working undercover and his network of sources kept him informed about what was happening on the streets of Quincy.

Jeannie died of an overdose. Tony died in prison. Most of the others were sentenced and some got probation. Others cleaned themselves up or died on the streets, A few of the more serious people did hard time.

The Soldado Family of Columbia and the Borgazino Family of New York City would continue to be THE PREYERS on society, until they meet Ernie and Eddie again.

~*~*~*~*~

Meet our authors

Ernie Lijoi, Sr.

Ernie Lijoi Sr.
Http://www.thepreyers.com
Http://www.erniesr.com

Larry Matthews

Larry Matthews
http://www.larrymatthews.net

Other books in the Eddie Pannoni thriller series
By
Ernie Lijoi, Sr.

*****

Destructive Obsession
*****

Meth or Myth
*****

The Butcher of Boston
*****

The Cash Mule
*****

The Tunnel

Eddie Pannoni

www.ingramcontent.com/pod-product-compliance
Lightning Source LLC
Chambersburg PA
CBHW051539260626
47170CB00003B/1007